"I should check on the fire."

Clay's mouth was so close to hers she could feel the warmth of his breath on her lips.

"Yes…fire," she agreed. She had felt embers glowing in her midsection even before he'd mentioned the fire. She met his lips and took them with a hunger she had never known.

He suddenly broke the kiss. "I am not making love to you here."

"Talking to me or yourself?" Vanessa whispered, smiling her wickedest smile.

"Both. I just want to hold you."

"Liar."

He pulled the blanket up around them swiftly as they lay side by side. "If I ever make love to you, I want it to be perfect, soft light—"

"The fire's pretty low," she interrupted, snuggling closer.

"Sweet music…"

"Crickets will do."

"Satin sheets.

"Two out of th   han anything I've   ere. Right now."

Dear Reader,

Take a break from all the holiday shopping and indulge yourself with December's four heart-stopping romances from Silhouette Intimate Moments.

New York Times bestselling author Maggie Shayne kicks off the month with *Dangerous Lover* (#1443), the latest in THE OKLAHOMA ALL-GIRL BRANDS miniseries. An amnesiac seeks the help of his rescuer, but the bewitching woman might just be a suspect in his attempted murder. Next is Lyn Stone's *From Mission to Marriage* (#1444), the new installment in her SPECIAL OPS miniseries. A killer vows revenge, and as the chase heats up, so does Special Ops agent Clay Senate's desire for his sexy new hire.

In Nancy Gideon's *Warrior's Second Chance* (#1445), a determined heroine must save her family by turning to the man she left behind years ago. But will her secret douse the flames of their newly rekindled romance? And be sure to pick up *Rules of Re-engagement* (#1446), the final book in Loreth Anne White's SHADOW SOLDIERS trilogy. Here, a wanted man returns to save his country…but to do so he must reunite with the only woman he's ever loved— his enemy's daughter.

Starting in February 2007, Silhouette Intimate Moments will have a new name—Silhouette Romantic Suspense, but we will continue to deliver four breathtaking romantic-suspense novels each and every month. Don't miss a single one! Have a wonderful holiday season and happy reading!

Sincerely,

Patience Smith
Associate Senior Editor

Please address questions and book requests to:
Silhouette Reader Service
U.S.: 3010 Walden Ave., P.O. Box 1325, Buffalo, NY 14269
Canadian: P.O. Box 609, Fort Erie, Ont. L2A 5X3

Lyn Stone

FROM MISSION TO
MARRIAGE

INTIMATE MOMENTS™

Published by Silhouette Books

America's Publisher of Contemporary Romance

SILHOUETTE BOOKS

ISBN-13: 978-0-373-27514-4
ISBN-10:   0-373-27514-5

FROM MISSION TO MARRIAGE

Copyright © 2006 by Lynda Stone

This edition published by arrangement with Harlequin Books S.A.

® and TM are trademarks of Harlequin Books S.A., used under license.
Trademarks indicated with ® are registered in the United States Patent
and Trademark Office, the Canadian Trade Marks Office and in other
countries.

Visit Silhouette Books at www.eHarlequin.com

Printed in U.S.A.

Books by Lyn Stone

Silhouette Intimate Moments

Beauty and the Badge #952
Live-In Lover #1055
A Royal Murder #1172
In Harm's Way #1193
*Down to the Wire #1281
*Against the Wall #1295
*Under the Gun #1330
*From Mission to Marriage #1444

*Special Ops

LYN STONE

loves creating pictures with words. She paints, too. Her love affair with writing and art began in the third grade when she won a school-wide contest for her colorful poster for Book Week. She spent the prize money on books, one of which was *Little Women*.

She rewrote the ending so that Jo marries her childhood sweetheart. That's because Lyn had a childhood sweetheart herself and wanted to marry him when she grew up. She did. And now she is living her "happily ever after" in north Alabama with same guy. She and Allen have traveled the world, had two children, four grandchildren and have experienced some wild adventures along the way.

Whether writing romantic historicals or contemporary fiction, Lyn insists on including elements of humor, mystery and danger. Perhaps because that other book she purchased all those years ago was a Nancy Drew.

This book is dedicated to my grandfather,
John David Perkins,
a man of few words, wry humor and a good heart.

Prologue

"This one's mighty little. Maybe we'd better throw her back."

Clay Senate wondered if his new colleague was serious. He glanced again at the photos and dossier of Vanessa Walker. The pictures were just in, a news photo of a smiling Walker receiving her badge and a mug shot, with height lines for a background, showing she measured sixty-three inches. She looked pretty. Young. Perky. Obviously Native American. "You know what they say, Cate. Good things often come in small packages."

"I'm not touching that comment," Cate teased, laughing as she looked at Danielle Sweet, who was barely five-five. "But okay, I say give her a shot."

Clay nodded at the vote offered by the first hire for the new COMPASS team, an adjunct of Sextant, the Civilian Special Operations team now being organized by Homeland Security to investigate and neutralize threats at home and abroad.

Cate Olin stood six feet tall and had the strong-shouldered, small-breasted, slim-hipped body of a long-distance swimmer. He watched as she raked a lock of straight white-blond hair back behind one ear. Cate had a degree in criminal justice, was fluent in several languages and had put in six years with the National Security Agency.

Jack Mercier, the agent who would act as director for both teams, had handpicked her. Mercier had the contacts necessary to identify and appropriate personnel. He also had an infallible knack for choosing personalities that would mesh into a cohesive unit.

"What do *you* think, Dani?" Jack asked Danielle Sweet, the latest hire, a former army brat who could kick some serious butt on the mats at the gym. She was a deceptively dainty brunette with a master's in international relations from Georgetown. Though people generally underestimated Dani because of her looks, Sweet's IQ was off the charts, her powers of reasoning were outstanding and she could charm her way into or out of anything.

She graced Mercier with a benign smile. "Excellent credentials. She's awfully gung ho, isn't she? Who grins like that for a mug shot?" Then she grinned herself. "But we like gung ho, don't we?"

"Absolutely." Jack turned then, silent for a moment as he regarded Clay. "Fine, we agree Walker's a possible. She's on a case, Clay, so if you go and give her a hand, you can see how she handles herself. You'll be pulling double duty here. Recruiting and investigating. I only found out about Walker's current case because I called to see when she might be available to meet with you. When I identified myself, her Agent-in-Charge assumed I was following up on the report submitted to his superior and promptly filled me in on what's going on."

"What kind of case?" Clay asked.

"A bomb detonated at one of the casinos on the Qualla Boundary."

"That's the Cherokee reservation in North Carolina?" Cate asked.

"Yes, and technically under federal jurisdiction, at least for a case such as this. Agent Walker was at the scene when it happened. Someone had called her and told her a friend of hers was in trouble at the casino and being held there by the manager. A ruse to get her there, of course. It's all in the report.

"I got the okay for you to partner with Agent Walker on it while you check her out, Clay. We'll go with your final recommendation about bringing her on here."

Clay nodded as he scooped up the folder of information and scanned it briefly for more details.

There wasn't much. Vanessa Walker had taken a phone call that had come in to the Asheville bureau. James Hightower, a former fishing guide and resident of Cherokee, had been convicted for manslaughter and had served four years. After his release, he'd returned to a small community just outside the boundary and had taken rooms with a woman called Lisa Yellowhorse.

Yellowhorse had made the call to Vanessa Walker, saying she suspected that her tenant was responsible for the bombing and might be planning something worse.

It shouldn't take long to round up this guy and find some proof, or at least some answers to the allegation. Clay just hoped he was there long enough to get some indication as to how their prospective hire performed.

"Mind telling me what Ms. Walker's claim to fame might be?" Even though he'd read her folder, he wanted to know her peculiar gift, the one that had prompted Mercier to suggest her above a number of others with equally impressive credentials. No doubt she would have some extra tricks that weren't in that file. They all did, ranging from excellent instincts to outright telepathy.

Jack inclined his head. "She's ingenious. Very inventive and thinks fast in a crunch. Her main talent seems to be staying alive against impossible odds. Vanessa Walker keeps cheating the grim reaper on a regular basis. Seems she has more lives than the proverbial cat."

"No reference to that in her file," Clay remarked, thumbing through it idly.

"I know," Jack said, not volunteering how he had discovered the information. He stood, signaling the meeting was over. "You'll need to determine whether her miraculous escapes are due to luck, skill or premonitions."

Clay understood what Jack meant. Luck could run out at any time. But if her skills or a talent for premonitions were what kept Walker landing on her feet, COMPASS had found the third teammate.

Chapter 1

Clay's ears ached, his head hurt and, after the flight, he was in no mood for a cheerful greeting. He could see he was about to get one, though. The candidate was waiting for him, wearing that same wide smile she wore in her photos. No one had told her yet that she was being considered for COMPASS. As far as she knew, he was only there as a rep from Homeland Security, come to assist her in the investigation.

She held up a hand-lettered sign with his name on it and looked straight at him. He nodded and strode over to her, his most intimidating glare daring her to be chipper.

She stuck out her hand. "Agent Senate? Thanks for coming, sir. I'm Vanessa Walker."

Cate had been right—this one was small, probably 105

pounds, and she looked about eighteen years old. He knew better, though. She was twenty-seven.

"Agent Walker," he acknowledged, shaking her hand. Hers felt delicate, but her grip was strong. Not surprising. She had graduated second in her class at the FBI Academy and weaklings didn't get through there.

She laughed self-consciously and broke the connection, tossed the sign into a nearby trash receptacle and tried to take his carry-on away from him. It weighed a ton, so he held on. She let go with a shrug. "Okay. Off to baggage claim. You have a nice flight?"

He grimaced ahead of them at the young mother dragging the five-year-old with the whine and the twitchy feet, who'd performed a horizontal River Dance on the back of his seat. "Not really."

"Turbulence?" she persisted, following his line of sight to the kid. She didn't bother suppressing a chuckle.

"You might say that."

"Sorry. Would you like a drink?"

He stared at her as if she had lost her mind.

"Can you? Drink, that is?" Perky. Too perky.

"Of course I can drink."

"Do you?"

"Not much. Why?"

She shrugged. "Some people have a problem with alcohol. I like to identify the ones who do and avoid them in working situations. Got shot once when I didn't. Friendly fire, too."

Clay mumbled a curse.

"Don't get touchy. It's a fact. Do you smoke?"

"An occasional cigar, never around loaded weapons."

She laughed, a low sensual sound that did something salacious to his insides. "Ah, a sense of humor. Here we are!" As if reaching the baggage ramp were a feat to celebrate.

They stood silently as they waited for the baggage to begin making its slow circle. But silence seemed more than she could stand for long. She took a deep breath and released it. "So, where are you from?"

"Why?"

Her lips tightened with exasperation. "I'm making polite conversation. Is it a secret?"

He focused on the empty baggage ramp. "McLean, Virginia."

She raised an eyebrow. "Conoy, Manahoac or Delaware?"

"Do you really need the family history?" God, he sounded grumpy, even to himself. He tried to temper the question with a smile. It wasn't her fault he was exhausted.

"Nope." Again she shrugged. "Just wondered. My mother was Italian, by the way. Daddy met and married her when he was in service. Most of us aren't full-bloods. And with those eyes of yours, it's pretty obvious—"

Clay couldn't believe her lack of tact. "Why would you care?"

"No reason. I just think it's good they sent an Indian. You'll understand what I mean when I say I've got a feeling something's gonna pop."

"Oh, right," he said cynically. "That mystical thing we have going. How could I forget all those movies I watched?"

"You like to scoff, don't you? But you know it's so. My boss thinks my informant's just a woman taking potshots, trying to get this guy locked up because she found out he was an ex-con and he scares her. Me? I take it seriously when somebody discovers a possible threat and bothers to call it in."

She took a breath, something he was beginning to wonder whether she ever needed. "I believe her. Bad vibes on this one."

"Vibes. Lovely," Clay muttered.

Her smile had disappeared. "I know Hightower. He's capable of this."

"You know him personally? Should be a piece of cake then."

"Don't bet on that, but we'll get him sooner or later. Just hope it's sooner."

Clay closed his eyes, pinching the bridge of his nose, trying to relieve his headache. With a resigned sigh, he opened them and saw he had missed his bag and would have to either run after it or wait for it to come around again. "Damn."

"Was that one yours?" She chased it down before he could answer. All that energy of hers was making him tired.

Watching her struggle with the heavy suitcase suddenly struck Clay as funny. Since he'd just returned from an assignment in Seattle, maybe he was spazzed out from lack of sleep. By the time she had thumped it down on the terminal floor, he had sobered. He walked over and picked it up. "That's it. Let's go."

"You won't need a rental car, by the way," she told him. "We have an unmarked you can use, or I'll cart you around since we'll be working together. I like to drive."

Yeah, she looked young enough to have just taken her first driving test. Her tailored red pantsuit fit a body any sixteen-year-old would envy, breasts high and firm, waist tiny and hips slender. She wore her ink-black hair slicked back into a braided knot. No jewelry besides the small silver studs in her earlobes. Her nails were bare, short and beautifully shaped. She wore no makeup that he could discern except for a touch of lip gloss.

Either she was a natural beauty or very skillful with the war paint. He suspected the former and approved her apparent lack of vanity. Oddly, that made him wish he could compliment her, but he didn't. It would be highly un-PC to say anything that might be considered a come-on to a prospective hire or a fellow agent.

His dark mood had improved by the time they reached her vehicle. It was a tan Ford Explorer with only a couple of years on it. Comfy and cool. He stretched his legs, leaned his head back, closed his eyes. To his surprise, she remained quiet for a good half hour. A really good one, during which he grabbed a few z's. He wasn't interested in scenery and sleeping kept him from staring at her.

When he woke up and checked his watch, he realized he felt a little better. At least his headache was gone and his ears had popped so he could hear normally again.

"Had you rather go straight to your home away from home or the office?" she asked, sounding a bit tired herself now. She was no longer smiling, no longer perky.

"Office. Might as well get the show on the road. Will I be able to interview your caller today?" It was already midafternoon.

"No problem. She lives in Cool Spring on the way to where you'll be staying."

Clay noted the change in his new temporary partner grow even more marked as they approached her place of work. So marked that he felt compelled to ask "Is something wrong?"

"Agent Roan sent me to pick you up but he'll offer you one of the guys to work with instead of me. Count on it."

"Because you're female? That's ridiculous," Clay said vehemently. Vehement only because he had already entertained some reservations about her himself since meeting her. Her size, her flagrant optimism, her lack of broader experience in law enforcement. But she was a well-trained agent, and according to her record, beyond simply capable. He hated any kind of discrimination and would not be a party to it. Walker was getting her chance.

He had to work with her. How else would he determine whether she would fit in COMPASS? Even if she wasn't quite ready, she would have months of extra training to prepare her for that job if he did recruit her. As for her boss trying to edge her out of this investigation, Clay set her mind at rest. "Don't worry. I'll take care of it."

She shot him a wry glance. "It's not the boy-girl thing if that's what you're thinking," she admitted. "See, I sort of overstepped my bounds by conferring with the chief out at Qualla about the case. It was hard not to since we're related. The boss is still ticked off that I discussed it. We butt heads pretty regularly."

Clay smiled at her moxie. "Nothing scares you, I guess."

She treated him to a blinding white smile that showed dimples. "Not much, no, but I have to admit, you're a little scary. I'm glad you're on my side. You got a wife?"

Damn, she kept throwing him curveballs. "No," he said. "No wife."

"Not surprised," she commented just as they parked. She popped her seat belt and hopped out of the car, energy crackling around her like static electricity. "You're the best-looking man I've seen in a long time, but that scowl of yours would terrify the bejesus out of most women."

But not her, obviously. Clay could only shake his head in wonder. The girl was outrageous, without a smidgen of diplomacy, and sort of exhausting to be around. He imagined the local Bureau would be delighted, or at least a little relieved, if he did steal her away from them.

"Agent Walker?" he called as she started up the steps, intending to advise her to let him do the talking when they went inside.

She stopped to wait for him at the top. "Might as well call me Van," she said, pausing with her hand on the door. "Everyone else here does. I think they like to pretend I'm a guy." She wrinkled her nose.

"Then they must have excellent imaginations," Clay said, without thinking that the comment sounded sexist until it was already out there.

"Thanks. May I call you Clay? Not in there, of course," she assured him, gesturing at the door with a quick lift of her chin.

"No problem." What else could he say without sounding unfriendly, even pretentious?

A glance at his watch told him it was nearly four o'clock. "Let's get this out of the way and then get busy. If that informant of yours is not jerking us all around, we don't need to lose any time on useless networking."

Her smile flashed again. "Hey, my kind of man." She swept open the door and indicated he should precede her.

A quarter hour later, Van cradled her coffee cup and sat with one hip hitched up on her desk, trying to hear what was going on in the boss's office. The walls were thin, but not thin enough to catch the words, only to hear that the argument to replace her was subtle, noncombative, but intense.

Two of her fellow agents, Buddy Dean and Joe Middlebrooks, listened with her unabashedly, watching for her reactions.

In defense of her boss, Vanessa knew half his reasons for disliking her were probably valid. He would be telling Agent Senate how she was too outspoken, too ambitious and that she tried entirely too hard. How those things caused resentment.

Dammit, she had to be an overachiever. How else could she prove herself? Everybody in the world knew that a woman had to work twice as hard to prove herself in a male-dominated field. In a same-case scenario, a man was applauded for his initiative while a woman was labeled overly aggressive and presumptuous.

Not that they meant to be chauvinistic around here. The men she worked with were good people, dedicated and conscientious. They worked hard and made a difference. All she wanted was to keep up with them and gain their respect.

She tried to keep a low profile. Not that she was all that modest and certainly not lacking in ambition, but Van was afraid the boss would think she was trying to beef up her participation into something that might get her promoted. This time she was going all out, begging for the lead on the case, even if it meant working with another agency on it. This threat was very real.

Hightower wasn't finished. But even with that considered, it had been a homemade bomb, not even a large one. Even she knew it was a local problem, technically not warranting FBI intervention. She wouldn't be in on it if Lisa hadn't called her directly and gotten her involved. So Van had to wonder why the powers-that-be had sent Agent Senate down here to assist. Scary as it was, this was not a national threat.

The door opened and Clay came out wearing that scary frown she hoped to have a chance to get used to. Vanessa stood and put down her coffee cup, ready to bow out gracefully if Roan had changed Senate's mind. Buddy and Joe stood, too, fully expecting to be called to duty in her place.

"We're burning daylight, Agent Walker. Let's go," Senate said, looking straight at her. She caught the almost undetectable hint of a smile in his eyes.

Van gave herself a mental high five and barely contained a whoop. Instead, she calmly picked up her purse and slung it over her shoulder. "Yes, sir."

The urge to wink at Buddy and Joe almost overwhelmed her, but she refrained. Decorum had suddenly become important, at least until she was outside the building.

On the way to the car, she gave him a pat on the arm and thanked him. He cut those steely gray eyes at her and Van got the distinct feeling she had overstepped again. Maybe he didn't like to be touched.

On the sixty-mile drive to Cool Spring, she kept her mouth shut except to thank him again, briefly and more circumspectly, for going to bat for her. He muttered that she was welcome and then concentrated on studying the written report of her interview with Lisa Yellowhorse that the chief had provided. Man, could this guy focus.

He had great hair, wore it long and tied back neatly. Though he looked better than presentable in a business suit, she could easily imagine him on horseback, flying like the wind, dressed in feathers, loincloth, leggings and moccasins. She'd seen way too many movies. This guy could definitely play a Hollywood Indian.

His features looked less Iroquois than Plains—sharp angles, square jaw, high cheekbones and a very slight hook to the nose. As large as he was, at least six-two and heavily muscled, he might even have Viking blood for all she knew. His size, height and those cool, gray eyes of his didn't come out of the Indian gene pool. Neither did the five o'clock shadow he was wearing.

She realized all of a sudden that she was physically attracted to him. Okay, more like bowled over. No point revealing that to him, however. He didn't like her much and she was definitely not interested in mixing it up with a superior who probably could burn her career if she made a wrong move.

Oh well, he was great to look at and she could enjoy that without feeling bad about it. She kept stealing glances while he was busy reading the report.

He thumped the page with the back of his fingers. "Very detailed. Good work."

"Thanks." Van enjoyed the unaccustomed thrill that came with praise, not something she had basked in very often since her college days. "Any questions?"

"Your AIC isn't convinced Hightower's behind this. Are

you certain Ms. Yellowhorse is being straight? Maybe she's a disgruntled lover or just scared to have him living with her."

"Gut feeling," she replied with a succinct nod. "And it all fits. Circumstantial at the moment, I know, but you'll see I'm right."

He turned to look at her fully, remaining silent for a minute. "Tell me about your escapes."

She laughed. "My what?"

"Roan told me you've pulled yourself out of the fire so many times, he feels the urge to bury you under a mountain of paperwork so you'll survive to see thirty. Details, please. Start with the robbery you interrupted six months ago."

"He's exaggerating," she said with a scoff. "I dodged a few bullets, that's all. The perps were lousy shots."

"But you're obviously not," he remarked with the ghost of a smile.

Van shrugged. "I have a good eye. It's probably inherited, but I've practiced a lot, too. My grandfather was a sniper in 'Nam. Taught me a few tricks."

"Enough to qualify for the Olympic team, apparently. What about the fire after that bomb went off in the casino? They thought you were trapped."

"It was jump off the roof or burn and it was only two stories, not necessarily a fatal leap. What would you have done?" Van hated talking about that. Fire was her worst nightmare and had nearly finished her off. She rubbed the back of her neck with one hand and flexed her left leg. "No serious injuries, thank goodness."

"And you saved two people by pushing them off that roof."

She shook her head impatiently. "Yeah, but I had to coldcock one and shove him off unconscious. Poor ol' Bobby Rock has a bad fear of heights. I worried that the fall would break his neck, but it was that or let him go up in smoke."

"What about last year, the hostage thing at the school? You

did okay, Roan said. Hard to think with a gun to your head, but you managed to talk the perp into surrendering."

She made a face. "He was just a kid."

"With a .45 full of hollow points. You've faced death square in the face several times now. I'm interested. Which time destroyed your fear of it?"

"Who says one did? But I will say this, I believe I've survived for a reason. I just don't know what it is yet."

His look was intense when she glanced over at him.

"Are you a loose cannon?" he asked quietly.

She faced the road again. "No. If we get into a dicey situation, you can count on me to react appropriately. Are you worried?"

"If you're convinced that you're destined to do something so great that a higher power is keeping you alive against all odds, then, yes, I am definitely worried."

She laughed. "Get real. Don't you think I know God helps those who help themselves?"

"So you're religious?"

"Most people in law enforcement are. Aren't you?" she asked.

"Let's not get into that. Sorry I brought it up."

"Well, you did, so brief answer, please. Do you believe in that higher power you mentioned, yes or no?"

He paused. "Yes, but if God's a woman, she could change her mind on a whim. Maybe decide to let someone else perform whatever task you think you're programmed to do, so I wouldn't trust fate too far if I were you."

Van laughed, but it was a little bitter. "My, my, here I was thinking you're so politically correct and then you come out with something weird like that. Women are inconstant, gods or not, huh?"

"It was a joke to get you off the topic of religion."

"Well, you can forget comedy, my friend. Some chick dumped you, right? Now you're down on the whole female gender."

He was hiding a smile, she could tell. "I'm thirty-six and unmarried. How do you know I ever liked women to begin with?"

"Because when you checked out my breasts, your expression did not indicate envy," she explained, her reaction deadpan.

He laughed out loud. The sound was new and Van liked it. She was shaking up that stoic warrior image to hell and gone. It was what she did best, making men laugh. Even the boss unbent a little when he wasn't ready to throttle her about something.

"See? You're no match for me," she told him, turning the Explorer down the dirt road outside Cool Spring that led to Lisa Yellowhorse's house. "We're almost there. I'll introduce you, but you do all the talking. I have her on tape and we'll compare notes later."

From the corner of her eye, she could actually see him morph into agent mode again. She suspected that was his usual state. She hoped her joking around had helped him to relax a little. After the interview, he had another surprise coming, so she definitely wanted him in a good mood.

On impulse, and because it was more convenient than stashing him in one of the tourist traps, she planned to book him at Hotel Walker, her grandparents' house.

She had figured that a stranger from D.C. might enjoy soaking up a little Cherokee culture while he was here. She hadn't known ahead of time that he probably was already steeped to the eyeballs in it. Who would have thought they would send an Indian?

That was okay, though. She would pass it off as hospitality of the People. No way he could refuse that.

* * *

Clay found Lisa Yellowhorse to be a plain woman, round-faced and a bit sullen. She wore a mismatched shirt and slacks, a pair of tube socks that had seen better days and no shoes. She had obviously been in the process of braiding her hair after a shampoo; he caught the scent of apples wafting from it. She greeted them cordially and offered them a chair.

She was a practical woman who made her living renting out the upstairs rooms and the basement apartment of the old clapboard her mother had purchased twenty years ago. Clay wondered whether she was the type to take up with a man like James Hightower, and, if she had, was she vindictive enough to frame him for something after a breakup? That scenario didn't seem likely, but he wasn't discounting it yet.

Ms. Yellowhorse proceeded to describe her reasons for calling Vanessa. Small bits of what appeared to be detonation cord and other discarded paraphernalia had led to her suspicions. There were empty boxes that had once contained a garage door opener and a set of screws, an empty roll of duct tape and an actual piece of fuse. You had to wonder where a woman like Yellowhorse would get this sort of stuff simply to use for a frameup. No, Clay believed she was legit and had the public's best interest in mind when she'd called this in.

The woman had called Vanessa because she was aware that Vanessa worked for the Bureau and had been instrumental in Hightower's former conviction.

"I wanted to stake out the Yellowhorse place just in case Hightower comes back, but Roan didn't think it was necessary," Vanessa said as she drove back to the main road.

"He told me what he thinks," Clay admitted. "You want to fill me in on your history with Hightower?"

"He killed my cousin."

Clay nodded. "Roan mentioned you might have a little vendetta going against Hightower because of that. Do you?"

"Well, it's not as if I know Lisa Yellowhorse well enough to conspire with her to frame James for this. If Roan seriously believed that, he wouldn't have agreed to let me investigate."

Clay noted she didn't appear to be upset by his questions, so she'd probably defended herself before on this issue.

She seemed confident. "After the bogus call that got me to the casino for the big blast and Lisa's finding the fuse pieces, things just sort of fell into place." She shot him a wry smile. "He's the one. He has no compunction about killing, I can tell you that."

"What's the story on the murder?"

She sighed, her fingers tightening on the steering wheel. "After four years of getting knocked around and refusing to report him, Brenda had reached her limit and was talking divorce. Surprise, surprise when she accidentally fell out of a raft in white water." A pause ensued as Vanessa swallowed hard, then she glanced at him with her dark eyes narrowed. "She was not wearing a life jacket. She was not dressed for rafting. She was six and a half months pregnant. What would you conclude?"

"Sounds like premeditation. First-degree homicide," Clay muttered a curse, shaking his head. "He only did four years?"

She shrugged, still gripping the steering wheel as if it were Hightower's neck. "Yeah. The D.A. went for first degree, but the jury couldn't agree on the premeditation. The thing was, she didn't die right away. Some other rafters happened along, got her out of the water and got her breathing again. But she had a head wound that put her in a coma. She stayed on life support until the doctors thought the baby could make it."

Clay didn't ask, but she answered his unspoken query.

"Little Dilly's alive and well, thriving."

"Thank God. Her name is Dilly?"

"Delinda," she explained, smiling for real now, pride showing. "Our beautiful blessing." She went on about High-tower. "The first bombing is only the beginning. James hasn't done his worst. That was just to get our attention. He's out for blood. Mine and probably others who were responsible for his conviction."

"You didn't put that in the report," Clay remarked.

"Because I only put down the facts, not supposition. Even though I know beyond a shadow who did it and why, I can't prove motive. But I *will*," she assured him.

For the first time, Clay saw the determination and drive he was looking for. Gone was the Pollyanna attitude and the youthful exuberance that had characterized her before. Here was an agent with a mission she would die to complete.

"He had the schedule for the annual Indian Fall Fair in October and a layout of the fairgrounds, Lisa said," Vanessa reminded him. The woman had dwelled on it during Clay's questioning. "Thousands attend it and they won't be spread out. Everyone I know and love is involved in one or more of the events, exhibits or concessions. For spectators, we have a festival in May," Vanessa explained. "This one is usually the first week in October and sometimes called 'the fair.' It's like a country fair, sort of, only we have many more exhibits, local crafts, fancy dances and drumming, stick ball games and so forth. It's mainly for the residents, but we do have some tourists and dignitaries."

"Should you even be on this case?" he asked.

"Why not, because I have a personal interest in nailing him to the wall? Nobody minded that we were related by marriage when I found him after Brenda's death. I took him down and I testified against him, too, for all the good it did. Four lousy years!" She huffed in disgust.

"Are there any other suspects?" he asked, wondering whether she had even considered it.

She shook her head. "Hightower's our best bet, but I'm keeping an open mind."

"Good, that's what I wanted to hear. All right, back to business. Extra guards will be hired for a round-the-clock watch on the fairgrounds for any suspicious activity. Can the local force handle that?"

"Yes, and we'll run the dogs through to sniff out any explosives before anyone's allowed in, then do gate checks."

Clay nodded his approval. "Let's get with your chief and the council, maybe round up a contractor to put in cement barriers to prevent crashing the fences with a truck bomb."

Vanessa remained quiet, but the air in the car was thick with unspoken argument.

"Okay," Clay said. "What?"

She cleared her throat and flexed her hands on the wheel as she drove. "We need to locate Hightower *before* he strikes again, not just set up to react. Word's already on the grapevine that everyone should keep an eye out for him and notify us when he's spotted. That's one great advantage to living in a community with only a few thousand people. Like *Cheers*, everybody knows your name."

"Clever, involving the citizens." Clay smiled. She was rapidly justifying a chance with COMPASS. So what if she was mouthy, nosy and had a warped sense of humor? He had put up with worse from the Sextant crew. He didn't know the members of the COMPASS team very well yet, but she'd probably fit right in.

"Hungry?" she asked, braking as they reached the paved road and waiting for his answer.

"I am. Is there somewhere around here we can grab a few burgers before you take me to my hotel?"

She put on the left blinker and began to turn. "Oh, we'll do better than that. How about barbecue, beans and fry bread? My grandparents eat at five, a blood-sugar thing, but there'll be plenty left."

Clay frowned. "That won't be necessary."

"Not feed you and put you up? What are you thinking? If I don't bring you home, the tribal council will haul me into court for sedition or something, not to mention that the grans would skin me alive." She shook her head fiercely. "Uh-uh, no way you can get off the hook, so deal with it."

"Put me up? Stay with them? No, I couldn't—"

"You don't understand. You *have* to unless, of course, you want to insult the whole tribe. And discredit yours while you're at it."

"No, *you* don't understand," he said, knowing the time had come to make things clear to her. "I don't *have* a tribe." It was true. He could not remember his mother's people and his father refused to tell him who they were. The first few years of Clay's life were a blur, spent at a place only God could identify, because Clayton Senate Sr. had gone to the grave with that secret six years ago.

She flashed a saucy grin. "Well, you have one now, brother, whether you want one or not. *Tsi lu gi.* That means *welcome.*"

Clay huffed out a breath of resignation and muttered, *"Wa do."*

"My God, you speak Tsalagi?" she asked with a laugh of delight. "You're Cherokee! Why didn't you say so?"

He didn't tell her he also knew Navajo and several other Native American tongues. He had a way with languages and these were simple to learn, a relative hobby, compared to Russian and Arabic.

Wherever you went in this business, it paid to talk the talk, or at least to be able to listen to it.

He normally kept his mouth shut and did just that, but this woman had a strange effect on him. In one afternoon, she had slipped under his guard, caused him to reveal a hell of a lot more about himself than his best friends knew, and had even made him laugh out loud.

For the first time, Clay sensed how dangerous Vanessa Walker was going to be to life as he knew it. And yet, he also realized he would not avoid her even if he could. Running scared was not his way. Father had called him a brave countless times and, while it had been meant as more insult than compliment, Clay did his damnedest to live up to the name.

Chapter 2

After driving for about half an hour, Vanessa turned off on a nearly invisible, unpaved side road that led up one of the mountains. "The grans are expecting us. I phoned them about it this morning," she explained while easily negotiating the twisting path with its overhanging branches and low visibility.

"Take me back to a hotel, will you? I really need to process these prints and fax those and Hightower's old license photo to—"

"No problem. You can fax from the grans place. They love company. Today is barbecue day. Maybe goat, maybe pork, maybe both."

Clay's apprehension grew. Primitive accommodations and food cooked over an outdoor fire didn't bother him in the least, so he didn't quite understand this niggling sense of unease in his gut.

"Don't worry. I promise you won't get the third degree.

Now you might if they got the idea I was bringing you home to get their approval as a potential husband. The tribe's pretty strict on consanguinity rules, so they'd politely insist on your background if that were the case. But I'll explain you're only here on business. I'll make that very clear."

"Consanguinity?" He knew what the word meant, of course, but what the hell was she talking about?

"Oh yeah," she said with a chuckle. "No relatives considered, goes without saying. Also, I can't marry within my own clan whether there are blood ties or not. Usually there are, to some degree, but it's not a problem."

"Yet you aren't married," he observed. "Must cut down on the number of potential candidates."

"Not really. There are seven clans to choose from. But I've never felt the urge to go looking."

"Why not?" And why did he insist on prying into her life as if it were any of his business?

She shot him a saucy look. "Ambition outweighed lust. Simple as that."

That raised his eyebrows. "A virgin, at your age?" God, he hadn't meant to say that out loud. He bit his tongue. "Sorry."

She laughed again, this time a low, seductive sound that sent a ripple of desire straight to his groin. "I never claimed *that,*" she quipped as she wheeled around a curve and pulled up in front of a two-story log house. "But they probably think so, so let's end that topic before we get out of the car."

She tooted the horn, unfastened her seat belt and opened the door all in what seemed one motion, exiting before Clay could pry any further.

Not that he would. What business of his was it if she had a lover? He didn't even want her to tell him. He'd known the woman barely half a day and had already violated every rule he'd ever made about conversations with the fairer sex.

He couldn't get over how different she was from every woman he had ever known, how off balance he felt around her. This was not good, and still he knew he would seek her out again, even if something separated them right this minute. If Mercier recalled him and ordered him never to come back here, Clay knew he would disobey orders just to see her, to explore this weird, unsettling connection or whatever it was. It made no sense at all.

"Hey, Du-da, my man! What's cooking?" Clay heard her cry as she took the stone steps two at a time. He watched as she embraced a gray-haired man who was frowning at Clay over her shoulder.

This wasn't what Clay had expected. The house impressed him with its charm, slate roof and sturdy construction. The Walkers weren't poor, that was for sure.

Wind chimes tinkled in the breeze. Oak rocking chairs and a swing graced the porch. The view up here was fantastic, the air sweet, the landscape lush even this late in the year.

The old man didn't fit Clay's preconceived image, either. Though probably pushing seventy, he looked like an aging adventurer who kept in excellent shape.

Vanessa turned and beckoned Clay up on the porch. "A-gi-du-da, this is Clay Senate, an agent from Virginia who has come to help me out on one of my cases." Her manner was polite now, bordering on formal. "Clay Senate, meet my grandfather, John Walker."

Clay extended his hand and gripped the gnarled one, several shades darker than his own. "Mr. Walker, my pleasure."

"Welcome," the man said simply. No questions, just as Vanessa had promised. Well, none yet, anyway.

"Where's E-ni-si, in the kitchen?" Vanessa asked, linking her arm with her grandfather's. The man grunted and nodded, gesturing for them to accompany him inside.

Clay held the door for both of them and entered last. Vanessa threw him a reassuring smile over her shoulder. "Smell that? Du-da's been cooking it out back in the pit for a couple of days. Mouths are watering in the next county, I bet."

The grandmother stood in the doorway of the kitchen regarding Clay with frank curiosity. She was a beautiful woman, probably around sixty-five, though her face was virtually unlined and her hair barely striped with strands of silver. This was how Vanessa would look in about forty years, Clay thought. He offered the woman his best smile.

"Clay Senate, my grandmother, Rebecca Walker," Vanessa said. "E-ni-si, Clay and I will be working at Cherokee for a week or two, at least until the festival."

"Then you both must stay here," the woman said with a decisive nod. "Please make yourself at home, Mr. Senate. We will feed you first, then my granddaughter will show you where you will sleep." Then she looked directly at her husband, a question in her eyes. The old man shook his head.

Clay assumed the unspoken query had to do with his reason for being here, that he had not come to offer for their beloved Vanessa. He experienced a surprising little stab of regret at their obvious disappointment. He seriously doubted Vanessa brought many men here, probably for that very reason.

A sharp tug on the back hem of his jacket distracted him. Clay turned slowly, expecting to see a dog. Instead it was a child. Bright brown eyes peered up at him, disappeared behind impossibly long black lashes for a blink, then reappeared. "You Daddy?" she whispered.

Clay's heart melted. He squatted to her level to answer. "No, not Daddy. My name is Clay."

She frowned. "Like red dirt?"

He smiled. "That's right."

She poked her pink-clad chest. "I'm Dilly."

He nodded. "Delinda. Like *beautiful?*"

She smiled back. "That's right."

Vanessa scooped her up in a hug and swung her around. "Hey, squirt. What's happening?"

"Bitsy had kittens. You wanna see?" She twisted in Vanessa's arms and craned her neck at an impossible angle to include Clay. "You can come, too, but you can't touch 'em."

"I promise," Clay assured her. He had never met a cat he liked and touching one was about the last thing he would want. Still, he followed Vanessa to one of the outbuildings with her little cousin riding on her shoulders, listening as they sang a silly little song about counting cats.

"She's charming," he commented to Vanessa as the little girl squatted to run her fingers over the mother cat's head. "So she lives with your grandparents?"

"Not all the time. She stays the weekends with my cousin Cody and his wife, Jan. Cody is Brenda's brother. When I take a few days off, Dilly stays with me."

"Who has custody of her?" Clay asked.

Vanessa frowned. "We do. All of us." Then she shrugged. "Oh, if you mean legally, on the books, Cody and Jan, but they both work. I guess when she starts school, she'll stay with them most of the time since they live in town. For now, though, this is a good place for her to spend the bulk of her time."

Clay could not imagine the child not having a permanent home. Strange that he should feel such an affinity for this kid, only having just met her. Maybe it was because they had something in common—mothers who had died too soon.

"She's lucky to have family," he said, wondering what it

would have been like if he had been absorbed into his mother's tribe after her death. For one thing, he probably wouldn't be feeling like such an outcast at the moment.

"Here," Dilly whispered, rubbing his hand with a tiny ball of fur. "Don't squeeze, though."

Instinctively, Clay opened his hand and accepted the tiny white kitten as she laid it in the palm of his hand. "I thought you said we couldn't touch them."

She tilted her head to one side, her small fists resting on her jean-clad hips. Then she reached up and placed her small hand on his wrist, just touching. "Me and Bitsy trust you. Put her back at her mommy's tummy when you get done. That's her dinner." In a bouncing flash of pink and denim, she skipped away and disappeared.

Vanessa relieved him of the wriggling fuzzy kitten and placed it back in the nest with the others. "I'm guessing you're *done,* Mr. Red Dirt?" she said with a laugh.

Clay brushed his hand against his coat. "I guess so. Is she always that mercurial?"

That question raised her eyebrows. "Mercurial? What a perfect description of Dilly. And most four-year-olds, come to think of it. You haven't been around kids much, have you?"

Not ever. There was the Cordas' new baby, but it was too small to be called a kid yet. It looked so fragile, he always declined to hold it when the opportunity arose. Joe and Martine might trust him with their lives on a mission, but he sort of doubted that faith extended to their infant.

He rubbed the area just below his shirt cuff that still felt the featherlight imprint of the little girl's fingers. Somehow, the child had touched more than his wrist with that gesture of her trust.

As they walked slowly back to her grandparents' house, Clay found himself wondering what the future would hold for young Delinda and whether she would ever feel stigmatized by sins of her father. Was it in anyone's power to save her from that?

The meal was superb and the food plentiful. Clay had to work hard not to overeat. The tender pork with its spicy sauce went well with what tasted like German-style potato salad and the fried, flat bread he couldn't seem to resist. He had thought the food might be totally comprised of Native American fare, but it was a delicious mix of what he was used to and what he had only heard about. Fry bread, for instance. Until today, he had made it a point never to go where they made it. Perhaps he'd had it once when he was very young and the memory was lost.

"Eat more, please. A large man needs filling." Rebecca Walker expressed her pleasure in his enjoyment of her cooking with a warm smile. "We have pie. Do you like peaches?"

"Peach is the best," Dilly declared, jumping with anticipation.

He didn't like peaches at all, but said he did just to keep the smiles going.

Mrs. Walker was so like Vanessa, but minus the almost frenetic energy, the endless pressing for information and the ready laughter of the younger woman. And the concentrated version of Vanessa that was little Dilly.

Had his mother been like Rebecca Walker? Clay hoped so, because she appeared the soul of contentment.

He finished every crumb of the pie and found it delicious. Had he only imagined an aversion to peaches? These were different, wonderful. "My compliments, Mrs. Walker," he said sincerely, placing his napkin beside his plate. "That is the best meal I've had in years."

"Years?" she repeated with a soft chuckle. "Doesn't your wife feed you well, Mr. Senate?"

He tossed Vanessa a sly look that said, *Here it comes, that third degree you promised I wouldn't get.* Out loud, to her grandmother he answered dutifully, "I'm not married. In our business, it is difficult to maintain a normal family life. We travel too often." Had the woman sensed his concealed interest in her granddaughter? He hadn't betrayed it by so much as a look in Vanessa's direction. At least not *that* sort of look.

Rebecca inclined her head and poured him another glass of iced tea. "A shame there is no one for you to come home to. Maybe someday you will find this. My husband liked the comfort of it." The old man nodded indulgently and shot his wife a knowing grin.

"You traveled a lot, sir?" Clay asked politely.

The old man nodded. "War. Then business school. I used to buy up inventory for some of the trading posts. Retired now."

Vanessa sipped her tea and expounded on her grandfather's meager answer. "He purchased lots of stuff from some of the smaller reservations out west and up north who haven't the tourist trade we have here." She smiled at her grandmother. "E-ni-si and other locals with creative talents make baskets, pottery and paintings to sell. I'll take you by the co-op shop so you can see."

"You're an artist?" Clay asked Rebecca. He could not believe how many questions he was asking. He rarely did that unless it had to do with investigations, but found himself interested enough to break a few more rules.

The grandmother ducked her head in a show of modesty. "I make baskets."

"Those ones," Dilly said after gulping her mouthful of pie. "Up there, see?" She pointed.

Clay reevaluated the row of baskets sitting along the top of the kitchen cabinets. One particularly beautiful, intricately woven example sat on the granite countertop holding a bunch of green apples. He decided he would buy one like that from her before he left. Something priceless to remember these people by.

"Well, come on with me if you've finished eating," Vanessa ordered. "We'll get your things settled in your room, then take a walk to wear off some of these calories."

She dropped a kiss on her grandmother's head as she passed by her chair. "Thank you, E-ni-si. Great meal, as always." She winked at her grandfather who solemnly winked back.

Dilly laughed with delight as she tried unsuccessfully to wink and instead, gave Vanessa a playful swat as she passed the youth's chair.

"It's bath time for you, button nose. Better be clean and have those dollies in bed by the time I come in to say night-night. There's a bedtime video in it for you if you don't flood the bathroom, okay?"

"Yes, ma'am," Dilly agreed. "Ni-si will make me behave."

Clay felt his eyes burn a little as he witnessed the open affection among these four. A pang of envy struck him like an arrow through the heart.

The child was precious, a true ray of light, and so secure in the love that surrounded her. So was Vanessa, he realized. He envied them that.

How would that feel, being accepted and loved so unconditionally? He wondered where Vanessa's parents were and if she had been raised by these two from an early age. But he wouldn't ask. Maybe some of the manners of the elder Walkers had rubbed off on him.

Vanessa's natural bearing and self-confidence attracted him almost as much as her lithe figure and her lovely, animated features. The swing of her hips wasn't meant to be enticing, but her unconsciousness of that made it all the more so. He was sweating like crazy.

He followed her out to the Explorer where they retrieved his two bags. She insisted on hefting his carry-on. She led him up the stairs to a bedroom containing a large dresser that looked handcrafted and a queen-size four-poster. It cried out for testing his weight. Along with hers. Clay sucked in a deep breath and released it with a huff of self-disgust. He had to stop this. Stop thinking about her *that* way.

"Bathroom's in there. We'll be sharing that. My room's on the other side. The grans' room is downstairs, and Dilly's, too, so you needn't worry about noise."

Noise? Oh, and didn't that just plant a vision in his head?

"No TV up here," she said, pointing, "but there's a radio with a CD player and a few CDs. Mostly flute music, I'm afraid. Cousin Eddie plays and we have to support the family endeavors."

"Flute," he repeated. Apparently he was to get a good dose of native culture whether he wanted it or not. "That's fine."

But it wasn't fine. Not the flute, the fry bread or the unfamiliar customs like tribal hospitality and ingrained politeness. He knew now why he had felt so apprehensive about coming here, aside from sharing a house with a female agent who stirred him up the way she did.

Since he could remember, Clay had flaunted his Native American heritage, though he knew very little about it. Raised by his white father, away from any vestige of his mother's culture since she had died, Clay had used his Native American looks as a form of rebellion against the man who had given him no choice about his upbringing and refused to discuss his mother or their marriage.

Clay had grown his hair long and adopted an attitude of

stoicism and silence that he knew very well was stereotypical. Early habits died hard. Even when it no longer served any purpose to provoke Clayton Senate Sr., Clay had not let up. The image had suited him. Until now.

Vanessa and her grandparents made him feel whiter than the Pillsbury Doughboy. That was what bothered him. He had no mask to hide behind when it came to these people because they knew that his mask was about as authentic as a Sioux war bonnet on a Cherokee chief. He did not want Vanessa to see him as a caricature of their people. Or rather, *her* people. He wasn't precisely sure he could, in all good conscience, claim either side of his family.

He felt a sharp need to fit in that he had not admitted to since he was eight and had realized he was rapidly forgetting what little he knew of his mother and her people. He had lost any stories, dancing, religion, belonging. His very identity.

"C'mon, let's go meet Brother Billy Bear," Vanessa said, catching his hand in hers as she strode past him to the door. "You can give him his daily Coke."

Clay followed wordlessly, afraid to ask.

Vanessa giggled shamelessly as Clay held the old soft-drink bottle she had filled with the vet's equivalent of Ensure for her grandfather's pet. Billy accepted his daily dose with a grunt, bracing the bottle between his paws and sucking down the contents with expertise.

"I'll be damned," Clay muttered as he stepped back from the fence. "Where did you get it?"

The old bear was so rheumy-eyed and arthritic he offered no threat at all, but Clay obviously was a city boy with a healthy respect for what he saw as a wild animal.

"Old Billy did his time downtown back in the day, performing for the tourists until Mack Bowstring decided to close up shop. Since Billy was my very favorite attraction, my grandfather offered the man five bucks to take the bear off his hands and give him a good home." She didn't confess that she'd been required to work off that five bucks washing and drying dishes for a month in addition to feeding Billy every day until she'd left the mountain at eighteen.

"How old is he?" Clay asked.

"Over thirty now and thirty-five's about the max for black bears."

"Better he's here than in a zoo, I guess," Clay commented.

"Definitely. He was too domesticated to release in the wild and nobody could stand to have him put down. Gran pulled some strings to get permission to keep him. Uncle Charly's a vet and keeps a close check on him."

"I take it you have a large family," Clay said as they watched Billy licking the bottle, exacting every last drop of the sweet nutritious liquid.

"Huge," she admitted. "You?"

"Not so huge. I guess you'd never want to leave here, your family, this place."

Vanessa turned, wondering why he'd ask such a thing. "I already left. I went to college, then the Academy and the job. I have an apartment in Asheville. I make it back most weekends to visit the grans. You thought I lived here?" She glanced back at the house, not minding the junky old mower, overgrown flower beds and the listing tree of gourd birdhouses. Rustic was the look and she loved it.

Clay tore his gaze from the bear and walked a few steps away, his back to her, his hands in his pockets. "I'm here to recruit you."

Vanessa stared at him, lost for words. Recruit her? For what?

As if he'd read her mind, he answered, "We're organizing

a team of agents and you've been recommended for it. COMPASS, or Comprehensive Analysis of Stateside Security is affiliated with Homeland Security and deals with terrorist threats within our borders. I'm supposed to observe how you perform, see how you'd fit, both professionally and personally. If you're not interested, I need to know."

"So you can leave and not waste your time?" Vanessa asked. She made him uncomfortable and she knew it. She hadn't made it to this age without recognizing the signs of physical attraction. She had probably been throwing out a few signals herself. He was ready to get out of here and this was his opportunity. All she had to say was no, she was not interested.

He turned, his expression unreadable. "No, I won't leave until we've concluded the investigation. The thing is, if you can't see yourself as a candidate for the team, then it's merely business as usual and I won't need to do an assessment on you."

Vanessa considered that. "Where would I have to live?"

"In McLean, Virginia. At least for the first year. There would be extra training involved, connections to make. It would mean travel, but mostly to your southern sector, with occasional calls to other areas to assist fellow agents. We follow the trouble wherever it goes. Sometimes overseas."

"I see. Is McLean where you live?"

"Yes."

"It's expensive there, isn't it?" she asked.

"More so than here." He looked off toward the mountains, her beloved Smokies. "You'd jump a couple of pay grades, get a cost-of-living increase and a hefty clothing allowance." He sighed and shrugged as if he didn't expect her to care about all that, as if he didn't himself. "Same basic benefits as you have with the Bureau. Hazardous-duty pay for certain assignments."

"Would I be the token redbird?" she asked without any bitterness. She knew all about equal-opportunity employment by the government. Had to have those minorities and women.

He smiled. "That plays into it, sure, but your qualifications weigh much more heavily in this instance. Not just any old Indian will do to meet the quota, if that's what you're asking. Nor would any female who could shoot straight and speak three languages. The requirements on paper are quite specific and you meet them. Interested?"

She paused for a full minute before she spoke. "You know some people aren't crazy about being called *Indian* anymore. Think it's not politically correct."

"Does it offend you?" he asked, really curious.

"The majority of people called *Indian* are satisfied with it. Know why?" Her dark eyes shone with mischief.

"Why's that?"

"Because the *majority* really are *from* India," she said, laughing. "Gotcha!"

"Cute. Seriously, what do you prefer? Native American? Indigenous person?"

"Cherokee works for me. I guess you have a problem there, don't you, since you don't know which tribe to claim."

"Yes, but I don't obsess over it. You know we're digressing here, and I think you're doing it on purpose. You want time to consider what the job entails, right? But you're not saying no."

She frowned as she nodded reluctantly. "I'd be a fool to say no."

"Would you?" Again he looked around them, taking in the wildness of the landscape, the beauty she usually took for granted, and drew in a deep breath, releasing it slowly. She saw this place through his eyes now. Could she leave for good?

"You're worried about living so far away from your people?" he asked.

She nodded. "A little. I feel I have a responsibility to the tribe. If I stay in Asheville, at least I can act as a liaison when something like this pops up."

His steel-gray eyes both challenged and warmed her with that piercing gaze of his. "Have you ever thought that maybe the world could be your hunting ground, the people of it, your tribe? They need you, too, Vanessa. Be a Cherokee, but be a world citizen, too. Could you handle that?"

"Interesting thought. How long do I have to consider it?" she asked. What he said intrigued her. Maybe he was right and she did need to broaden her horizons, give more than she was giving here.

"Until we finish this," he replied.

"Then I guess you'd better take some notes on me just in case," she advised. "Could be that I'm not what you're looking for after all."

"I think you're *exactly* what I'm looking for," he replied. For some reason, Vanessa thought that sounded personal. Or maybe she was just reading her own fantasies into it. This guy really was every woman's dream. Unfortunately, all she could afford to do was dream that fantasy, not act on it.

His eyes met hers, their unusual steely color warming. "You could try bribing me with another piece of that peach pie. Maybe a cup of coffee to go with it? I'd probably support you for president."

She grinned. "Whoa now! Don't tell me you're still hungry."

He nodded, smiling, though his expression faltered a bit, leaning toward sadness. His cynicism and professional distance seemed to desert him all of a sudden. He looked vulnerable to her, almost lost, before he turned away, pretending to focus on the empty birdhouses.

Vanessa could sense his hunger, but it wasn't for food. It appeared to be a soul-deep need she wasn't sure she knew how to feed, but she wished she could try. Her grandmother had warned her time and again that she took things too much to heart, that she shouldn't think she had to try to fix everything and everybody.

Maybe, like old Billy, this man just needed someone to show him they cared and that he had a place in the world. She could do that much, surely. It had worked wonders for the bear.

Chapter 3

Clay felt the change in Vanessa's attitude since telling her about his real reason for being here. It wasn't anything abrupt, just an obvious softening. He would have thought it might intensify that eagerness to please she had exhibited earlier, but somehow it had the reverse effect.

Now she seemed more at ease with him, and as if she were trying to take him under her wing or something. The odd thing was, he didn't mind.

They sat in her grandparents' den where earlier he had used the fax to send the information to McLean. The child had been in bed for hours and the older folks had retired at ten, leaving Clay and Vanessa alone.

"We'll go into town in the morning," she was saying, verifying the thought he'd just had. "You'll need to meet the chief, the council and our local force. Jurisdiction's not much of a problem, because we keep the lines of communication open."

"*Cooperation,* that's the new byword, isn't it? That's what my team is all about. We have agents from six different diciplines and so far, it has worked out to our advantage."

"Things are improving at the top levels, but also on the local scene," she said.

He leaned back in his chair and watched her dark eyes shine as she continued in earnest, obviously proud of her role in law enforcement.

She had beautiful eyes, large and black fringed, beneath perfect eyebrows. Her voice had a quality about it that fascinated him for some reason he couldn't quite explain. He could listen to her forever. Why had he ever thought she talked too much?

"Generally speaking, we go by North Carolina laws here on the boundary, but we have our own court system, our own police and everything. As I've told you, I spoke with the chief already and touched base with the sheriff. But even though you and I are already on it and will handle it anyway, protocol dictates that we be invited to run this investigation. It's a formality I think we should observe."

Clay nodded, attempting again to focus his attention more closely on her words instead of her mouth. It was bow-shaped, naturally rosier than her skin, not too full or bee-stung, but refined, sort of ethereal. Malleable. Kissable. With a sharp shake of his head, he yanked his thoughts back to the business at hand. "It will be your op, Vanessa, but I agree. You should go by the rules, even the unwritten ones, whenever possible."

And so should he. Especially that one about not coming on to fellow agents, Clay decided.

He had a great deal of respect for her already. She was determined to share all she knew in order to help him understand how things were done here. Listening to her and getting her personal perspective sure beat having to research all of that.

She should be the one to set things up, show him how she interacted with local law enforcement, which she would certainly get plenty of if she took the job with COMPASS. Cooperation was the cornerstone of success in a multilevel investigation.

Along with the politics, she continued to salt in local customs and unwritten rules the Eastern Band lived by. She bragged about the tribe's success in establishing the current constitution, their thriving new compost business and the added revenues from Harrah's casino. A woman so proud of her community, she glowed with it.

"And that," she said, clapping her hands once as she leaned forward, facing him over the ottoman, "is enough of local history for now."

Clay leaned forward, too. And he kissed her.

Surprised at first, she stilled, then slowly began to participate. Her lips tasted exactly the way he'd expected, soft and generous, flavored with peaches, which he now loved, and hot, sweet coffee.

For all of two blissful seconds, she responded, opening to him like a flower to rain. Suddenly she backed off, breaking the kiss, her dark eyes wide.

"I didn't mean to do that," she rushed to say, touching her fingertips to her bottom lip. "Really!"

"You didn't do anything," Clay said with a gusty sigh of regret. "I did." He sat back, hands carefully clasped in his lap. He wished he'd grabbed a sofa cushion to better hide the evidence of his feelings. "And I didn't mean to, either. I apologize, Vanessa. It was…just an impulse. A mistake."

"Yeah, huge error," she breathed. "We'd better not do it again, huh?"

Clay released a self-deprecating chuckle and shook his head. "No, unfortunately. Better not."

She scooted back in her chair and tucked her feet under her. "If I kissed you—seriously, I mean—you might think I was trying to persuade you to choose me for that team of yours."

"No, I wouldn't. But you could think I was offering the job in exchange for sexual favors. Which I am definitely *not* doing," he added with emphasis.

"No sex on the table, huh? Well, flattering to know the thought occurred to you somewhere along the way. But you're right." Her lips turned up at the corners. "Boy, we sure know how to gum up a situation, don't we?" She sighed. "Okay. No kissing. No sex. We should just forget this happened."

Fat chance of that. Clay could not believe what he'd done. Mercier would fire him on the spot, probably see he never worked in the field again if he found out about this. But he then remembered how Mercier had met his wife on an op in France. That was different, though. Solange had been a civilian.

Same deal with Joe and Martine Corda. Then there were Holly and Will Griffin, who actually were fellow agents and partners on some assignments. Their getting together had almost caused a serious flap and they still had problems to iron out because of it. No, no good precedent in favor of his pursuing Vanessa Walker existed. He had to leave her alone. Besides, he wasn't looking for a relationship. Never had, really. Bad time to start.

His own composure was so rattled right now, he had the urge to run out of here and down the mountain as if his pants were on fire. In fact, that was close to the truth. But despite the wrongness of it all, he wanted nothing more than to crawl across that damn ottoman and kiss her again, harder, longer and without stopping.

"Well, I guess I'll say good-night now," she said, hopping up from the chair and pulling the lapels of her jacket together. But not before Clay saw the beads of her nipples, erect as they could be, showing through her shirt and bra. No way he could hide his response to her. So with as much aplomb as he could muster, and without standing, he simply said, "Good night, Vanessa."

Clay's cell phone chirped at five o'clock in the morning, waking him. He fumbled around on the nightstand for it and answered. It was Mercier. "Don't you ever sleep?" Clay asked, rubbing his eyes. "What's so urgent?"

Ten minutes later he was dressed and knocking softly on Vanessa's door. When she opened it, he almost forgot why he was there. He watched, breathless, as she hitched the thin strap of her nightgown back onto her smooth, bare shoulder and raked a wealth of silky black hair off her brow. Her dark eyes were slumberous and a little unfocused.

"Clay?" she murmured, "Anything wrong?"

He cleared his throat and looked past her into the room, trying to regain his equilibrium. "I got a call from my office. About Hightower." Clay put his hand on her arm, touching her before he thought about it. "He's former military, you knew that, right?"

She frowned and stepped away from his touch, raking both hands through her hair and fanning it out around her shoulders. "Sure, he went in the army right out of high school."

"Guess what he did while in the service," Clay said rhetorically, then answered, "EOD."

Her gaze locked on his. "Explosive Ordnance? That I didn't know. I thought he was a ground-pounder."

"Apparently he knows his stuff. Not the amateur I wish he was," Clay admitted.

Clay braced his hands on the door frame, needing the support to remind him not to take her in his arms to reassure her. She was a woman, yes, but a professional in law enforcement, one whose strengths he was supposed to be evaluating, not shoring up.

He spelled out his greatest concern. "There was a reported theft last month, a shipment of C-4 used in training exercises at the EOD school over in Alabama. No viable suspects until now. Hightower trained there and would have known the probable location of the substance and how to gain access to it."

She nodded slowly. "So he's saving the good stuff for the big bang. The little homemade device with the dynamite was only the prelude."

He gave the only answer that made any sense. "He's probably got things wired to blow that we haven't even thought about yet. He has a boatload of this stuff, Vanessa. He could blow this whole county off the map, little by little or all at once."

She looked so small and vulnerable. And way too sexy. "I bet he wants the judge, jury and everyone else who had a hand in punishing him." Her shoulders drooped, causing the gown to slip dangerously low.

Clay cleared his throat and tried to look away. His eyes just wouldn't cooperate. She quickly caught up the front of her nightgown in a fist. "So get out of here and let me get dressed. We've got to go find the bastard and take him down."

Clay reached to close the door even though she had already turned and was striding to her walk-in closet. "I'll meet you downstairs."

In the mirror of her dresser, he caught her reflection. Her back was to him and she had already shucked her gown. The glimpse of her totally naked, pale light from the window bathing her in its soft glow, nearly did him in. With a major effort, he pulled the door shut and closed off the sight.

Rubbing a hand harshly over his face, Clay attempted to

erase the tactile memory of her lips on his, the vision of her nude and the raspy sound of her sleepy voice when she had murmured his name. Waking dreams weren't that easy to banish.

The real nightmare they faced ought to do it, but it didn't.

Two hours later, Clay stood in the background and remained silent while Vanessa spoke with the Eastern Band chief, the sheriff and three deputies.

He noted how she laid out her plans for the bomb search as if they were only suggestions, then carefully listened to everyone who wanted to give input. She nodded and made changes on her notes.

"You are certain James Hightower is the man responsible?" the sheriff asked.

"No proof yet, sir," she answered. "But he is the most viable suspect at this point. We need to find and interview him at any rate."

He detected no patronization on either her part, due to the fact that she was FBI, or on theirs, because most were her elders and had probably known her as a child. Her quiet deference surprised him a little. Their obvious respect for her did, too. This was a matriarchal society, but guys the world over were well-known for wanting to control the ball no matter what history dictated.

"Vanessa's blessed," a quiet voice said in a confidential whisper. Clay turned slightly and saw the stern visage of Lance Biggins, one of the senior deputies who stood beside him at the back of the room.

"How so?" Clay asked.

"Look at her," Biggins suggested. "We haven't seen a woman like her since Nancy Ward."

Clay was familiar with the tales surrounding the Cherokee

heroine from the early nineteenth century who'd taken up arms for the People. "That's some comparison," he commented.

"Yeah, Van's quite a girl. Even back in grade school, nobody messed with her. She'd kick your butt in a heartbeat."

Clay smiled. Apparently, the deputy was still nurturing a schoolboy crush combined with a heavy dose of heroine worship. "I hear she still kicks."

Biggins nodded, pursing his lips. He looked straight at Clay then with a warning in his jet-black eyes. "So don't mess with her. Okay?"

Clay turned back to watch Vanessa and decided not to answer. He had already sort of messed with her and maybe he needed a butt-kicking for it, but it wouldn't be by this guy.

He understood Biggins's protective urge, though. Clay felt the same way about her and imagined most men did, especially those she was conversing with right now.

They might look on her as blessed somehow, given the number of her recent narrow escapes, but no one discounted the possibility that she might take one chance too many and the gods would cease to smile.

Vanessa continued with her proposal for the manhunt. Clay noted the sheriff's reluctance to commit all his resources to searching for Hightower. His response to Vanessa's suggestions was cool. He didn't argue, but he didn't agree, either.

Clay sauntered to the front where Vanessa and the sheriff were standing, going over the plans. "You have doubts, sir?" Clay asked, since Vanessa was barreling ahead with her orders as if she had full backing already.

The dark, fathomless eyes of the older man examined Clay's curious expression, probably for any antipathy. Clay felt none of that. The sheriff seemed capable enough, just hesitant. Vanessa paused, too, when Clay asked the question. Both waited for the sheriff to speak.

He took his time, worried his upper lip with one finger for a minute, then shook it at Vanessa. "You were responsible for Hightower's arrest before. We know he got much less time than you thought he deserved for what he did. Now you seem to have convicted him of these bombings already. Suppose he's not the one you should be after."

Vanessa blew out a breath of frustration, then shook her head. "Sheriff, I *know* he's the one. Who else would be doing this?"

"There were a couple of guests at the casino who might have been targets that had nothing to do with Hightower. As a matter of fact, we know they are loosely tied to organized crime here in the South. I think they were hoping to muscle in on our action, or at least check it out to see if it was worth their while. They certainly have enemies within their organizations. I asked your people to pursue that line of investigation since it falls within the Bureau's domain."

"That's in the works," she assured him. "But it's considered a real long shot, Sheriff. I'm telling you, James Hightower has plenty of reason to do something like this and he did. I'm sure of it."

The sheriff pursed his lips and inclined his head. "Okay, I'll give you the manpower to do the search, but let's try to keep an open mind. Hightower's got no business being back here on the Boundary anyway, but unless you can prove he's committed some crime, all we can do is send him packing. Even that will take some doing."

Clay could see Vanessa working up to an argument and quickly intervened before she could let it fly. "Thank you, Sheriff, that will be fine. Just catch him and let us question him. We'll take it from there."

The sheriff raised a dark brow and gave Clay another once-over. "You are convinced he's our man? Do you have some information you haven't shared?"

"No," Clay admitted, "but Agent Walker's concerns seem legitimate to me. We need to find this man and we need your help."

He nodded. "All right, but I can't commit every man available. I'll give you six deputies and three cars."

Vanessa looked outraged, but she knew when to hold her tongue. She realized that was as much cooperation as she was going to get. Clay added prudence and self-control to her attributes and would mention those in his report on her to Mercier. She also knew how to make do.

It was sometimes necessary in the business to work with what you had and make the most of it. Bureaucracy and limited manpower and funding often altered an operation and agents had to adjust and compensate for that.

"Thank you, Sheriff," she said, schooling her features into a more pleasant expression. "We appreciate it."

Clay wanted to reassure her. He kept getting the urge to do that for some reason. Why? She was just as capable of understanding all the ramifications of this op as he was. Why was he seeing vulnerability in her that probably didn't even exist?

She began laying out a plan for the use of the limited resources available to her.

If he had his way, she would become a great addition to COMPASS, and Mercier would be thanking Clay for his assessment before James Hightower even came to trial. And he would, Clay thought. Vanessa would get her man one way or another. For what it was worth, her gut hunch about Hightower seemed right on the money to him.

He just hoped for all he was worth that personal prejudice wasn't creeping into his evaluation of Vanessa. The pride he felt in her didn't seem wholly of the professional variety and it bothered him more than he wanted to admit. He truly liked her as a person and that was okay. But he was also power-fully attracted to her as a woman. And that was not okay. He would need to ignore that. If he could.

She nodded to the sheriff and the others who were present, thanked them again, then closed her notebook. "Okay, that does it. Sheriff, if you will divide up the search teams and assign areas to be canvassed, I'd appreciate it." She turned to Clay. "You and I are on the radio and will act as control. That okay with you?"

Clay shrugged and followed her out the door, closing it behind them. "It's your op. I'm just here to advise and lend a hand."

"And grade me," she added with a wry grin. "They're setting up a small conference room over at City Hall for a command post. I asked one of the deputies to outfit it with maps, get a copy of James's trial transcript and mark where his possible targets live and work. The EOD and other visiting personnel can use the place to coordinate."

"A-plus, so far," Clay told her. "I like the way you handled everything, how you interface with local authorities."

She rolled her eyes. "I wasn't handling *them* if that's what you think. They're wise people with good ideas. It pays to listen and learn, even when you don't fully agree. I do wish the sheriff had bought into this a little more, however. We're going to be stretched pretty thin."

"You show respect where it's due," he said with a smile. "I like that."

She replied with a succinct bob of her head. "Now, if you want, I'll take you to Karen's Kitchen and we'll get some breakfast. I'm starved."

He followed her out to the car and got in. "Don't tell me. Karen's another cousin of yours?"

She hopped in the driver's side and slammed the door. "Nope, but she cooks the best hominy you ever had."

"Hominy? Is that like grits?" Clay wasn't sure he wanted a taste of that, but Van hadn't led him wrong so far when it came to food. "I'm going to need some way to work out," he told her. "If I don't watch it, I'll soon be too overweight to keep up with you."

"We'll run off some calories this evening," she promised, wheeling the Explorer to the left and crossing the bridge to the other side of town. "Nothing like hauling it around a mountain for about five miles to keep trim."

"Five miles?" He wanted to wheeze already. Because of his Seattle assignment, it had been over a week since his last run and he felt out of shape.

"Don't tell me you're a candy-ass, Senate," she teased, laughter sparkling in her dark eyes as she looked over at him. "I had you pegged for going at it nonstop until I cried for mercy."

He rolled his eyes and sighed at the picture her words painted. He surely didn't need *that* image in his head.

"About the grits or whatever it is," he muttered, trying to change the subject before he betrayed what he was imagining. "What else is on the menu?"

She laughed merrily and wheeled into the parking lot of a glass-fronted diner. With a flourish, she pushed the gearshift into park and sat back, looking at him with an impish expression. "C'mon, man, where's your sense of adventure?"

"Okay, okay, I'm working up to it," he said, feigning resignation. He liked it when she snickered. Or when she frowned. Or when she looked pensive or delighted or disgusted or uncertain.

Lord, he was in trouble and hadn't a clue how to avoid the train wreck that was certain to happen when they both stopped fighting whatever this was arcing between them like summer lightning.

* * *

The search that day netted nothing. Clay had hoped against hope they would find Hightower, he would confess and this would be over. Then he could go back to McLean and give his report. If he stayed much longer, he knew there would be trouble that had nothing to do with the job. And everything to do with it.

The Walkers made him feel welcome that evening, treating him exactly as they would a member of the family instead of a guest. They obviously didn't know any other way. He ran with Vanessa, marveling at her endurance. How could she look so damn fragile and possess such strength? She just fascinated the hell out of him, though he was careful not to show it in any way. But his dreams that night drove him crazy.

When morning came, he found himself in the midst of a family gathering that started immediately after breakfast and looked as if it might last all day.

Clay stood on the back deck of the Walkers' home feeling totally out of place. The house and yard had filled with family. They were celebrating a month's worth of birthdays all at once. Apparently, this was a tradition. He had counted three cakes on the kitchen table before he'd been gently ousted by the women and herded outside.

Poor Vanessa seemed to be everywhere at once, looking harried but happy. She looked about fifteen in her low-slung jeans, orange tank top and short denim jacket. Her long dark hair, usually confined in that sedate little bun, was caught up in a ponytail today.

Clay had watched her dart across the yard hauling a tray of meat for her grandfather to put on his grill, then dash back inside to help her grandmother and the other women.

She had been pausing frequently, as she was doing right now, to carry on cell-phone conversations with the search teams looking for Hightower and the explosives. She frowned as she tucked the phone back into her jacket pocket and hurried over to him for the current report.

"Still nothing," she told him. "You know what I think?"

"That he's deliberately waiting until the last minute?" Clay guessed.

She drew her dark brows together. "You think so, too?"

Clay shrugged. "In his place, that's what I would do. Wait until everybody stops looking. By that time, you won't have much credibility left with the locals. He's letting you cry wolf."

She pounded a fist in her palm. "Dammit, I'm playing right into his hands. But how can I *not* order searches when we know he's got the C-4? There are so many places he could plant it. The concessions, the exhibits, even turtle-shell rattles carried by the dancers! Who knows where he'll choose?"

"Want a suggestion?" Clay asked, planning to give it anyway.

She nodded enthusiastically since she wasn't a prima donna who insisted on calling all the shots. He really appreciated a woman who was willing to listen.

"Use the Explosive Ordinance Disposal teams to search the vehicles, homes and workplaces of those involved in his trial and conviction. He'll set those first. Do the fair only after everything's set up and ready to go."

"That's pretty much what they're doing now, except that I asked them to go ahead and clear the bleachers." She shifted from one foot to the other, obviously antsy. "I should be over there, doing something myself." She threw up her hands in frustration.

"Not today. Not unless they find something." Clay handed her a soft drink from the cooler on the deck. "Here. If you hover, they'll be insulted and feel like you think they don't know what they're doing."

She was already nodding, muttering the word *delegate*

to herself. Clay smiled, knowing that was her weakest point, the ability to relinquish even a little control. But she was working on it.

Her cousin, Cody, wandered over. "What are you two looking so grim about? Am I interrupting something?"

"You *live* to interrupt things," Vanessa teased. Laughing slyly, she poked his concave chest with her finger. "Look at him. He's got a coyote-mischief look on his face, doesn't he? That wicked, sneaky little look!" She poked him again, harder, then handed Clay her drink can. "I can still take you, cuz. Show me what you got!" She backed off and beckoned, taunting him. "Scared of little girls, cuz…zin?"

To Clay's surprise, Cody rushed her. She grabbed his arm and, using his momentum, flipped him neatly onto the grass. He rolled to his feet growling in mock anger and rushed her again. They fell in a heap, laughing like loons.

Clay cleared his throat and looked away, checking to see what her grandfather and the others milling about the yard thought of the horseplay. He didn't much like it himself. Undignified, he thought. Then he wondered if that was really what he thought. Maybe he just didn't like seeing her make physical contact with another guy, especially one who seemed to be enjoying it so much.

Cody Walker was whipcord lean, not much taller than Vanessa and they were pretty well matched physically. Still, Clay didn't like how the man had grabbed for her as if he meant business. Twice. Because of his own size, Clay was used to pulling his punches when he trained with women. He avoided doing so whenever possible.

"How about you, cowboy?" she asked him, jumping to her feet, dusting the grass off her jeans. "How's your hand-to-hand?"

Clay pursed his lips and raised an eyebrow as he assessed her size. "I'll pass. It wouldn't be much of a contest."

"Ah, come on, scaredy-cat. Give it your best shot," she said. "Afraid to get those new jeans dirty? Or are you afraid I'll hurt you?" She was biting her bottom lip and grinning. "You lead such a sedentary life, Senate! How do you keep your job?"

Clay grabbed for her, intending to toss her over his shoulder and show her how easily he could overpower and sweep her off her feet.

She ducked, whirled one leg, hit the backs of his knees and, in a blink, was on top of him with the heel of her hand right under his nose. With a sharp shove, she could have easily embedded the bones of it into his brain. He looked up at her and smiled. "Uncle."

With a roll of her eyes, she got up. "Well, you're no fun at all!" She shook her head in disgust. "And I am not paying any taxes ever again if you're the best the government can hire."

They had drawn quite a crowd. A snickering, pointing crowd. Clay thought maybe he'd better get into the spirit of the thing before he dishonored male agents everywhere.

He slowly rose to his feet, gave her fair warning, then went for her again. This time, he figured precisely what she would do, blocked her move and had her over his shoulder in less than a second. She cried out as if wounded. Clay quickly set her on her feet to see if he had really hurt her and found himself flat on his back before he knew what had happened.

She pranced comically around the yard, preening in her victory, bowing low to the boos and cries of "Unfair!"

Clay was laughing at her antics along with the others, not minding at all that his jeans were grass-stained and the sleeve of his shirt was ripped. "This is worse than touch football," he complained.

"Football?" she asked, then turned to the others. "This boy hasn't seen a ball game yet, has he, folks? Want to show him a little stickball?"

"No, thank you!" Clay exclaimed. "My dignity has suffered enough today." He had no desire to strip down to his shorts, fight over a ball hardly big enough to see and get his brains dashed in with a stick. He had seen the game played and it made football look as tame as croquet.

Their audience dispersed, drifting off to play their own games now that the show was over. Vanessa grabbed her drink off the edge of the deck and took a hefty draft.

"Yeah, you do strike me as a tennis sort of guy," she said then, affecting an uppercrust accent and showing him a prissy expression of distaste.

"And you strike me as a bloodthirsty little savage." Too late, he realized she might construe that as a racial slur. "Wait, I didn't mean that the way it sounded."

She frowned for a second. "I guess I had it coming, didn't I?" Then she smiled. "Sorry about the tennis crack. That was a lie."

"Do you lie a lot?" he asked, hoping to lighten the conversation or at least change the subject.

"Not much," she said thoughtfully. "Do you?"

"Often and well," he admitted ruefully. "On my last op, I presented myself as a Middle Eastern bodyguard. Once I even passed myself off as a prince."

She cocked her head and studied him for a minute. "Yeah, I can see how you might. You can be such a *royal* pain."

Clay suffered a stab of hurt. "I can?"

"Oh, good lord, Senate! I was *joking!* Don't you ever tease? A minute ago I thought you were with that lying thing. You had it going pretty good there and I thought there might be hope for you, but I don't know…" She started shaking her head. "So literal. So *serious!*"

"I joke," Clay declared, frowning down at her.

"You lie," she accused, looking a little sad for him. "And sometimes you don't do it as well as you think."

Clay knew she was right. He had very little in the way of a sense of humor. Sometimes he envied the others he worked with, especially Eric and Joe, when they started horsing around. Maybe it wasn't something that could be learned, but was inborn.

He looked at Vanessa's family, talking and laughing with one another, and wondered if living in large groups developed that sense of play.

She had done her best to include him in it, though. That was something. He had played a little and he had liked it. Maybe it could be learned. He offered her a smile of thanks and loved the way she winked back and toasted him with her drink. Was there another woman like her in the world? He wondered.

The next morning they had barely finished breakfast when her cell phone erupted with Beethoven's Fifth. "Walker here. What have you got?"

"A possible sighting of the suspect over near Cade's Cove," the voice responded.

"We're rolling. ETA, seventeen minutes."

They made it in fifteen. Two uniformed officers stood by the squad car speaking to a tall lean man who was pointing and gesturing. Van hustled to join them and Clay followed.

"It was like he knew I'd be here and wanted me to see him," the witness declared, flapping one long hand at the small village set up to simulate for tourists what life had been like when the cove had first been settled. "He went in one of the cabins, stayed a few minutes, came out and then drove off in an old black pickup. Went north."

Vanessa included Clay in the conversation by introducing

the witness. "This is Cleve Little. He works here in the cove doing maintenance. Hightower knows him, knew he would be here, wanted to be seen." She turned to the officers. "Order all visitors out of the cove, rope off the parking lot and put up a closed sign," she said in a clipped voice and watched one of the cops take off immediately to do that.

Then she addressed the witness again. "Cleve, you know for *sure* it was James?" Van asked.

The man nodded. "Sure I'm sure. That's why I called the station. Heard you were looking for him. Shame about him killing Brenda. Wish I'd a been on that jury."

"Thanks, Cleve," Vanessa said, giving the man a reassuring pat on his arm. "Did you get the tag?" She smiled her approval when he rattled off the number and made a note of it while the local officer did the same.

She was a toucher. Liked to make a connection with whomever she was talking to. Clay wasn't sure he approved of that, but he had to admit it probably encouraged better results than he ever obtained with intimidation.

He ought to include her penchant for familiarity in his report to Mercier. However, he had to consider that she knew these people. They were her friends, people she had grown up knowing. Still, she had touched *him,* too, when she hadn't known him from Adam.

Her brisk tone interrupted his thoughts. "Soon as they arrive, let's get the EOD guys to that cabin and check it for explosives.

"Come on," she said to Clay and headed back to the car.

"What's the plan? We giving chase?"

She shook her head. "He has too great a head start. With all the side roads, James could be anywhere in the mountains by now and there are scads of places to hide the truck."

Clay silently applauded her focus, ability to form quick decisions and her willingness to delegate. Definitely a team player, but possessing good leadership qualities, too. Vanessa seemed the perfect candidate for COMPASS.

She more than met the eye, that was for sure. Her pal in uniform had been correct, she had an indefinable quality about her that made her seem somehow "blessed."

Clay was not a toucher, that just wasn't his way, so it really struck him as odd the way he really needed to touch her now.

Without dwelling on it, he reached out tentatively and placed his hand over the one she rested on the knob of the gearshift. He gave it a light squeeze.

She took her eyes off the road long enough to shoot him a look of surprise and a soft little smile. "What?"

Clay quickly looked away and slowly moved his hand off hers. "Nothing," he replied, blowing out the breath that had caught in his throat.

She chuckled, a sweet seductive sound coming from her. "Okay."

He felt ridiculous, exposed, but strangely gratified at the same time. She knew he'd lied when he'd said it was nothing.

He wanted to classify that uncharacteristic gesture as professional, the reassurance of one partner for the other. Respect. Encouragement. Admiration.

Hell, who was he trying to kid? "You did just fine back there, the way you called the shots. Everything right by the book."

She sighed, her smile dimming a little. "Thanks. I guess I forgot you were observing my performance of duties. It wasn't for show."

"I know that. You took care of business without second-guessing yourself. That's how it should go. As I said, I'm just here to watch, and assist if you need me."

"If I need you…" she repeated under her breath, then shook her head and laughed wryly. She made a left into the parking area of the precinct.

Clay turned his head and met her gaze as she braked and slipped the gear into park. He didn't even want to guess what she was thinking. The look in her eyes spoke of something a hell of a lot more explosive than the C-4 Hightower had stolen.

By mutual, unspoken agreement, they abandoned that subject of need then and there. He figured it would come up again, probably like clockwork, until this operation was over.

Chapter 4

The phone call from Mike came less than an hour later. Vanessa and Clay were in the chief's office going over Hightower's arrest records while waiting for search results.

"They've cleared everything." Vanessa pondered what other locations Hightower might have wired. "I wonder why he was there? And why he made sure Cleve saw him."

"Maybe he was leaving a subtle message."

"Right. He's saying *Look what I can do and you can't stop me.* Setting off a bomb there would have cut down considerably on tourism and hurt the economy. The casino bombing has had an effect, but most everyone thought it was a random act, or that it was planted by someone with a grudge against gambling or something. I think he's going to go after the community now. Did I mention he's banned, not supposed to return here because of his crime?"

"You mentioned it briefly. Is that standard?"

"Pretty much for any crime that a perp might repeat. He's half Cherokee and was raised here. I guess he feels he's being denied something he's entitled to. He's not entitled, of course. You do a certain crime, you get punished, then banished." Yet there was not much the police could do to enforce it other than apprehend the violator and escort him out of the Boundary.

"What's in the works concerning protection of the individuals involved in his apprehension and conviction?"

"I arranged for protection," she assured him. "Well, except for me."

"You think he'll go after you personally?"

"I'm sort of hoping he will," she said with a grin.

"Don't even joke about that," Clay ordered, his tone of voice sharp. "What about little Dilly?"

Vanessa shrugged. "James has never shown the slightest hint of interest in his daughter, never seen her or even asked to. But maybe I should ask a couple of guys to keep an additional watch on her when I'm not around."

"Won't the force searching for the explosives be stretched pretty thin with all the protection surveillance necessary?" Clay asked.

"These aren't cops. We're a close community here. We look out for one another."

"You're involving civilians?" Clay demanded. "You know that's—"

"Necessary in this case," she informed him just as curtly. "The chief deputized everyone who had the right experience to deal with something like this. We've got ex-military, retired law enforcement and so forth. They know the town and sur-rounding areas. If we borrowed officers from outside the Boundary, they'd be virtually useless."

"Good point," he said. "And just for the record, I've got your back."

"I know." Vanessa scooped up her phone and car keys and slung her purse over her shoulder. "Let's get out of here for a while. I'll show you around town. You might as well get familiar with the landscape, what there is of it."

She drove by the museum, offering to give him an inside tour. "I worked there one summer."

"That's all right. I'm not much for museums," he said, declining.

She pulled in the parking lot anyway. "Well, I need to check in with them, see of anyone's seen James," Vanessa told him.

"Why? How likely is it he would take a tour of the museum?"

Vanessa looked at the building, the pride of the community, the tribe. It held their history, the record of their culture, priceless artifacts. "If he wants to deal us a blow, this would be the place. And there are any number of places to stash a bomb. It won't hurt to have a look around."

Clay nodded, still appearing reluctant to accompany her inside. Vanessa couldn't understand his reticence, but figured it had to do with something in his past.

"Let's go then," he said, unbuckling his seat belt. He got out, adjusted his tie and buttoned one button of his jacket. For the first time, she thought he looked a little self-conscious.

She led the way in and smiled a greeting to Jolly, who was selling tickets. "Hey, how's your mama?" she asked.

"Arthritis is acting up, but she's still going like a house afire. What's up, Vanessa?"

She turned to Clay. "This is Agent Senate. We're on the lookout for James Hightower. Wondered if he had been around here lately."

Jolly nodded and shot Clay a speculative look. "Nice to meet you. What's Hightower done now?"

Vanessa didn't want to panic Jolly and the rest of the

employees by mentioning a bomb. "Just need to talk to him. Who else is around today?"

"Clerks in the gift shop," he said, inclining his head to the brightly lit set of rooms that held the souvenirs and books. "Only one docent, Mollie Osprey. She's somewhere in the back if you want to talk to her."

Vanessa stuffed a twenty in the donations glass and beckoned over her shoulder for Clay to come along.

She detoured through the shop and spoke with the two clerks working there, then took Clay on the set route through the museum. She noted every nook and cranny that might afford a hiding place for a bomb. There were too many to list, unfortunately. She would have to send in a team to do a thorough search.

Clay lingered at the pottery, studying the glassed displays with a keen eye. Trying to recognize patterns? she wondered. The costume exhibit seemed to fascinate him, so she slowed as they passed through it. When they got to the language bay, he hesitated, then lifted a set of earphones and put them on.

Vanessa smiled to herself, imagining how the soft, sibilant sounds of her native tongue sounded to him. She loved to listen. Almost no one spoke the old language fluently enough to use it in everyday conversation anymore. It was making a comeback, though, in the schools. At least it wouldn't be lost forever.

She saw Mollie and held up a hand in greeting. The girl was the daughter of one of Vanessa's grade-school teachers. At nineteen, Mollie Osprey represented all that was beautiful about their people, both in looks and attitude. She and Vanessa had had many talks about the possibilities for Mollie's future. Vanessa liked to think she had a little to do with the younger woman receiving a scholarship in history from the University. "How's school, kiddo?"

"Fine, thanks," Mollie told her, sliding a curious glance at

Clay, who was still listening to the earphones. "Looks like you're doing okay, too." She mouthed, "He's hot! Who is he?"

Vanessa laughed. "Down girl. That's Clay Senate, agent from D.C. who's helping me out on a case. We just dropped in to see if anyone's seen James Hightower around here."

Mollie frowned. She was a little young to have followed the case when James had been sent away and probably didn't even know the man by sight. Then her lips rounded and she nodded. "The one who was married to your cousin, right? I don't know what he looks like. You think he's going to come around and cause trouble?"

"Could be," Vanessa admitted. "If I get you a photo, will you pass it around and let me know if anyone's seen him? And if he turns up, I need to know about it immediately."

"Can do. Gosh, I never thought I'd get to help out in a real investigation. That's what this is, isn't it?" Again, she glanced at Clay.

"You bet." She gave Mollie's arm a pat. "Thanks. Come on over and I'll introduce you to the guy since you can't keep your eyes off him. He's too old for you, though."

"Not for you. I say go for it," Mollie teased.

Vanessa laughed, but secretly wished she could *go for it*.

Mollie didn't help matters. After the introduction, she sang Vanessa's praises to the skies, crediting her with single-handedly orchestrating Mollie's higher education and inspiring her by example. Clay must have been wondering how much Vanessa had offered to pay the girl for the character reference.

Later, when they left the museum, Clay remained quiet, thoughtful, maybe even a little disturbed.

She pointed out some of her grandmother's baskets in the window of the culture center across the street where arts and crafts of the locals held the spotlight. He nodded, gave the objects a cursory glance, then suggested they go to the stadium where the fair would be held.

"How about some free tickets to see *Unto These Hills?* That's the play, the story of the People. Season's over for this year, but you could come back in the spring when we resume. I had a role when I was in high school."

"Thanks, but I can't make plans that far in advance. Could be out of the country. Anyway, I'm well acquainted with the history of the Removal."

Why did he continue to act so disinterested in any symbols of their culture? Vanessa wondered. She would think he'd want to explore it a little more, given that he'd been raised as white. "What's the matter, Clay? Afraid you'll trip over something familiar?"

He met her eyes as she stopped at the red light. "I know how proud you are of your heritage," he said, his voice gentle. "Maybe it's just that I'm a little envious."

"Maybe so," she said. "But don't say I didn't offer to share."

He gave her a smile that looked a little too practiced. "Face it, I'm a loner by nature and I like it that way."

No, he didn't like it, she thought. He *suffered* it. Maybe she should leave well enough alone. But she knew she couldn't.

Clay knew he had insulted her, though he hadn't meant it that way. He only wanted to avoid getting caught up in the community. He wasn't geared for it, and he would be expected to give something in return. Unfortunately, he had nothing to offer.

He had no political pull in Washington that would benefit the People. He had no right to expect any woman, especially one with such close family ties, to enter into a relationship with him when he wasn't even sure who or what he really was.

Besides, Vanessa definitely was not his type. He invariably

chose women who were quiet by nature, lacking in curiosity about his job or background, and sophisticated enough to be satisfied with the status quo. They demanded no more than he offered, which was never more than a mutually satisfying encounter, repeated only if they didn't seem overeager for a second date. Vanessa was the absolute antithesis of all that.

So why did he want her so intensely? Why would it enter his mind to start anything with her in the first place?

And what kind of ego trip was he on that made him think she would even be interested? One kiss was not something to base that on, especially when he was the one who had initiated it.

He mentally switched off that troublesome line of thought and forced himself to think about the very real problem of the bomber. Was it James Hightower? Stood to reason it was. He had motive, the means, and was out there probably looking for more opportunity.

It shouldn't be that difficult to find him. Everyone knew the guy and was looking for him. Sooner or later, he would turn up. Like Vanessa had said, Clay hoped it was sooner, not later, for more than the obvious reasons.

"There's the casino he bombed," Vanessa said, pointing to her right. Clay observed the former crime scene as they passed by it. It wasn't Harrah's, but one of the tribal casinos built before the giant had come here to roost with its multi-storied hotel and bright lights. This was a modest, two-storied structure that was only a fraction of the size of the chain.

The damage must have been repaired already. It appeared they were doing business as usual today.

The report said the damage had been significant, mostly due to the resulting fire. The bomb itself had been small, home-made with dynamite and set with a timer. That probably meant Hightower was saving the C-4 for a bigger project. Or projects.

Surprisingly, no one had died in the casino. It had happened in the early hours of the morning when there had been few customers, all of whom had escaped right after the blast. Those trapped on the second floor in the offices and observation rooms, including Vanessa, had been most at risk.

"Whatever possessed your cousin to choose a man like Hightower to marry?"

She shrugged. "Oh, James can be charming when he puts his mind to it. And he's handsome as homemade sin, no question about that. I figure it was probably the old bad-boy thing that got her hooked."

"What do you mean exactly? I've heard of that before, but I just don't get it. A woman knows a man is trouble, but is actually attracted to that quality in him?"

"Oh yeah." She nodded, a small frown marring the smoothness of her brow. "It's an inborn need to fix them, straighten them out."

Clay couldn't suppress a laugh of disbelief. "You can't just make up your mind to *fix* a man and change him. People are what they are. They don't change. Not really."

"Bring out the better qualities in him, then," she explained. "Help him realize his full potential." She shot him a sly look. "Sort of like me, attempting to make you laugh. You hardly ever do, I bet, yet I dragged one or two chuckles out of you and you loosened up a little. Ergo, I made a small fix."

He studied her, wondering whether she was teasing him or dead serious. "You felt a need to fix *me?*"

She grinned. "Oh yeah, can't help it. You've got a bad-boy streak yourself, Senate. I think it's that scowl. Maybe the way you sort of swagger when you walk."

"Swagger?" Clay scoffed, but realized that he felt a little flattered by the thought that Vanessa considered him worth fixing. She had changed him to some degree, he had to admit that. He had never unbent enough to kiss someone he was working with. "I have never swaggered in my life."

She laughed. "Okay, I made that up. Actually you move with the grace of a dangerous cat. How's that? Everybody knows cats are bad. I could remedy that walk of yours. Teach you a little klutzy stumble."

Clay cleared his throat to hide his amusement and put on that scowl she was talking about. "We should get back over to the office and see how the search is going," he said in an attempt to direct the subject back to the investigation.

"They'll call if they find anything or he's spotted again. Did I answer your question?" she asked as she drove. "About my cousin's choice of husband, I mean?"

"She was young, impressionable and badly misled."

"And compassionate," Vanessa told him. "There's a powerful incentive to try to reform a guy. Too bad it didn't work."

The radio interrupted. Mike reported that officers questioning employees at local stores had turned up a sighting of Hightower at one of the Jiffy Marts less than an hour before he'd been seen at Cade's Cove. "He purchased gas, a case of cold drinks, candy bars, milk and a couple of boxes of cereal," the officer informed them. "And a stuffed toy."

Clay's senses tingled with apprehension. "If Hightower thinks he's so entitled to everything he's lost, he might be including fatherhood in that."

For the first time, Clay saw fear in Vanessa's eyes. She took a sharp right at the next intersection and sped up, heading in the direction of the cutoff to her grandparents' home. "Get my folks on the phone and give my grandfather a heads-up," she ordered. "Speed dial two."

"Take it easy," Clay warned when she narrowly missed clipping the bumper of a delivery truck. "Hightower's headed north. Dilly will be safe until we can get her relocated."

She flashed him a look of fright. "These roads coil around like a damn snake. He could easily get to the grans from the north side of town." She banged the heel of her hand hard on the steering wheel. "Damn! Why didn't it occur to me that James might—"

"It *did* occur to you," Clay reminded her gently. "You said yourself you warned your grandfather. He's armed and on alert. She'll be fine, Van. Now slow down before you get to that freaking section without a guardrail or we won't get there at all!"

The hair-raising ride took less than twenty minutes. Vanessa's approach was direct. She wheeled right across the front yard, braked at the steps and jumped out. Clay barely beat her to the front door. Gun drawn, he entered ahead of her without knocking.

Vanessa's grandmother appeared in the hall, clutching a dish towel to her chest. "What is it, dear? What's wrong? Why are you—"

"Where's Dilly? With Du-da?" Van demanded.

"Down at the creek fishing. Is it James? Is he coming here?" Rebecca gasped. "Oh lord!"

"Go to the cellar. Lock it and stay there until we get back," Van told her.

Clay hurried to escort the woman when she began to protest. He slid an arm around Rebecca's shoulders and guided her to the cellar door leading down from the kitchen.

"We'll be right back," he promised, offering her a hug of reassurance. Her shoulders felt fragile as she looked up at him. "We don't know that Hightower's headed this way. This is just a precaution."

The front screen had slammed and he knew Vanessa was already outside.

Rebecca grabbed his arm. "My husband is armed. He

always carries a pistol for snakes and such. Look after Vanessa," she ordered, giving him a firm push. "You go, go with her! I'll be fine."

Clay turned and ran. Vanessa wouldn't hang around waiting for him and he knew it. He saw her sprinting into the woods just as he reached the porch. Damn, the woman had no sense of caution. He took off after her.

The Walkers' truck was the only vehicle he had seen. Was there another way up the mountain? He waded into the undergrowth wishing for his boots and a machete. She appeared out of nowhere. "This way," she commanded. "Become the cat."

Clay knew exactly what she meant. He had been pressing through the woods with all the stealth of a wounded bear. He began following her actions, parting the brush more carefully, trying to do it as quietly as possible.

The sound of rushing water grew louder. "Up ahead there is Du-da's favorite fishing hole."

"Does Hightower know that?" he asked.

"I imagine so. I'm hoping we were wrong and he's halfway to Gatlinburg by now, but what he bought at the store has me really worried."

"Where would he have left his truck? Is there another access road?"

She nodded. "On the other side of the creek. It runs out at the old cabin about a quarter mile from here. He does know that for sure. He and Brenda lived there for a few months after they were married."

"There's your grandfather!" Clay exclaimed. The old man was poised behind a huge boulder, facing away from them, his weapon in his hand. Dilly was nowhere to be seen.

"Oh God, James already has her!" Van moaned.

"Do you see them?"

"No, but she'd be with Du-da."

Clay had to clasp her arm to keep her from rushing down to the creek. "Stop and think, Van! Your grandfather would have hidden her somewhere safe, wouldn't he? He'd never have her in the potential line of fire."

She gave a jerky nod and released a rush of air from her lungs. "Yeah. You're right. Okay, okay. I'm good." He watched her suck in a deep breath and release it slowly, along with her panic over Dilly.

Suddenly something snagged his peripheral vision.

"Over there. Across the creek," Clay whispered next to her ear. "I saw a flash of blue. He's in that thicket at our two o'clock, moving too fast to have Dilly with him."

"I'll go upstream and get behind him," she said. "You stay here and cover Du-da if they confront."

"Be careful," Clay rasped, knowing how useless the warning was even as he said it.

More than anything, he wanted to go with her, but knew she stood a much better chance of retaining the element of surprise if he stayed where he was. She moved like a wraith and he lost sight of her quickly.

Luckily, she was wearing dark green, a short jacket and slacks that blended into the surroundings. He, on the other hand was wearing a damned white shirt with his suit and would stand out like a flag in this terrain.

He wished to God he could get down there with her grandfather and warn him not to fire in that direction, even if Hightower stepped out and invited it. Van would be over there within minutes.

He whirled around when something tugged on his pant leg and narrowly missed hitting her with the side of his weapon. "Dilly?"

"Hey," she said, peering up at him with eyes wide. "You have a gun, too!"

"Shh. Lie down on the ground, sweetheart. Can you do that for me? Just as flat as you can make yourself."

"Like a li'l bunny rabbit," she said, sounding excited about what she must think was a game. "Du-da said not to move out of my leaf bed over there, but I didn't want you to be by yourself and scared if he shot at that warthog."

"Uh, thanks, Dilly. Be quiet now. Like a bunny," he added. "Don't get up again until we get the…warthog."

"Okay. Du-da will barbecue that rascal tomorrow."

Clay would like to do that right now. He just hoped they could maintain the fiction about the predator and never let Dilly find out the wild animal they were after was her father.

That was when a shot rang out and the firing commenced. Two shots, then another. In horror, Clay watched Mr. Walker stand up behind the boulder, raise his pistol and take aim.

"Hold your fire! Van's over there!" Clay shouted, hoping his voice would carry over the rushing water. And that the old man's hearing was up to par.

Walker spun around, glanced in Clay's direction, then lowered his weapon. He bent down, moved around the rock and headed for the far bank toward the thicket where Hightower had been when Clay spied him.

"Did Du-da shoot it?" Dilly asked.

"Don't think so, honey. Stay down."

He patted her on the back, his weapon still trained on the far bank, even though he knew that hitting anything at that distance would be pure chance. And he might accidentally hit Van or Walker.

Clay ached to rush over there. Van could be in trouble. Hell, Hightower could kill them both and get clean away. But it wouldn't do to leave the child here alone. She could decide to leap up at any minute, not realizing the danger.

Chapter 5

After ten excruciating minutes, Clay heard a motor in the distance. The urge to tear across the creek and follow that sound almost undid him, but he waited, his worried gaze trained on the far bank. Mr. Walker appeared near the trees where Clay had spotted Hightower earlier. He tore down the bank and into the shallow rushing water, wading across as fast as he could. Halfway across, he motioned for Clay to meet him.

Clay gave Dilly another pat. "Du-da is almost here. I'm going to help him. Stay right here, okay?"

"Yes, sir," Dilly said in a small voice.

"Where's Vanessa?" Clay demanded as soon as he grasped Mr. Walker's hands to pull him up the bank.

"She was tearing through the woods after she fired, so I don't think she was hit. Sounded like he got away. I left Dilly over—"

"She's fine. By that big hickory." Clay jerked his thumb

in the child's direction, bypassed the old man and hurriedly splashed through the icy water to see about Vanessa.

She appeared out of the underbrush just as he exited the creek. Clay rushed to her, running his hands up and down her arms. "You hurt?"

"Just winded," she gasped. "I called for a car to intercept him, but they probably won't reach the cutoff in time. I lost him, Clay. I missed."

"It's all right," he assured her. "We'll get him. At least Dilly's safe and no one was hurt."

She didn't look mollified in the least.

"You did everything possible."

"I should have nailed the bastard and ended this," she said bitterly. "So much for my marksmanship skills."

Clay kept an arm around her shoulders as they waded back across the stream. "Well, it's different when the target's shooting back. Don't beat yourself up about it."

"He was armed. I saw the pistol, but he didn't return fire. The shots were mine."

He could see her strength was spent and wished he could just lift her and carry her the rest of the way to her grandparents' house. As if she'd allow such a thing. Instead, he simply boosted her to dry land and climbed up behind her. "Let's go get dry. We'll join the hunt after you rest a little."

She shot him an angry glare. "I'll rest when he's caught. Let's go!"

Her grandfather and Dilly were waiting for them. She quickly hugged them and made certain they were okay. "Did he see her?" Van asked her grandfather.

"No, I saw him first. He was over there coming through the trees. Soon as I hid Dilly, I thought I'd lead him away from where she was. I made a lot of noise getting down to the water, he ducked back into that thicket and I took cover."

Vanessa frowned. "You should have run back to the house, Du-da."

"Nope. He would have caught up to us for sure. Figured he was armed, but he hadn't fired on me yet. I stayed behind that rock, between him and Dilly. That's when I heard Clay warn me not to fire, that you were over there."

"I saw him," Vanessa said. "I got close, but he's fast and I wasn't exactly geared for pursuit. Won't make that mistake again."

Clay noticed she was barefoot and wet up to her hips from wading. Her feet were scratched and bleeding. She had ditched her low-heeled pumps. They had looked like sensible, comfortable shoes, but were not made for splashing through muddy, rock-bedded creeks or trekking through underbrush.

"You're sure he was armed?" Clay asked.

"The warthog has arms?" Dilly asked, biting her bottom lip, looking up suspiciously from one to the other of the adults around her.

Clay scooped the child up in his arms and tapped her playfully on the nose. "You don't need to worry about it, Dilly. He's long gone."

Her dark eyes examined his for the lie. "Can I fish now?"

"Not today. Let's go and see if your grandmother has something yummy to eat. I'm starved, how about you?"

Vanessa tossed him an appreciative look. "Yeah, Dilly, we could go for some cookies and juice, right?" She started back toward the house.

Clay put Dilly up on his shoulders and followed, amazed by Vanessa's sudden renewal of energy and the speed with which she moved. He understood it. Her family was threatened and that gave this chase a different sort of urgency.

"Van, you know personal involvement can cloud thinking and wreck your normal sense of caution," he warned as he caught up to her on the porch. He set Dilly down and watched as she dashed into the house, intent on cookies. "I ought to have you taken off the case," he told Vanessa.

She gave him a shove in the chest. "Don't do that to me, Clay," she snapped. "Don't you do it!"

He recognized that look in her eyes. She wouldn't quit even if ordered off it. She'd only take vacation time and go after Hightower on her own. He might as well leave things as they were and stick to her like duct tape until this was over.

Clay couldn't fault her when his own personal involvement equaled hers. And no way would he lay off and let someone else look out for her safety.

He sighed. "Then show me some objectivity. I don't want you haring off like some fired up vigilante. As it stands right now, we don't have anything concrete on this guy. If you shoot him, it won't look good for you."

She nodded once, took a deep breath and arranged her features so that she looked totally serene. "Go dry off and change, Clay. Your shoes are squishing and—"

Her grandfather interrupted. "Want me to put together a couple of packs for you?"

"Thanks, Du-da," she said with a grateful smile. "That sure would help a lot. After you do that, I want you all to drive to Asheville and stay at my apartment until this is over. Give Cody and Jan a call and arrange for them to go with you. They might be targets, too, since they have primary custody of Dilly. Our local force is already stretched to the max and you'll be better protected at my place. I'll call in a couple of agents I work with to give you added security."

"Where are *we* going?" Clay asked.

"Warthog hunt," she said, flipping his tie with one finger and giving his suit a cursory once-over. "Dress is casual."

* * *

Vanessa reluctantly decided to wait until the next morning to go after James. For one thing, she had to convince her grandfather that he shouldn't go with her and Clay. Though he might come in handy on the hunt, she needed him to go with her grandmother, Dilly, Cody and Jan to Asheville and keep them safe.

Clay agreed on the delay. "You need a good night's sleep," he told her. "I'll keep watch."

She busied herself constructing sandwiches for all of them since her grandmother was occupied packing their clothes for the next day's trip. "We'll take turns on watch," she argued. "You really have to stop babying me the way you do. It's not very flattering, you know."

He smiled. "My chauvinistic streak. I know it's a problem and I'm working on it. Holly, one of my fellow agents, keeps on me about it and, believe it or not, I have improved."

"What? Now you let her make the coffee by herself?" Vanessa retorted.

Clay laughed and snitched a piece of ham from the plastic tray of cold cuts. "Don't be nasty."

She handed him a knife and shoved the jars of condiments across the counter to him. "Here. Let's see if you have any culinary skills. Make Dilly one with just mayo."

"She's a little love, that one." He settled on a counter stool. "Smart as a whip."

"Too smart sometimes. She's reading a little already."

Clay grinned. "Maybe you should think about putting her in advance classes. What about Montessori? I've heard that's good."

Vanessa shook her head. "Nope. Regular old classes with the three Rs."

He shrugged. "You know if you took the job in McLean, there would be lots of opportunity for Dilly up there."

"Man, you are trying to entice me, aren't you? She's not mine to raise, Clay. I do my part, but Dilly belongs to all of us. I could never take her away from here."

"Not even for her own good? You could convince the others, I'm sure."

Vanessa's heart warmed toward him for his concern, however misguided it was. "*Her own good* is a matter of perspective, Clay. Dilly is a smart kid. She'll do well wherever she's educated. There's also the cultural aspect of her education to consider."

His expression darkened and he didn't answer right away. He finished making the sandwich and laid it aside on Dilly's small plate. "Of course she will," he said, then added, "and I suppose it would be difficult for you to have a child and give full attention to your job. Single parents have it rough, especially if they travel a lot."

"There is that, but if she had no one else but me, I wouldn't hesitate. Family is way ahead of everything else in my book."

He nodded and stood up, going to the back window to look out into the gathering darkness. "After meeting your grandparents and Delinda, I can see why you feel that way. Though my father and I were never very close, I can remember just enough of my early years with my mother and her people to know how comfortable I was with them, how accepted and loved."

Vanessa felt his pain. It was almost tangible. "Can't you recall any details of your life then?"

He shrugged again, propped his hands on his hips and turned. "I remember a goat and how the damn thing terrified me. And there was a small drum I practiced on because I wanted to drum at ceremonies. You wouldn't believe how many recordings I've listened to since, trying to recognize something familiar."

"Do you remember any of your people besides your mother?" Vanessa asked.

Clay shrugged and smiled. "I can't say that I really remember her. I have the impression that she was beautiful, but I guess all little boys believe their mothers are that, don't they?"

"You lived with her and her family?"

"For a while. I don't know how long. There was a man there. He seemed very old. I called him grandfather, but I don't know if he was. And a woman, but I don't recall her voice or how she looked or what I called her."

"Their clothes," Vanessa suggested. "What did they wear?"

"Regular clothes, I guess, or they would stand out in my mind. No feathers or beads," he said with a touch of impatience. "I've been over and over it and there's nothing to indicate who they were or where they lived. I was only seven. They might have been an hour or a continent away from where my father lived."

"And he lived in Virginia?"

"Boston. That's where I grew up. When he came to get me, we flew there. I do remember that I wasn't afraid. I already knew him, I think, and when we arrived, the house was not unfamiliar." He squinted at her. "Why all the questions?"

She stirred uncomfortably in her chair. "I don't know. It's just interesting that your past, up to the age of seven, is nothing but a blur. I remember tons of things that happened to me before I was that age."

He held up a finger. "Ah, but I'll bet many of those stories were reinforced by family anecdotes told again and again, right?"

She thought about it, then nodded in agreement. "Did the old grandfather teach you things?"

"Not to climb on the cliffs," he said without thinking. Then his gaze snapped to hers. "God, that's the first time I've thought of that. He warned me."

"Cliffs?" she asked, looking as excited as he felt about the new information. "There's a clue!"

Clay shook his head. "I don't know. What popped into my mind just then was more a visual memory than auditory. He pointed at these rock outcroppings and looked stern. His words escape me, but his meaning doesn't. It *is* a clue, isn't it? You are one shrewd interrogator."

"That's me!" she said, beaming.

"At the rate you're going, I'll have total recall next time I set out to find myself." His laugh bordered on bitter and he wished he could call it back. She was only trying to help.

But Clay had spent more time and money than he wanted to admit, trying to fill in his past, with no results. His father had made quite an effort to erase those seven years and all the records that had existed regarding the marriage and Clay's birth.

If he didn't have the Senate eyes just like his dad's and a build that was nearly identical, Clay would have sworn he'd been adopted. But Clayton Senate Sr. would never have picked him if he'd had a choice and Clay knew it. The one thing his father had tried so hard to deny for almost thirty years always was and continued to be the most apparent. Clay looked Native American.

The sad thing was, if he had looked any different, he knew his father might well have been successful. The fact that his looks set him apart had made Clay what he was. Independent, introspective and sometimes irascible. For the most part, he liked himself and who he had become. At other times, he yearned to know the rest of himself.

He looked at Vanessa now, so secure in her skin, so confident and self-assured. Is that why he wanted her so?

* * *

Vanessa continued setting the table, sensing that if she stopped and paid too close attention, he would close up and stop sharing anything of his past. "What was her name? Your mother?" she asked conversationally.

"Margaret. That's all I know about her and only that because I heard my father curse her once when he didn't know I was listening." He sighed. "Her name was Margaret."

"When did she die?" Vanessa asked.

"The year I turned seven. It was sudden. One day she was there and the next she wasn't. I don't think it was an illness that took her."

"An accident? Surely they would have talked about that, don't you think?"

"They never speak of the dead," he muttered. Then he turned, his eyes wide. "I just remembered that."

"Another clue," she said, smiling. "But not much of one, I'm afraid. Many tribes avoid speaking of the deceased by name. How much digging have you done into your past, Clay?"

He came back to the counter and sat down, propping his chin on one hand. "A lot. Do you know how many Indian women there are on the rolls named Margaret?"

"Quite a few, I'd guess. Well, at least you know that she loved you. That's very important, don't you think?"

"Yeah, very," he agreed. "It's what has saved me when I felt lost in the white world. I know that somewhere, at one time, I was a part of a family who cared about me. I like to think they're still there somewhere."

Vanessa laid her hand over his. "You made a place for yourself, though, didn't you? Your friends in McLean accept you. And I'll bet you made peace with your father before he died, right?"

He shrugged. "More or less. We had great differences I don't believe we'd ever have ironed out, but we didn't hate one another. The Sextant agents are the closest thing to family that I have now. They tolerate me pretty well," he said, grinning, turning his hand over to clasp hers.

"Good for you," Vanessa said. "Now, if you'll excuse me for a minute, I'll go and see if the others are finished packing and ready to come and eat. You get to put ice in the glasses for tea while I'm gone."

He accepted the task and began as Vanessa hurried up the stairs. She needed to jot down a few notes on his background before she forgot any of the details.

"I have a job for you while you're at my place," she told her grandmother.

"Not organizing your closets, I hope."

Vanessa laughed out loud. "I'd never saddle you with that. This is much more important and calls for your special skills."

When they came to the table, Vanessa's hopes were high that eventually they could give Clay a gift greater than one of her grandmother's pretty baskets.

Dilly commandeered the conversation at dinner. Her excitement about the coming trip to Asheville had eclipsed her former curiosity about the day's events and the warthog. She dimpled every time she looked at Clay. "You're a good horsey player," she told him while busy licking the mayo around the edge of her sandwich. "Your shoulders are way high up."

"Everyone's always asking how the weather is up there," he commented. "Glad to give you a ride any old time."

"Now?" Dilly asked, already wriggling to get down from her youth chair.

"No, no, not now!" he said, laughing. "Later, after we eat. Horses need hay and I'm starved, aren't you?"

She giggled and reached across to smack his hand playfully. "You don't eat hay, Uncle Clay! You silly boy."

Vanessa noted the way Clay's eyes softened at being called *uncle*. It was something Dilly did naturally, drawing everyone into her little family circle. If he knew how many uncles the child had claimed since she'd learned the word, he probably wouldn't be quite so thrilled.

"You don't know what you've started now," Vanessa warned him. "You'll be galloping around all evening. Better you than me, though," she added with a grin. "Dilly's putting on weight from all those cookies!" She gave the little girl an affectionate poke on the tummy. "Will you be good when you go to stay at my place? Stay out of my makeup?"

Dilly hung her head, looking up guiltily from beneath her long lashes. "I'll try."

"Just stay out of the nail polish and you can have my pink lip gloss, okay?" Vanessa told her.

"Yes, ma'am," Dilly agreed.

Vanessa tried to keep the conversation light for Dilly's sake. She knew her grandparents were extremely worried about James's return to Cherokee and especially the fact that he had shown up today looking for his daughter. They should be safe in Asheville. Reprisals from perps that agents apprehended were always a risk, so the locations of apartments were a well-kept secret. No one gave out her address. Only the family and her fellow agents knew where she lived.

Unless James followed them there, he would not be able to find them. She meant to insure that they weren't followed. Then, once the family was away and safe, she and Clay would continue their search for James in earnest.

She wanted him found and incarcerated before they returned here.

The evening passed with happy laughter from Dilly and the

others. Vanessa enjoyed every minute and felt especially warmed by Clay's participation. The man was obviously hungry for interaction with others, but he had to be pushed a little even so. What sort of life had he led that made him feel so isolated?

Vanessa couldn't imagine. She had lived among her people all her life and by the time she'd left, had a solid sense of self and her place in the world. Clay had clearly missed that. Maybe that was why she felt so inclined to wrap him in her family. Or maybe there was another, deeper reason she wasn't ready to admit.

Dilly wasn't the only one determined to find homes for her strays. The kittens were almost all spoken for already, thanks to her persistence. Even now, she was working on the last one, trying to persuade Clay to take it.

They sat on the floor by the fire, coloring in Dilly's Cinderella coloring book. "Give me the purple," Dilly ordered. "Why don't you want Snazzy? She's the prettiest one. Won't your mama let you have a kitten?"

Clay shook his head and picked up another crayon. "My mother's gone to heaven."

"Mine, too," Dilly said in a matter-of-fact tone. "Maybe they're together. Is your daddy there, too?"

He hesitated only a few seconds. "I expect so. Swap me the purple so I can do this robe. Do you have all your things ready to go in the morning?" he asked, deliberately changing the subject.

Dilly nodded. "Are you coming, too, Uncle Clay?"

He stopped coloring and smiled. "No, not this time, but I'll be here when you get back. We'll have another ride around the yard, okay?"

"Better get to bed now, sweetie," her grandfather said. "We need to get an early start." He got up from his rocker and held out his hand to Dilly. "I'll tell you one quick story."

Dilly jumped to her feet and flung herself at Clay, wrapping her arms around his neck. "Night, Uncle Clay. Sweet dreams!"

"Thanks," he replied, his voice gruff. "Same to you. See you in the morning." His eyes followed Dilly up the stairs, then settled on Vanessa. "She's an amazing child. Just brilliant."

Vanessa had to laugh. "She's an average, rambunctious four-year-old who has wrapped you around her little finger, that's what she is."

He grinned. "You're jealous! Just because I'm in love with Dilly, you're green with envy," he teased.

Vanessa smiled back at him, happy to see him so happy. "Sucker," she said. "Next thing you know, she'll have that kitten in your suitcase with holes poked in it for air. You will have a cat, *Uncle* Clay, whether you want one or not."

"Well, I'll be getting the prettiest one. Dilly said so."

"So you will. Okay then," she said, standing and stretching. "Want first watch or shall I?"

"I'll take it," he said, glancing at his watch. "Shall I wake you at two?"

Vanessa nodded. "Good night," she said, unable to resist looking at his mouth, wishing she could just stand on tiptoe and kiss it.

"Sure is," he replied, meeting her gaze with one of longing she recognized. "Sweet dreams," he said, echoing Dilly's wish for him.

Vanessa knew they would be sweet, probably X-rated, too. Whew! The man really stirred her up. She needed to watch that because she wasn't altogether sure he was keeping his guard up the way he should.

Early the next morning, after seeing her grandparents and Dilly off to Asheville, Vanessa instigated the search for

James. They covered quite a bit of ground, but found no sign of him.

She tried to keep her mind on driving. She'd had trouble with that all day long. Clay wearing jeans and boots, minus that outer layer of sophistication provided by a business suit, turned her on big time. The dark gray pullover he wore emphasized the steely color of his eyes and the pushed-up sleeves granted her the chance to admire those muscular forearms again. *Wow.* That was the only word for him.

He kept shooting her looks of approval, too. She had to admit that she'd spent very little time deciding what to wear. And her decision had been solely based on comfort and how appropriate the attire for possibly having to chase a suspect through the wilds. Clay obviously liked her favorite straight-leg jeans and the chocolate-brown V-neck sweater.

She glanced over, caught him studying her breasts, but pretended not to notice. She blew out a long-suffering sigh and determinedly focused on the road.

"We'll find him," Clay said, totally misinterpreting the reason for her mood.

"I know," Van replied. "The question is, will we get him before he wreaks more havoc?"

Unfortunately, no one reported spotting Hightower or his truck. Vanessa worried he had changed vehicles, taken to the mountains on foot, or maybe even left the county to wait for the search to die down. The latter option would be most like him, she figured.

"We can't keep up the intensity of the search effort for more than a few days," she told Clay. "Regular police business is already taking precedence."

"The casino bombing's a couple of weeks old now and no one was hurt. I get the feeling some are thinking this was simply a prank to cause some property damage. When we checked in at one of the roadblocks, one of the guys admitted to me he thought the bomb could have been planted by a competitor out to eliminate the competition."

"That's just…stupid! People could have been killed in that blast, very nearly were! I *know* it was James."

"He's the most likely suspect, I agree. We should bring in more people. Use my resources to find him," Clay suggested yet again.

She was already shaking her head. "No good. Those on duty now know all the side roads and the people who live in the isolated areas. Anyone up the mountains who had seen James probably wouldn't give that up to a stranger."

After riding around and checking in with the various teams all day, she wasn't entirely sure those on duty now were looking all that assiduously. But she knew she was right about bringing in strangers. The community was pretty tight and was set on solving its own problems. She was just worried that they might not be considering Hightower as a high-priority problem. Even if he had planted that bomb, no one had really suffered in the end. The place had been insured, no one had been killed and the casino was repaired now and back to business as usual.

The thing was, James could not have planned for it to work out that way. People could have died in that blast and had probably been meant to die. She had been lured there with an anonymous lie and caught up on the second floor with several people she'd had to throw off the roof to save. And he wasn't through yet. Catching him was certainly high on her list of priorities.

"Well, I guess we should call it a day," she said, feeling dispirited. With the sun nearly down, the beauty of the fall colors was enough to take your breath away. Darkness would fall quickly. For now, there was nothing to do but get a good night's rest and start fresh in the morning.

"I'm beat," she said, "yet I feel like I haven't really accomplished a thing today. Almost home," she said with relief. "And I'm looking forward to a long soak in the hot tub."

"Not exactly what I need," Clay muttered.

She knew what he meant. Maybe she would opt for a cold shower, too. She admitted to herself that she was a little worried she might do or say something totally out of line to Clay unless she avoided him for the entire evening. He just looked too damn scrumptious. And if the way he had been looking at her was any indication, he was definitely more interested than he thought was prudent.

They'd just have to play it by ear and see what happened, she thought with an inner shrug. Maybe they should just go with the flow, but Vanessa knew that was just her hormones thinking. She wondered what *his* were recommending.

With the last turn up the mountain, her grandparents' house came into view. Vanessa braked abruptly. Their car was gone from the driveway beside the house since she had sent them to Asheville. But in the place of the green Jeep her grandfather drove sat a black Chevy truck. And James Hightower was perched on their front porch as if he owned the place.

Vanessa grabbed her weapon. Clay was one step ahead, already out of the car and rushing the porch, pistol braced in a firing stance. "Get down!" he shouted.

Chapter 6

James had missed seeing his daughter, but he hadn't really expected to get that close. Later, after he had gotten rid of Vanessa and the rest of the Walkers, getting the kid would be a cakewalk. This attempt had been mostly to sucker Vanessa into crying wolf to the locals. The more she railed against him, the more they would believe she was out for vengeance.

If he blew up enough people and places who had nothing to do with his former arrest, they couldn't tie the bombings to him. Of course, he meant to get that judge, above all. And Vanessa, of course. First he had to discredit her and show her up. If it hadn't been for her, he would still have Brenda and the kid. He wouldn't have been forced to get rid of his wife and spend four years of his life in that hell hole.

Maybe losing Brenda had worked out for the best, though. Now the Walkers, including Vanessa, had no one to leave everything to except his little girl. He knew from all Brenda had bragged, that her grandfather had a fortune in bonds stashed away for retirement. The old man probably had a fair amount in trust for Delinda's education, too. James could sure use that.

All he had to do now was set up an alibi and throw suspicion off himself. Not a problem. Vanessa was about to help him do just that.

Vanessa exited the car and skirted left, ready to fire. Hightower smiled at her, his fingers locked behind his head. He continued rocking in her grandfather's chair. "Hey, Vanessa, what's up?"

"Down on the ground, James!" she ordered. "Hands behind you."

He kept rocking. "You and your bud here plan to arrest me, honey?" he taunted. "What for?"

Clay grabbed him and thrust him face first onto the boards of the porch. In seconds, he had him cuffed and was reading him his rights. Hightower offered no resistance at all.

Vanessa rolled her eyes and shook her head, exhaling with relief as she holstered her weapon. "Dammit, James."

"Hoping I'd run so you could shoot at me again?" he asked with a chuckle. "I haven't done anything. Just wanted to see my little girl was all. Where is she?"

"A bit late to be showing fatherly solicitude, don't you think?" she asked, taking one of his arms to help Clay lift him to a standing position.

James hadn't changed all that much in the last four years. His Indian heritage didn't show except in the high cheekbones. He was tall, almost as tall as Clay, of a wiry build and handsome, but in a too-slick, creepy kind of way. His dark blond hair had grown longer, its sun-streaked length caught at his nape with a braided leather thong. His lazy grin showed even, white teeth, a nearly perfect smile.

James would be a normal, good looking guy, she thought, if not for his eyes. The color of weak tea, they had no depth, no expression at all, unless he got too angry to hide the evil in them. Then he could be downright scary. Brenda had been terrified of him.

"*Solicitude*, Vanessa? You always did impress me with your vocabulary. How about the term *probable cause*, or *evidence?* Heard of those?"

"Shut up, Hightower," Clay advised as he searched him. "He's clean except for this." Clay tossed Vanessa the small bone-handled pocketknife he had located.

She had hoped there would be something more incriminating in James's pockets. "What made you think you could waltz in here this morning and snatch Delinda away from my grandfather?"

"Hey, I just went up to the old cabin and while I was there, decided I'd walk on over here and see how the kid turned out. Just wanted to see who she looks like. You're the one who started shooting. Scared me to death." He grinned up at her.

"Let's go and get him locked up," she muttered to Clay.

James gave a protracted sigh. "Now, Vanessa, what you got on me, huh? Prints? No. Eyewitnesses to place me at your little crime scene? No. But go ahead and make yourself look stupid if you feel that cocky."

"You ignored the banishment order," she said. "Officially you are trespassing."

"I'll plead guilty to that," he agreed, nodding enthusiastically. He glanced at Clay. "Tell her what will happen then, Tonto." He squinted in the twilight. "By the way, do I know you?"

Clay smiled. "Not yet, but if they do turn you loose, we're destined to become very well acquainted."

Hightower twisted to look at Vanessa as she walked behind them. "Ooh, this one scares me bad, Van. Where'd you find *him?*"

She didn't answer, merely opened the hatch of her vehicle and helped Clay stuff James in the back. "Cuff his ankles to his wrists," Clay ordered. "Let's get this hog to market."

Vanessa didn't miss the worried look Clay wore because hers probably mirrored it exactly. Hightower was right about the charges. When they took him in, they would have the devil of a time holding him for long with only circumstantial evidence that he was involved in the bombing.

He would argue that Lisa Yellowhorse could have planted what she'd said she had found in her trash. There was nothing but Vanessa's own gut feeling, James's former military training in explosives and a probable motive for revenge that could link him in any way to the bombing at the casino. And she couldn't prove he had fired at her in the woods by the creek yesterday. She still had to justify firing her own weapon. He had been armed, but it was her word against his that he had been.

Her gaze locked with Clay's as they got into the car to take James back to town. "What do you think?"

Clay glanced at the back of the vehicle where James lay, obviously listening. "Well, at least we'll know where he is for a while."

There was that. But why had he shown up here, virtually turning himself in to them? Judging by the sly looks and verbal taunts, he had something already in the works, something he thought they had no chance of stopping. Or had he come to her grandparents' house in hopes of catching the older couple alone with Dilly?

"Better have EOD step up that search," Clay advised, "and have a look in some less obvious places."

Vanessa nodded as she drove down the mountain with their prime suspect. Clay had come to the same conclusions she had. The suspect was entirely too willing. Something was set up.

When the authorities had held James for as long as they could for merely trespassing, they would have to release him. In the meantime, half of Cherokee County could get blasted off the map and he would be home free with nothing to tie him to it.

"I wonder what he's got up his sleeve," she muttered.

Clay gave her a look that advised silence on the subject until they knew for certain Hightower couldn't hear them.

Could she keep her people safe from this monster? She had not been able to save her cousin, and as hard as Vanessa had tried to get justice for her, James had only received what amounted to a slap on the wrist for Brenda's murder. Four measly years. Now he must think that with a little more prior planning, he could get away with anything.

Questioning Hightower proved futile. Clay silently approved Vanessa's decision to cut short the interrogation and use the time to try to discover what he had been up to. They left him in custody and went over to the city hall where a sort of command post had been set up in one of the small conference rooms.

There, Vanessa arranged for several canine teams to report in and deployed them to the homes and businesses of everyone involved in Hightower's arrest and trial. She got search warrants granted for every place she could think of that he might have stayed since his release.

She was getting cooperation on all fronts, but no one seemed to view the investigation with the urgency that she did. Hightower was playing the role of repentant ex-con who only wanted a little peace in his life. No one paid him much attention.

Clay added help on another avenue. "My people at Sextant are looking at anyone he might have connected with in prison, all visitors, and also reviewing the records of all outside calls he made or received while he was behind bars."

"Thanks," Vanessa said, offering him a weary smile. "I just wish we knew exactly what he plans. That smirk of his tells me he's got it lined up, whatever it is." She glanced up at the wall clock, wondering how much time they had to foil disaster. It was nearly 3:00 a.m.

"Let's go," Clay told her as he pushed out of his chair. They were still at the command center where they'd been going over all the search data and adding their reports. "You're dead on your feet and there's nothing else you can do until something's found or they can't hold him any longer."

With a final look at the county map with all its flagged pins denoting possible targets to search, she rose, too. "You drive?" She tossed him her key ring.

He deftly caught it and opened the door for her, ushering her through with a palm at her back. His touch warmed her, a brief spot of comfort in a dark and dreary night. She could do with more contact like that, she thought with a sad smile. Wasn't likely to happen though, and that was probably for the best.

She didn't like to lean on people and he obviously didn't like to be leaned on. They were partners on this op, but she wouldn't be pulling her weight if he had to hold her hand.

If he had any further suggestions, he would offer them. If he saw her making a misstep with running the investigation, he would be the first to set her straight. That, in itself, reassured her. He was giving her all the assistance anyone could ask for in a situation like this. But a genuine hug sure would be welcome.

Vanessa slept in the car on the way up the mountain to the cabin. Slightly disoriented, she woke when the engine cut off.

"Wait in the car," he ordered. "I'll have a look around before we go in."

"I'll come with you." If James had set a charge here, he'd

had plenty of time to do it before they'd arrived to find him sitting on the porch. The search teams had begun already, but this place was farther out of town than most of the others.

Clay went one way around the outside of the cabin and Vanessa took the other. The heavy beams of the powerful flashlights they carried lit up the night in streaks as they searched high and low. When they met at the back porch, she was satisfied that James hadn't gone crazy enough to wire the cabin, then wait for them to show up and take him in. Finding C-4 or dynamite here when he had such recent access wouldn't exactly qualify as circumstantial evidence.

"All clear," she said. "Back door key's the odd-shaped one." She watched him unlock with her keys and flip on the light switch. The bright yellow of her grandmother's kitchen flooded her senses with badly needed comfort. Home. It smelled of chocolate-chip cookies and coffee.

"Hungry?" she asked, washing her hands in the sink. "I'm suddenly famished. We never did get around to eating. Let me see what we've got."

She pulled a casserole out of the refrigerator and stuck it in the microwave. "Lasagna," she told him, and with a wiggle of her eyebrows, punched the heat-up button.

Clay laughed. "Real Native American fare."

Vanessa found paper plates and peeled two off the stack while he opened the cutlery drawer.

They were almost finished when she remembered. "Oops, I forgot to feed Billy. Want to come with me?"

He nodded and Vanessa thought she noted a look of anticipation on his usually stoic features. Come to think of it, that expression of stoicism had become fairly rare when they were alone together. It did her heart good to know he felt comfortable enough with her now to let some of his feelings show. Anticipation…worry…lust. She almost laughed at herself for being foolish enough to think about his wanting her. Even though it was true and she knew he did, that wouldn't mean squat when it came to doing anything about it. He had already stated his views on that and they couldn't be clearer. No more kisses and no sex.

She only wished she didn't know he was attracted, or that the lust was not one-sided. Realizing his difficulty with abstinence made it a little harder for her to handle.

But she could be friends with him and ignore the sparks if he could.

They walked out to the fence. She carried the bottle she'd made up for Billy, and Clay shone the flashlight to light their way. The bear lumbered up, rising on his hind legs for the treat. "There you go, you greedy ol' teddy."

"What about the cats in the barn?" Clay asked.

Vanessa smiled. "The kitties are too young to do anything but nurse and the mama cat is an excellent hunter. She mostly feeds herself."

"Any other mouths to feed?"

She collected the bottle Billy dropped at her feet. "No, that's it. Guess we'd better turn in.

He raised his hand and brushed back the strands of her hair that had worked free. "You are so—"

"Scatterbrained," she interrupted, drawing away from his touch and starting back down the path to the house. "I should get more organized now that I need to look after things around here. Poor old Billy!"

Clay grasped her hand and halted her in her tracks. "Vanessa, I don't know if we can ignore this." He slid his arms around her and drew her close.

She knew he was going to kiss her. Lord, what temptation! If she allowed it, she knew what would happen next. Either Billy Bear would get the facts-of-life show right there on the path, or she and Clay would be racing one another for the nearest bed. She'd bet on the path thing.

With every ounce of willpower she possessed, she pushed Clay away from her. "I should act coy and say I have no idea what you mean, but I *do*," she admitted, taking another step back, hoping to lessen the temptation. "You'll hate yourself in the morning."

He shrugged, planted his hands on his jean-clad hips and lowered his head. "Right," he muttered. "I know you're right. It's just that—"

Vanessa broke in again. "Keep it up and you're gonna talk me right into something, Clay. We need some sleep. Neither one of us is thinking straight. Let it be for now, okay?"

He nodded, shining the light back on the path and gesturing for her to precede him.

"You know I'm right," she argued, feeling the need to justify her rejection of him and maybe explain to her unruly body why it couldn't have what it definitely craved.

Suddenly the sky lit up in the distance and what sounded like a sonic boom reverberated the air a half second later. Vanessa halted immediately and grabbed Clay's arm to steady herself. "Oh, God! Somewhere in town! Let's go!"

Clay kept an eye on Vanessa as he surveyed the damage to the strip mall that had housed several souvenir shops and an art gallery, now smoking rubble.

"Definitely not a gas leak," Officer Mike Haygood said as he ambled over and joined Clay in the littered parking lot. "All electric here. No mains nearby."

Merchandise littered the area. Clay crouched to pick up a small doll in a white leather-fringed costume. Dirty, but otherwise undamaged, the brown plastic features stared back at him. He tilted it so that the eyes blinked.

Had Vanessa played with one like this as a little girl? He had seen a bow-and-arrow set stapled to a cardboard target lying nearby. That would have been more her speed, he thought. She had to be frantic with this happening in her hometown. You'd never have known it to look at her though.

"Well, Hightower's got a solid alibi since he's sitting in jail," Haygood said.

"If there's anything left of a timing mechanism, he doesn't," Clay said.

"Van could be wrong about him."

Clay didn't think so and he didn't believe Haygood thought so either. "You know anyone else we should be looking at?"

"Not offhand," the cop admitted. "Just playing devil's advocate."

Vanessa joined them. She looked pointedly at the doll Clay was holding. "I'm surprised anything survived intact."

He handed the toy to her. "Want to go play good cop/bad cop with Hightower?"

"Only if I get to be bad cop," she replied, casting a frustrated look at the destruction around them. "He's responsible. I know he is." She looked at Haygood and must have recognized his doubts. "Mike, you like him for this, too, right?"

"I'm trying to keep an open mind about it, but in the long run it doesn't matter what I think, does it?" He nodded to Clay, then went about his business.

"Longtime pal of yours or yet another cousin?" Clay asked.

She grinned. "Friend. Asked me to marry him once."

Clay carefully concealed the spurt of jealousy that ripped through him. "Only once?" he asked, forcing a smile. "Gave up pretty easily, didn't he?"

She rolled her eyes. "Well, third graders don't set a very high priority on hooking up permanently. He forgot to check back with me after recess."

"Third grade, huh? No second thoughts about your refusal?"

"Oh, you bet." She nodded. "Several times in high school after he went from scrawny bookworm to hunky halfback, but he was already in love with someone else."

Clay thought he had detected an undercurrent of jealousy in Haygood. Maybe it was just a proprietary attitude because the man had grown up with her. Clay didn't know exactly how these things worked. He hadn't formed any attachments like that during his school years. Always the outsider, even now.

He held open the door of Vanessa's vehicle for her and watched her get in. Then he closed it and leaned against it, his face close to hers. "I'm glad you told him no."

She peered up at him, her beautiful dark eyes promising closeness even as she warned him away from it. "Don't say things like that. It makes me want to do things you and I have no business doing."

Clay backed off. He went around the car and got in, determined to rein in the need she stoked to fever pitch.

Why did he keep giving in to it when he knew better? Maybe it was that little touch of vulnerability hidden within her obvious capability. And how could she look so incredibly hot when approaching exhaustion, totally devoid of makeup and wearing clothes that made her look like someone's little brother?

"My mouth gets ahead of my brain whenever I'm around you," he grumbled as he slammed the car door and locked his seat belt with a little more force than was necessary.

"As confessions go," she said with a heavy sigh, "I could have done without that one. Let's get on with what we have to do, okay?"

"Okay." She wanted him, he wanted her and it was as simple as that. Plain old desire kicked into high gear by all this…togetherness. Not as if he had a lot of choice there.

Sooner or later they would be going back to the Walkers' house and spending the night together. Separately. Well, that was the official plan. Until they faced that particular trial, he was going to do just as she suggested and try his best to forget about it.

They reached the police station within minutes. Cherokee was a small town and the traffic was negligible in the early hours of the morning.

He walked in behind her, deliberately keeping his eyes off that nicely rounded backside of hers. Damn, he couldn't ever recall being so *aware* of a woman before, every breath she took, every move she made.

"Which cell is Hightower in?" she asked. They had left the man cuffed in the interview room with two of the locals ready to lock him up.

"He left with his attorney about fifteen minutes ago," the officer told her.

"He what?" Vanessa shouted. "How did this happen, Gary?"

She was as near to losing it as Clay had ever seen her.

The desk sergeant actually stepped back, his dark eyes rounded in surprise. "Hey, your charge was trespassing, a simple misdemeanor. The attorney paid the fine for it and got him released. Promised to escort him off the Boundary."

"Where's the sheriff?" she demanded, pounding her fist on the counter.

"Gone over to see about that explosion. You must have crossed paths on the way. It was another bomb, wasn't it?"

"What'd it sound like, Gary? A firecracker? Of course it was a bomb! And you… Never mind," she huffed, grabbed Clay by his sleeve and stomped back outside to the car. "We have to find him again. And this time, I don't think he's gonna be sitting on the front porch waiting for us to haul him in."

"I think he'll be where you can find him. I'm almost sure

of it. He's setting you up, Vanessa. Bring him in again and I'll bet he'll file a charge of harassment against you. He's got his alibi. Even if he used a timer on the bomb, you can't charge him without proof that he set it."

"If he used the C-4 that was stolen—"

Clay shook his head. "That he took it is still only supposition. Besides, I have a feeling this bomb was a simple IED, like the one at the casino, indicating an amateur made it. Anyone can get plans for those on the Internet and buy the stuff to make them at any hardware store."

"Improvised explosive device," she muttered, frowning. "But *why* when he's got the heavy stuff?"

"He's saving that for the finale," Clay told her. "First he wants to make himself look like the victim in your little crusade for justice."

"I am not a vigilante!" she cried. "I'm *not!*"

"I know that, but if you play into his hands, your boss and probably mine, along with the sheriff and the council here might begin to think you are."

She looked near tears, frustrated, feeling helpless, but to her credit, she was keeping it together. Clay took her hand and rubbed it between his. "We'll get him."

Vanessa stood on tiptoes and kissed him on the chin. "Thanks."

He kissed her back, catching her lips open and taking advantage of that. She didn't pull away, but he did when he heard a car engine rev and his common sense kicked in. All they needed was for the sheriff to drive up and catch them necking in his parking lot. Any credibility they had would be blown to hell if that happened.

"Well, I see interagency communication is progressing right along." Mike Haygood got out of his patrol car and slammed the door.

Clay cursed himself for getting so involved in the kiss. He hadn't heard the vehicle approaching until it was too late.

He watched Haygood amble over to them, thumbs hooked in his belt, one eyebrow raised in speculation.

Arrogant, but not combative yet, Haygood looked a little pissed off. Maybe jealous.

The cop set Clay's teeth on edge, probably because he represented all that Clay hoped to steal Vanessa away from. Haygood was her past, a homeboy, part of her tribe. There was no point getting defensive. Clay had no defense. That didn't keep him from wanting to shield Vanessa from Haygood's obvious disapproval. "You have a problem with that?" he asked the man.

"Yeah, I *do* as a matter of fact," Haygood snapped, then cast a level look on Vanessa. "You need to watch yourself, Van. Rumors are sprouting on the grapevine already."

"So what's the word?" She had her chin thrust out and her eyes narrowed in challenge.

Haygood switched his gaze to Clay. "No one's quite sure what agency you're working for, Senate. When Van introduced you around, she was pretty vague about that and there's a lot of speculation." He frowned at Vanessa. "The wind has sort of shifted. They're saying you brought your secret-agent boyfriend here to help you nail Hightower for killing Brenda."

She smiled, but it looked forced. "I already nailed him for *that,* Mike."

"But not the way you wanted to and everybody knows it. There are some who believe Hightower's paid his debt and you're bound and determined to stick it to him again."

"You think that, Mike?" Vanessa asked, pinning him with a glare.

"Not necessarily, just wanted you to know what's in the wind." Haygood nodded to both of them and went on inside the station.

Vanessa's troubled expression said it all. "Cooperation is really going to be iffy from now on. They believe I'm on a witch hunt here."

Clay couldn't argue with her. That kiss had lost her some credibility, too. And that was his fault. Maybe he should apologize, but he knew she would take it the wrong way. To tell the truth, he wasn't sorry he had kissed her and would do it again in a heartbeat. Just maybe not out here in public. That was not wise.

"Let's go home and catch a couple hours sleep. Nothing more we can do here. I can't even put out an APB on him, can I?"

"You could, but I don't think it will be necessary. He'll probably be waiting for you to locate him so he can play up his role of victim. Call his lawyer in the morning."

It was already morning. Almost dawn. They had almost made it through this night without a personal catastrophe. Clay firmly reminded himself she was off-limits. However, when those luminous dark eyes of hers met his, Clay's resolve slipped a notch.

Chapter 7

It felt strange having the house to themselves. They had slept through breakfast and managed to avoid each other until lunchtime. Clay wished her grandparents and Dilly were still here to offer a buffer.

Vanessa looked way too enticing wearing those blue knit lounge pants and matching top. In spite of himself, he kept trying to decide whether she wore a bra beneath it. The azure color enhanced her burnished-copper skin. He ached to touch her and feel her smooth firmness on the pads of his fingers, on his palms, on his own body.

He really needed to get a grip and *not* on her person.

Vanessa chattered away about food as she warmed up a casserole and shredded greens for a salad. Clay busied himself setting the table, trying to ignore the graceful way she moved, the efficiency with which she performed each task, the exquisite line of her neck visible between her upswept hair and the neckline of her soft collarless shirt.

His lips warmed at the thought of pressing them there on her nape, tasting that finely textured skin with his tongue, sliding his arms around her and pulling her against him.

The cold shower hadn't helped at all. His appetite raged, the one that had nothing to do with food. Why her? he kept asking himself. What was it about the woman that warped his common sense all out of proportion?

"Excuse me," she said, her voice bright as she briefly brushed against him while placing the salad bowls on the table.

Their gazes locked and he felt her resignation, her surrender, the inevitable pull that drew them together. Powerless to resist her, Clay lowered his mouth to hers and lost himself in the taste of her.

Her moan of pleasure echoed his own as he deepened the kiss, crushing her in his arms, loving the feel of her moving sinuously against him. Encouraging, inviting…

Her phone chirped its tune, *dum-da da-dum*. She ignored it the first few times, then sighed and broke the kiss. Both of them were breathing fast, nearly hyperventilating. Her crooked little smile of apology did nothing to assuage his disappointment, but he let her go.

"Walker here," she snapped into the cell phone, her voice breaking slightly. She listened for what seemed a long while, her eyes closed as she absorbed the message. "Keep this quiet for as long as you can. We don't want a panic and I don't want our perp to know it's been found. Good idea. I'll stay put until then. Thanks, Gil. I'll be waiting here for the results."

She flipped the phone shut and sank onto one of the kitchen chairs, propped her elbow on the table and rested her head on her hand. "They located a bomb. Small one, set beneath Judge Eversalt's car."

Clay cleared his throat and tried to get his mind back in gear. "IED or something more sophisticated?"

"C-4," she said. "He's going to the heavy guns."

"Looks like," Clay agreed. "How was it set, for pressure?"

She shook her head. "Wired for remote detonation."

"Not good," Clay said, wincing. "I guess they're checking the vehicles of the others?"

"On it now. A couple of EOD guys are headed up here to check out my Explorer soon as the others are cleared one way or the other." She glanced at the cooling casserole. "Suddenly I'm not very hungry."

"Eat anyway," he advised. "We might get too busy later and energy could come in handy." He proceeded to serve both plates with generous helpings of the dish she had warmed.

"There's pie in the fridge if you want it," she said half-heartedly. But he could see her mind was not on that. "What am I doing wrong, Clay?"

"Nothing," he assured her as he dug into his salad. "He's obviously cleverer than we'd like, but he's also arrogant. Takes unnecessary chances." He pointed at her with his fork. "That'll be his downfall. You'll see."

"I hope you're right. Do you think I'm on the right track, going after Hightower? All of a sudden, doubt seems to be coming off everyone else in waves. Could I be wrong? Could someone else be responsible for the bombs?"

"Don't doubt your instinct," Clay advised her. "It's the best tool you have and what separates you from run-of-the-mill investigators. I trust it. I think he's the one."

Vanessa nodded. "Thanks." But he could see her doubt and wished he could magically erase it.

"Why don't you take a mental break from it, Vanessa? Step back and concentrate on something else. There's really nothing you can do with regard to the case until you get another call or the team shows up to check out the Ford. Even then, the bomb squad will handle anything they find and forensics will follow up."

"I know you're right. I'll try."

"Imagine that we have nothing more pressing to do than eat, watch a little television and get a nap this afternoon." *Alone,* he added to himself. "That's our goal for the day." He watched her nod in agreement and take a nibble of lettuce.

"Officially off duty," she agreed, bobbing her head. She concentrated on her food, studiously ignoring him as she ate.

Clay couldn't help thinking how normal this seemed, sitting here in the comfortable kitchen, surrounded by the trappings of her family life. Too normal for the likes of him.

What would she think of the house where he'd grown up? His old home place was cold, modern to the point of being clinical, though decadently expensive. And missing the key element that made a house a home. Love, of course.

Oh, he believed in that and had seen it applied in relationships he'd observed. He just didn't know how to go about getting it, or more importantly, giving it. Sex was about as close as he could get to it, but he certainly knew there was a whale of a difference.

He forked a bite of the greens tossed with the piquant and an unusual dressing she had stirred up from unfamiliar ingredients. As he enjoyed the unique taste of what she had prepared, he wondered whether she could blend a mix of feelings that effortlessly. She obviously knew how, had probably been born knowing how.

"You ever been in love?" he asked, keeping his tone light.

She stared at him as if he had belched out loud.

He shrugged. "You know, really invested in someone full out with no reservations?"

The stare remained as she added a jerky little shake of her

head and swallowed with some effort. "No," she admitted then. "Not really. What brought that up? You looking for advice or something?"

Clay laughed and laid down his fork. He picked up his wineglass and took a hearty sip. "No, I just wondered. I was thinking how much you remind me of someone I know back in McLean. The wife of a friend of mine. She's a Southern girl, too. Very open and affectionate."

"Sure you're not secretly in love with her?" Vanessa asked, rotating her wineglass, ostensibly focused on the *robe*.

"No, I just always admired her and…the way she is." He fastened his gaze on Vanessa's. "The way *you* are."

She stopped eating, sat back in her chair and crossed her arms over her chest, observing him with a tilt of her head. "You're pretty affectionate yourself."

"Me? No, I'm the quintessential cold fish."

She laughed out loud, that golden sound he craved like oxygen. What had he said that tickled her so? Only the truth.

She was shaking her head now and reaching for her wine again. "My lord, Clay, you are the most clueless individual I've met in a long time. Whoever described you as a cold fish?"

He thought about it. "No one I can recall. I guess that's how I see myself." That's how he saw his father. Was he becoming the old man?

"Clueless," she stated, nodding as if to herself. "I see right now some woman is gonna have her hands full straightening you out."

"I wish it could be you," he said honestly, wanting more than anything to break out of the mold in which he had been formed.

Her smile grew radiant. "Clay, that is absolutely the nicest thing a man has ever said to me. But you know that's impossible. We've already discussed it."

With that pronouncement, she got up and began clearing the table. Subject closed. "Go, watch a little TV. I'll be in when I get through in here."

He went into the den and turned the television on low. Now they were playing the avoidance game. How long could they last this time?

Clay suddenly felt a profound need to confess his overwhelming attraction to Vanessa. Not to her, but to someone. It was definitely coloring his evaluation of her and he knew it. Or maybe he just wanted to confide. That constituted a new experience, he thought with a wince of disbelief. He never trusted anyone enough to lay out his innermost thoughts.

Well, there had been that one time he'd all but declared himself to Holly to keep her from falling into bed with Will. That had been a huge mistake and it hadn't been all that effective, either. Too little, too late.

Not that he had been in love with Holly. Sure, he'd been attracted to her, cared about her more than any woman he'd known at the time, admired her and thought they would be a much better match than she and Will were. He had been dead wrong about that. Yet, if anyone would understand his present conundrum, it would be Holly, who had faced a similar situation.

Without giving himself time to rule it out, he picked up his cell phone and hit her speed dial number. She answered on the second ring. "Hey, Chief, what's up?"

Clay smiled. Holly was not the most politically correct person he'd ever met. In fact, she was the least so. "Hi. Nothing yet. We're still investigating."

She paused. "Something's wrong. Personal problem?"

Clay sighed into the phone. The woman might not be psychic, but came damn close. "I'm sort of…involved, for lack of a better word."

"A woman? Oh God, let me call Will. He'll never believe this. Ol' Senate the Stoic had flipped out over a skirt. Who is she?"

"Don't you say a word about this to that husband of yours. It's the candidate. Jack's going to have to replace me. I absolutely cannot find, or maybe can't admit to, any of her faults. I literally can't see them. This is…not working."

He almost clicked off then and left it at that, but she was making those crooning sounds she used with all of them when she went into Mama Mode. He realized he needed that right now. "What do I do?" he asked, feeling about twelve years old and lost in the throes of his first big crush. Come to think of it, this was his first Big Crush.

"That's it," he said, more to himself than her. "Infatuation. It'll probably pass, but it's interfering big time with my judgment and Jack should know that."

"Then maybe you should be telling *him*," she suggested. "Why are you calling me about it, hon? You had to know I'd say go for it. That's what I did," she reminded him.

She and Will had bucked the unwritten rules and had nearly had to choose which one stayed on the job at Sextant. Mercier had not been pleased that two of his agents were getting it on and even less thrilled when they'd decided to marry. There were still problems regarding assignments where their personal feelings might affect an operation.

Clay thought for a minute. "Maybe subconsciously that's what I wanted to hear from you."

"Don't overanalyze this, Clay. You're bad about that."

"If I do start something with her, though, it will seriously impact on her chances of getting hired. I can't do that to her. She's really capable, Holly. Perfect for COMPASS and deserving of it, too."

"Go for it, Clay. Don't be a dope," she said with a smile

in her voice. "Sounds like you're dead serious about her. If she's worth her salt and all that praise, she'll get what's coming to her one way or another. I happen to think *you* would be a much bigger prize than any job she could ever imagine."

Clay felt his heart swell with the praise. "Thanks, Holly. I'll think about it."

"Don't think so hard, hon," she advised. "I'm telling you, you think a thing to death. Go with your feelings on this. Want me to talk to Jack about it for you?"

"No, I'll do it. But later. First, let me try to ditch these rose-colored glasses I keep seeing her through. Even if I am falling for her like I've lost a parachute, I do need to see her as she really is, you know?"

"Lotsa luck," she said laughing wryly. "And Clay? Don't screw this up. The thing with her, personally, I mean. The job will take care of itself."

"Okay," he muttered. "Gotta go. I never called you about this, right?"

"Right," she quickly agreed and was gone without a goodbye.

Clay could picture her running straight to Will. He would be the joke of the office tomorrow. What the devil had he been thinking to call Holly?

Something inside him seemed to be opening up, welcoming in outside interference, asking for it. Hell, for a man who had always prided himself on being so self-contained, he seemed to have lost it in a hurry. Vanessa had changed him, was still changing him. In a way, he resented it, but in another, he felt a little relieved that he could change at all.

When rules collapsed, even rigid, self-imposed rules, that left a void, a wide-open field where there had once been a definite road with signposts to follow. How was he supposed to find his way?

"Want some fudge?" Vanessa asked from the doorway.

The way she stood, one slender hip cocked, her head tilted just so, made her as enticing as any confection in the world. He could almost taste her sweetness. "You made fudge?"

"Me? Nope, I'm not much of a cook. The grans keep a pretty good supply on hand. Chocolate cures everything," she declared as she came over, plopped down next to him on the sofa and tucked her bare feet beneath her. With a groan of pleasure, she proceeded to savor one of the squares from the saucer she had brought from the kitchen.

He frowned at the amount stacked on the little plate. "You must be *seriously* ill."

She licked her lips and grinned, her dark eyes as rich as the candy. "Have some."

Have some. Clay sucked in a steadying breath and dragged his gaze away from her delicious mouth. He was pretty sure fudge wouldn't cure what ailed him right now, but he took a piece anyway. It melted in his mouth, the sugar high hitting him almost immediately. Yep, just as he feared. Chocolate was not a cure-all. It was an aphrodisiac.

"I need to get out of here and get some exercise," he said, hoping for escape before he did something foolish. Even if he decided to *go for it,* as Holly advised, he couldn't just jump Vanessa with no warning. "I ought to change and go for a run."

"I could come with you!" she said. "Wouldn't want you to get lost."

It was way too late, Clay thought. The wide-open spaces beckoned with all sorts of possibilities he'd never allowed himself before. Who needed a road with signposts anyway?

With regret, he knew what he had to do. He leaned forward, resting his elbows on his knees. "Vanessa, I'm going to have to turn over your evaluation for the COMPASS team to someone else. Of course, I'll stay until you've completed this investigation, but I can't be objective about your performance. I promise this won't preclude your being considered. I'll make it very clear that the personal involvement is one-sided and all my doing."

She shoved herself up off the sofa. After pacing for a minute, she faced him directly. "I don't care about the position. Tell them I'm not interested."

"But you are," Clay argued. "I know that you are." He could see it so clearly in her eyes, even now. She wanted it. She also wanted him and he could see that, too.

"Okay, I admit it," she said with a one-shoulder shrug and took her seat again, this time facing him, one foot tucked under her. "But we don't have to let this… Whatever it is between us doesn't have to make a difference. You know as well as I do it's just a galloping case of lust. I find you wildly attractive and obviously you see something in me that excites you a little. Let's just come to terms with it."

Wildly attractive? Clay's pulse stuttered. "And how do you suggest we do that? You think if we lay it out in the open this way, it'll just go away?"

She pursed her lips, as if weighing their options. Then she came to a decision. "As it stands now, the *forbidden* factor makes it loom very large. All we can think about, right?"

He nodded with a wry grimace. "All the time."

"So we burn it out," she suggested, giving her knee a thump with her palm. Her fingers flared and then came together as she fisted her hand. "You know as well as I do that once the tension is relieved, once that seductive unknown is known, you'll see I'm nothing special."

He laughed. "Nothing special? You're kidding right?"

"Not at all," she assured him, shaking her head vehement-ly. "This will work, Clay. Once it's played out, you'll get your objectivity back and I can function a lot better. No harm, no foul. Just a very short fling to take the edge off and put things back in perspective."

Her naiveté drove him crazy. Crazy enough to tell himself what she suggested might work. But there was a danger here she didn't understand and he needed to warn her of it.

He reached across the table and took her hand in his. "What if it doesn't *play out,* Vanessa? What if one of us gets in too deep to let it go?"

"Me?" she asked with a nervous laugh. "No way. I'm not looking for any promise of commitment from you. Never even occurred to me."

Ah, the temptation to let it go at that, but Clay knew he couldn't, in all good conscience, do that. "It's not *you* I was worried about."

He could see he had shocked her speechless. With reluctance, he let go of her hand and sat back to see what she would do with the information.

Much to his surprise, she didn't run from it. Instead, she took a deep breath and asked point-blank, "So you're afraid to chance it?"

Clay couldn't be anything but frank now that he had opened this particular can of worms. "I'm terrified. Maybe sex with you would be enough. But what if it's not?"

He didn't simply want her, Clay realized that. He craved her with every ounce of his being, but not just her body. He wanted all that she was. Maybe it was not love, but envy he was feeling. She had everything that he didn't, was everything he wasn't, embraced everything he couldn't.

"I need you, Vanessa," he admitted, dropping his gaze from hers, unable to meet it any longer. "God, that sounded desperate and I didn't mean it to. I'm not desperate. If I left you right now, I could get on with things, maybe be better off for it, but…" He looked up at her, not caring now if she saw into his soul. "I would never be able to forget you or stop wanting the essence of what you are."

Her brown eyes softened even as they flared, but her tone was teasing. "Are you saying you're in *love* with me, Clay?"

"I don't know," he said, releasing a breath of frustration. "I can't say that, because I honestly don't know."

Her soft laugh sounded a little bitter. "Well, at least I can count on your being up front about it. I think maybe I'm a little bit in love with you. Or probably just fixated on what you are. Hard to tell."

"When in doubt, *do* something," he said with a sigh. "My father always said that. He was always wrong."

Now her laugh was sincere, though definitely dry. "When in doubt, *don't,*" she replied. "My grandmother always says that. And she's invariably right. So I'm not going to bed with you, Clay, as much as I would like to. Forget I suggested it. It was a bad idea."

"A dangerous idea," he said with a nod. "I don't blame you for changing your mind. But that still leaves us with the initial problem, doesn't it? What to do about the job. About us."

She shrugged. "Well, there's not an *us* as yet. Let's table it for now and see how the op goes. Nothing says we have to decide anything right now." She shot him a mock frown. "Just don't kiss me again. I tend to start justifying anything that might happen the minute our lips meet and I suspect you do, too. No hand holding. No touching."

Reluctantly, he nodded. "No kissing, no touching," he agreed, wondering if he could follow through on that. Even now he could still taste her, feel the firm ripeness of her mouth, the vibration of the moan she made in her throat, and the encompassing heat that any contact with her sent rushing through his body. The mere memory of it was enough to arouse him.

He wished he had kept his mouth shut and taken her to bed when she suggested it.

She wiped a palm across her brow. "Is it hot in here or is it just me?"

Clay burst out laughing and she joined him. The moment was incredibly intimate, he thought, probably more so than if they had given in to the lust. What the hell was he supposed to do now?

Concentrate on the op, do what he could to assist Van in wrapping it up and get the hell out of Dodge, that's what. She had him thinking along lines he knew he couldn't afford to consider.

This was precisely why he didn't do relationships. He didn't know how. When should a man be totally honest with a woman and when should he keep his big mouth shut? There was a question he had waited about ten minutes too long to ask himself.

The EOD team arrived, two guys, a sniff dog and a trunkload of gear. Buoyed by their earlier find in the judge's car, they did a thorough search. They found nothing remotely suspicious. Vanessa thanked them and sent them back down the mountain to continue checking out other vehicles and homes.

As long as the team had been there, she'd kept her mind on the investigation, but the minute they left, her thoughts turned right back to Clay and their earlier conversation.

He was the most unusual man she had ever met. He seemed wholly incapable of doing all those little dodges guys did when it came to discussing anything personal. She liked that about him, but it was disconcerting to say the least.

No playing games. No talking in circles. She was used to guys doing that. In her experience, she sort of expected to have to guess at a lot and read between the lines.

If only they had met under other circumstances. However, it probably wouldn't have made that much difference. She wasn't looking to get involved. Her main goal was to excel in her job, to make a difference and try to make the world a little less susceptible to crime.

She also wanted to set an example for girls with her background who needed a role model. Maybe that was pretentious of her, but Vanessa saw too many of them settle for less than they could be simply because they didn't know what that was or how to find out.

She liked giving talks in the school about fulfilling potential and, to be perfectly honest, enjoyed the way some of the students looked up to her and wanted to emulate her career path. She wasn't out to recruit for the Bureau, but to show how important it was for young minority women to make good grades, set goals, focus and follow through.

If she deviated from her current path in order to have an affair with a man she found attractive, or worse, to marry one, start a family and alter her goals, what would that say about her? Would she be setting a poor example? She needed to put things back in perspective and stop mooning over Clay like a lovestruck groupie.

From now on, she planned to keep her distance.

For two days, they behaved like strangers in a state of limbo. Nothing was happening with the investigation. No other explosives were found, much less detonated. And no sightings of Hightower were reported. She and Clay actively searched for the man, but it was as if he had fallen off the earth.

"He's waiting for things to die down," Vanessa said as she and Clay sat in the parking lot of the local Burger King and ate their lunch. "I think he'll strike when he thinks everyone's lost interest."

She grimaced and plunked her French fries back into the sack. "And I think that time has arrived. The mayor wants his conference room back."

Even though Vanessa had already released the EOD personnel the day before so that they could get back to their regular jobs and answer other calls, one four-man team from Redstone had elected to stay. They were calling it a training exercise. Three guys performing on the job training and one experienced man and dog to cover countless possibilities. The sheriff had to consider the available funds when keeping extra deputies on duty. They had already been dismissed. "I've lost almost all support."

"Cases go cold, Vanessa. You know it happens. If Hightower's given up on his original plans, there's nothing you can do but hope that he finally came to his senses."

"I know better. He's just waiting. I feel it in my gut," she argued.

"A premonition?" he demanded, his dark eyes alert, as if she had said something vitally important.

"Just a strong feeling that he's not through yet," she explained. "Why do you ask? Are you giving up, too? Going back to McLean?"

"Not yet," he stated, taking a huge bite of his sandwich.

"Why not?" He had been unusually quiet today and looked vaguely troubled. Vanessa couldn't think why he would stick around unless he believed she was right about James. She decided to come right out and ask him. He had been honest to a fault before. "You agree with me, don't you?"

He swallowed and took a sip of his drink. Then he crumpled up his trash and held it between his palms for a minute, looking at it as if it had the answers. He seemed to be trying to reach a decision about something, then looked defensive when he met her questioning gaze. "I had a vision last night."

His expression told her he wasn't joking about this. She got serious, too. "I'll bet that revelation cost you, didn't it?"

He smiled. "Yes. I generally don't mention that I have them, but if there's a chance it could help us, it would be wrong to ignore it."

"You continue to surprise me," Vanessa admitted. "You want to share what you saw?"

He shook his head. "Not until I try to figure it out." His gaze met hers. "But it was strong enough to make me determined to wait here with you until something breaks."

"Did you see me in your vision?" she asked. "Maybe if you tell me about it, we could try to interpret it together."

He pursed his lips as if debating about how specific he would get. He carefully disposed of the remains of his lunch, then propped his arms on the steering wheel. "You were there. A sly little fox darting through the trees and around rocks."

He sighed and closed his eyes, probably trying to visualize it again. "I ran to keep up with you. Thunder boomed and lightning struck, breaking everything beneath our feet. Chasms opened, earth crumbled."

"You were the panther," she told him, unable to look away from his face.

The gray eyes flew open and he stared at her. "What?"

"The panther," she said with conviction. "You see me as a fox, I see you as a panther. I tend to associate people with animals, too. You move like a panther. Graceful, agile, lethal. I can see you stalking, muscles bunching to leap, eyes narrowing as you plot the next move of your prey."

For a long minute, he said nothing, just continued looking at her in a speculative and intense way. "And Hightower, how do you see him?"

She grinned. "Well, the image of warthog sort of stuck in my mind after Du-da put out the pretense for Dilly. He's like one, don't you think? Razor-sharp, quick, unpredictable and very dangerous. Ugly. At least to me, he is."

Clay didn't agree or disagree, but changed the subject entirely. "How much stock do you put in the old ways of your people?"

"Which old ways?" They had changed a lot over the centuries.

"The ones dealing with harmony and balance. In particular, the one that requires a life for a life to keep things even?"

Vanessa's heart sank. Was he subscribing to the vengeance theory that some of the others were hinting at? She took a deep breath. "Studied us, did you?"

He nodded, running one long finger along the dashboard, creating a line in the film of dust there. "Before the whites intruded, that was the solitary reason for war among the Cherokee. Avenging a death or deaths. The warriors never fought about property, either land or goods. They simply exacted what they thought was due when someone was killed, retribution."

"I have no vendetta against James for killing Brenda. I just want to stop him from hurting or killing anyone else," she assured him. "You need to get over this obsession with the *ways,* Senate. I don't know anyone who's still living in the dark ages around here. One of the foremost attributes of the Cherokee is adaptability. We adjust to new ways of doing things. I took an oath as an agent and I didn't have my fingers crossed or add any silent *buts* in there."

He smiled at that and inclined his head a little as if he accepted her at her word. "Noted. Only asking. See, I didn't grow up with all the verbal history you must have had mixed in with your bedtime stories. For all I know, you could be a closet purist."

She smiled at that. "We'll put you in the Booger Dance at

the festival and make fun of you if you don't watch us. That's what we did with the other tribes and then the whites way back in the day. Anything strange, we sort of brushed off as ridiculous. That wound up killing off ninety-five percent of us when the Spanish came over and lost forty percent of what was left with the English settlers. We should have gone to war when we had the manpower and we should have fought over property rights. So, no, I don't hold with keeping things the way they were. We weren't right in some cases. Respecting culture is one thing, learning from mistakes is another."

"Would you kill him if you had the chance?" Clay asked point-blank.

Vanessa thought about it. "If it came down to him or me, I like to think it would be him, but I wouldn't shoot him on sight just because I could."

"Your people used to run the offender off a cliff. Or give him the necessary push." When she frowned at him, Clay added, "Part of the vision made me ask. Probably not significant. Most of the time, these little scenarios are so loaded with symbolism they're impossible to understand until after the fact."

How interesting. "But in retrospect, you can see what they meant? Is that how it goes?"

He nodded. "If I'm right, somehow it will come down to you, me and Hightower. No one else." His expressive lips twisted in a wry grin. "Unless it was just a nightmare. I didn't seek this vision. I rarely have sought one, and then only to explore the phenomenon. They're virtually useless for any prior planning."

"The thunder and lightning, though. Could that represent explosions?" Vanessa was buying into his vision, she realized. Maybe she had listened a little too carefully to all those tales the grandfathers told her.

"Maybe. No way to be sure about that."

She sat forward, excited now. "Listen, what if you really prepared? Suppose you did the cleansing, fasting, sweat-lodge thing and tried again. Maybe the vision would come clear?"

He laughed. "You think I haven't tried all that? The spirits seem to like confusing the hell out of me and it gets worse when I'm dehydrated or playing with peyote."

But Vanessa couldn't let it go. "Let's get Du-da here and do it right. And we don't use peyote. It's the Black Drink, a kind of tea."

"Oh great. A super-tannic acid trip." He made a face as he reached over and took her hand. "The visions are probably just a waste of time. Maybe we should just get everyone out beating the bushes to find Hightower and put a tail on him."

"That, too," she promised, squeezing his hand with both of hers, ignoring the no-touch rule she had instituted herself. This was not hand-holding. It was only showing her support and encouragement. "But in the meantime, let's do the other. C'mon, be a sport. You started all this about the visions and I'd like to see what comes of it. It couldn't hurt, could it?"

"I guess not. Will your grandfather take it seriously? I found out the hard way, this is nothing to play around with."

"Grandfather's no medicine man, but he's a real history buff. At any rate, I'll bet he knows the drill or can find someone who does."

She suddenly thought of Clay, naked, arms outstretched, rising out of the river as he readied himself to receive his vision. She wondered just what the spirits had in store for her to give her such a picture in her mind.

Chapter 8

"I'm not sure this is such a great idea," Clay argued, wrinkling his nose at the cup of foul-smelling brew. He had already had a spate of it earlier with the correct results, according to Walker.

The stuff was brewed of yaupon holly and used in almost every ceremony conducted by the Cherokee, right down to stickball games at the festivals. The strong emetic was chock full of caffeine. And probably other things he didn't want to know about.

"Well, you won't upchuck again, I promise." Walker's grin reminded Clay of Vanessa at her most devilish. "This time you just sip it."

Clay figured he should be pretty well cleansed by now, inside and out. "All right, but what if we're leaving out some important steps here?"

He had fasted for twenty-four hours, bathed seven times

in the stream where Mr. Walker had indicated and was about to enter the little hut they had constructed out of limbs and skins where a small fire burned to heat large stones. The steam bath planned in there ought to clean out his pores if nothing else.

The religious aspect of this didn't trouble him. Though he had been raised Presbyterian, he understood that had nothing to do with Native American spiritualism. It was a mindset, a way of living and being that he had embraced long ago, maybe even before he was old enough to retain memories. It was a natural thing.

So far this had turned out to be a fairly simple ritual compared to the one he had undergone out in the Midwest a few years back. That had netted him nothing but a raging headache and a jumble of meaningless hallucinations.

The older man smiled at his reticence. They were both stripped. Each wearing only the traditional loincloth. Walker would pour water over the stones to get the steam going once they got things underway.

Walker took the cup from him, held it and stood back for Clay to enter first. His deep voice followed Clay inside. "I think each of us receives messages from the Spirit World. Some people hear those messages more clearly than others. These careful listeners used to become medicine men."

"Well, I'd hardly qualify for that."

"You could have if we still had them," Walker argued. "People of the Longhair clan were often made medicine men even though many of them were of mixed blood or strangers adopted by the tribe. The Cherokee understood that others often see us more clearly than we do ourselves. The Longhairs were often called the Stranger clan. You are now of this clan among us." He closed the flap and sat cross-legged on the blanket he had spread within earlier. Clay sat, too, facing

Walker across the fire, and had the eerie feeling he had just been transported back to a primitive time when this event would not have been unusual.

"What if I really *am* Cherokee and was born to another clan and just don't know it?" Clay asked, wondering if not knowing would affect his chance of getting any more seriously involved with Vanessa. That wasn't something he ought to be considering, but it did occur to him and seemed vitally important at the moment.

Walker smiled knowingly, his weathered features thrown in relief by the firelight. "I do not believe you were born to us, son, but I do think you are here for a reason."

Clay shook his head in wonder. "I still can't believe you're going along with this."

"Why not? A greater understanding of the mind and the psychic connections between the human mind and the Spirit World could enable us to do greater things than we do. Things that most people consider impossible. We know of people in the past who could heal with a touch, travel outside the body, mentally communicate with others and see the future. What if each of us has the capacity to do those things but just don't know how?"

Clay felt humbled, a little taken aback and totally in awe of this man who was granting him and his visions such acceptance. He slicked back the damp hair that had fallen over his ears and rubbed his palms over his chest. "Should I apologize to the spirits for not knowing precisely what's expected?" he asked.

"The medicine people who might have taught us those secrets are gone so this is not your fault. To tell you the truth, Clay, I believe that you need to seek your vision using what you think will work for you. The spirits will probably appreciate your attempt, at any rate."

He poured more water over the hot stones, almost

eliminating all visibility with the steam as he rose to his feet. "I'm going now. We'll wait for you at the house. You know the way back?"

Clay nodded. He couldn't seem to put the guilt out of his mind. Vanessa was carrying the whole load of the investigation while he was camping out in the woods. How could he concentrate while worrying about her? Would it affect the success of this attempt? If a vision could help, even a little, he knew he had to give it his best shot. "Thank you, sir. If this works, it will be your doing."

"So you'll buy me a steak." He pushed back the flap of the hut and turned. "Drink the Black Drink now. And don't forget the tobacco." He pointed to a small clay pot that sat beside the blanket. "The spirits like that."

Clay downed the dark liquid, holding his breath against the god-awful smell. Then he took up a huge pinch of the sacred tobacco Walker had provided and sprinkled it over the fire.

Should he say any incantations along with this? He switched to the language of the Principal People for the sake of politeness. "Show me. Warn me. Guide my path. Keep Vanessa Walker safe." There. "And if you have to choose one, pick that last request," he added for good measure.

Already, he felt dizzy and a little out of it. He dipped more water and sluiced it over the hot stones, welcoming the fog that engulfed him. He felt both jumpy and exhausted. Sort of wrung out. He just hoped he didn't fall face first into the fire. What was he thinking, doing this? But since he had gone to such lengths already, he might as well give it his all.

He poured more water on the stones, inhaled the steam, leaned back and closed his eyes.

Twelve hours later, he crawled out of the hut, knee-walked to the nearby stream and fell in face first. His mind reeled and he still wasn't sure what to make of all he had seen. The only thing he was certain of was that he didn't plan to go back for the second show.

"Clay!" Vanessa cried. She grabbed the blanket she'd brought and rushed down to the stream. "Good grief, don't drown yourself. Here, let me help you." Thank God, he had finally come out. She had debated whether to interrupt him and had decided to follow her grandfather's orders to leave him alone.

He pushed himself to his knees and managed a weak smile. "What are you doing here?" With a squint, he looked up at the sky through the trees. It was midmorning. "Were you here all night?"

"A few hours," she admitted, feeling guilty for suggesting he do the ceremony thing. "Come on, let's go get you some breakfast. You must be starved." He hadn't had anything to eat for at least thirty-six hours and probably nothing to drink but water and the Black Drink. His nerves must be shot from that alone. The stuff was almost pure caffeine. That, taken on top of sleep deprivation was enough to wreck anyone. "How are you feeling?"

"A little disoriented." He got to his feet and she wrapped the blanket around him, patting his face and shoulders with the corner of the fabric. He pushed it away and stepped back. "I need to bathe. I smell like wood smoke and sweat."

She shivered as she glanced at the cold rushing waters of the stream. She knew her grandfather had left nothing of Clay's here in the way of clothing. The landscape looked totally primitive, almost primeval. "Come back to the house and soak in a hot tub."

"No argument there," he muttered.

Vanessa inhaled his pure maleness mixed with the wood smoke and the faint lingering essence of the Black Drink. His hair hung in wet strands to his shoulders and his eyes were bloodshot, but the effect was anything but pitiful. He looked like a warrior of old, clad only in a loincloth and blanket, his skin glowing like burnished copper. The sight, scent and feel of him next to her sent warmth rushing through her veins.

"I brought you some mocs, over there," she said, guiding him over to the tree where she had spent most of the night waiting. When they reached her little temporary campsite, she knelt before him and slipped the moccasins on his feet. He smiled down at her and she grinned up at him. "They're a tight fit. Du-da has smaller feet, but they should do." Somehow, slippers hadn't seemed right for the occasion. Though she figured Clay probably had packed some, she hadn't wanted to plunder through his things.

Silently they trudged together back to her grandparents' house. It was a good half mile. Clay seemed to gain strength with each step, though he kept one arm around her shoulders, both pretending this was for support.

Her grandfather greeted them from the back porch. "Bet you're ready for some breakfast," he said.

"A bath first to warm him up," Vanessa said, then looked up at him to see if he agreed. He nodded and they went together up the steps and on up to his bedroom.

While he watched, seeming a little removed from reality, she drew him a hot bath. Without a hint of modesty, he dropped the blanket, toed off the mocs and unfastened the leather cord holding his loincloth in place. Vanessa couldn't look away. She bit her lips together to keep from exclaiming. Every fantasy she'd ever had about the perfect man came to mind in that instant and nearly had her sinking to the floor in admiration. That would probably embarrass him.

He stepped into the tub and sank down with a sigh. Vanessa took the soap and began to lather his face and neck. He captured her hand before she got too familiar and smiled softly in admonishment.

"Shampoo!" she said, feeling her face flush as she turned away to get it. "I'll do your hair."

When he offered no protest, she poured out a bit of the gel and worked it into the soft mane. He groaned with pleasure as her fingers massaged his scalp and neck and Vanessa's blood heated even more. Lord, she would love to crawl into the tub with him, hold him, find out what kind of love they could make together. Never had she wanted a man this way. And how inappropriate was that when he was practically in a state of fugue?

She tried to shake off the need. They had business to take care of after he had recovered a little. So far he'd said nothing about a vision or lack of one, but they needed to explore it as soon as possible before he forgot the details. If there were any details. Maybe this had been a fruitless experiment after all.

He slid under the surface to rinse his hair. Then for the first time, he spoke normally, each word succinct and not allowing for any argument on her part. "Vanessa, go and wait for me in the kitchen."

With a sigh of regret, knowing it was the wise thing, she did as he asked.

Later, when he appeared fully dressed in jeans and a V-necked sweater, his hair slicked back and tied at his nape, she felt a little more in control of herself.

She watched as he ate, gingerly at first, then with gusto. Her grandparents smiled silently, perfectly willing to wait and let Clay relate whatever he had learned in his seclusion. He was the man of the hour just for trying to commune with the spirits. She hoped he had met with some success for all this trouble. He wasn't talking about it yet, though. Had it been so terrible?

"Stop frowning so," he muttered. "I'm all right, just hungry." He finished off his last bite of toast. "And confused," he admitted.

She couldn't stand it any longer. "Did you see anything? Learn anything?"

Slowly, he nodded and sat back in his chair, one long arm resting on the tabletop. "The vision was the same as before but with more clarity. Thunder, lightning. This time torrential rain." His eyes had a faraway look as if he were recapturing images. "The animal he is was not one I recognized, not real. Part wolf, part something else. Long arms. He ran upright and carried…bolts of lightning. Waved them like a threat."

Vanessa dropped her voice to a near whisper. "Were we there again?"

"The panther," he said. "It appeared, but I don't think it was me, not like you said it was. I should have been afraid of it, but…" He shook his head.

"Your spirit guide," her grandfather said with assurance.

Clay continued. "Hightower kept hiding things, the bombs maybe. Couldn't tell what or where he was, but there were many stops. We were rushing, never quite catching up."

"We?" Vanessa asked, leaning forward, excited. "Me, as the fox and you as the panther?"

He shook his head. "I don't know. Maybe. I sensed you there. And I was, but the panther was ahead somehow, leading the way. The chase was long. Grueling. Frustrating. And in the end, there was a falling away of earth. I felt a sense of…failure." His eyes were red-rimmed and his voice halting. "It's still not clear."

Then he turned abruptly and faced her grandfather. "The phrase *kick bird* or *kill bird*. Does it mean anything to you?" It kept running through his mind with urgency, an almost gleeful urgency. "Could the bird be Vanessa?" he asked her grandfather.

No, she knew what it meant. But Clay placed a hand on her wrist when she started to get up. "Wait. There's something else right at the beginning, that was new, that I didn't see in the other vision. His eyes…strange, even for him."

"James?"

"Yes. It was…like a madness overtook him. Suddenly he twisted something and killed it. Elation. Power. Then resignation. Dead resignation. I sensed he hadn't meant to do what he did, but it was done and he couldn't undo it. After that he began with the phrase running through his mind. *Kill…bird. The only way. Kill…bird.* What could it mean?"

Vanessa couldn't wait. "I know what it means! Killbird Mountain. That's where he's gone!"

"The death," Clay said. "It was a man, someone he had trusted. He felt betrayed."

Vanessa pulled out of his grasp and went to the phone on the counter and quickly dialed. Six rings and she got the answering machine. She hung up and dialed again. "Michael? Get over to Maggie Valley and check out Tim Sauk's place. See if he's there. If he's not, find him. I need to talk to him right away."

She replaced the receiver. "Sauk's his lawyer. I think we should warn him."

"You think James is planning to go up Killbird? That's some rough terrain. Why would he go there?" her grandfather asked. "Surely there are better places to hide."

Vanessa knew. She leaned back against the kitchen counter and looked out the wide picture window that faced the mountains. "I think it's probably a straight shot, perfect line of sight from the mountaintop down to Cherokee. No interference," she said, her worried gaze sliding back to her grandfather, then to Clay. "If he's planning to use a remote-control device to detonate the bombs, what better place to be?"

While Clay slept, Vanessa found and studied the terrain maps she had collected when she had worked as a camping guide. Her grandfather, guessing her intent, was busy making up backpacks with the necessary items. The only problem was he was making three.

She made it very clear he was not coming with them. "You have to stay here, Du-da. Keep the family safe."

He argued that Dilly was safe enough with her aunt and uncle in Asheville and her grandmother would want him to go along and look after Vanessa.

After a while, she convinced him he couldn't go. Or maybe he realized he would only slow them down. She brought up the vision and reminded him that neither he, nor his spirit guide, the bear, were present in it.

An hour later, she knew Clay's vision was true. Michael called. Tim Sauk, James's attorney, was dead. Michael had found him at his home, lying on the patio with a broken neck, ostensibly caused by a fall from the balcony above. Vanessa knew she would never be able to make Michael believe what had really happened. At least not until he had an autopsy report in his hands that would indicate homicide. They couldn't wait.

She and Clay would have to act on the vision alone then. No official backup could be secured with the nebulous information provided by what the authorities would term a hallucination. They still had nothing official on James Hightower, only her strong suspicion.

At least that bomb found beneath the judge's vehicle created enough of a question about James to keep the search teams busy looking for other explosives he might have set.

She went to wake Clay. They needed to get up to Killbird Mountain. She had no idea whether the outcome of his vision could be changed or if it was fated to end in the failure he had sensed, but she certainly intended to do everything within her power to put a better end to the situation.

Surely there was a reason why the visions had come to Clay in the first place. He was expected to do something about it, or what would be the point of the spirits warning him?

He had detailed the vision as much as possible. The early parts were crystal clear, he'd said. James planting the bombs in a hurry, Sauk's murder, James's thinking of Killbird. Clay, Vanessa and her grandfather had all agreed that this portion of the vision must have happened real-time, as events were going on.

What Clay had said had come off rather hazy and flashed in and out like a faulty strobe were the latter parts—the lightning bolts, the chase up the mountain and the so-called falling away of the earth. All that had to be prophetic.

An hour later, she and Clay were just now about to ascend Killbird. They parked her vehicle on a side road at the foot of the mountain, got out and shouldered the packs her grandfather had prepared for them.

"You did notify the sheriff's office exactly where we're going, didn't you?" Clay asked as they set off plowing through the brush.

"I did, but they thought that looking for James up there was pretty far-fetched. I had to tell them it was just a hunch we were going to check out. Admitting that we're following a vision might not cut much ice with most of them. Michael would laugh his butt off, I can guarantee that."

"And he might be justified," Clay muttered. "Who knows how much of what I saw was a real vision and not just my warped imagination?"

Vanessa scoffed. "You saw Tim Sauk's death. We know that's all *too* real. I almost wish I had told Michael about your vision when I sent him over there to check on Tim. Of course, then he might have decided you or I had something to do with killing him."

"If he *was* killed," Clay reminded her. "Maybe he did fall off the balcony and break his neck. A hell of a coincidence if he did, but entirely possible."

"No it's not," she argued. "And if you were just dreaming up stuff, how would you have gotten the name *Killbird?* It's not even called that on any maps you might have seen. Today they call it Wuh-Tehh Peak. Like you can rename a mountain any old thing you want."

They trudged along through the rough terrain near the foot of Killbird. There were no paths up the mountain since few people ever ventured up there. The climb was steep, rocky, tiresome and the view from the top totally uninspiring. True, you could see the rooftops in town with good binoculars, but there were also the ugly outlying shanties. No wild beautiful mountain vistas like you got from Clingman's Dome or some of the other elevations. There were simply better mountains around here to climb with breathtaking offerings at their peaks. Much better ones for the experts who liked climbing vertical rock faces for sport, too. Old Killbird was left pretty much alone.

James Hightower was well aware of that, Vanessa was certain. He'd probably be up there somewhere by now, though they had seen no signs of him so far. There was no point trying to track him. He could have begun his climb anywhere around the base of Killbird.

The trees, still in full leaf, kept most of the sun blocked. The brush and ground cover thinned the higher they got. Rocks, some enormous and part of the mountain itself, made climbing in a straight path impossible. Still, it wasn't a bad hike, Vanessa thought. She let Clay take the lead, mostly so she could feast her eyes.

He would be gone soon, but she did not intend to follow

him to McLean, Virginia. She would not accept the job with this COMPASS team, even if he did decide she was qualified.

Clay had gone into great detail during their two days of downtime and now she fully understood what the new position would entail. The prospect fascinated her, she had to admit. Working for this elite team would definitely be a huge step up in her career. She knew it was quite an honor to even be considered. But the trade-off troubled her and had played a large part in her decision not to accept the offer. Personal reasons played into it, as well.

She had done a lot of thinking about it in the early morning hours as she'd waited for him to emerge from the little hut and his visit with the spirits. Maybe they had spoken to her, too, in a way.

Clay had not yet come to terms with who he really was. Indian or white? Loner, or a part of something much larger than himself? He was struggling with this and likely had been all his life. Vanessa knew she confused the issue for him, but she couldn't help trying to make him fit. Finding himself was something a man—or a woman—needed to do alone.

Maybe she also needed to get a firmer grip on her own self before she even thought about getting somebody else in order. She was a buttinsky, a do-gooder, a fixer by nature. But, in the end, she was probably just as out of sync as Clay was.

Look at her life goals right now. They were to excel, to impress the hell out of her superiors in the Bureau and provide an example for young Indians who doubted they could make a career for themselves. How self-important was that? As if she had all the answers.

She should be focusing on something else, but she wasn't sure just what that was. Anyway, she had come to the conclusion that two heads not screwed on straight were, in no way, better than one.

Maybe sometime in the future… No, she couldn't think that way, or she would talk herself right into that job she didn't need to take, the one that would keep her in Clay's pocket. She was *not* going to Virginia.

Her eyes had settled on his strong back, the confident and graceful way he moved, that tight butt that looked so darn good in worn jeans. She released a little huff of appreciation followed by a groan of regret, then shook her head to clear it.

What wouldn't she give to share just one night with this guy and make memories to last forever? Would it ruin her for any future relationships? Vanessa wondered. That curiosity of hers would be her downfall if she didn't watch it.

Hours later, the sound of his breathing told Vanessa the altitude was getting to him. She was feeling a little light-headed herself. Clay shrugged off his backpack and tossed it on a flat rock nearby. "Let's camp here."

Hmm. More command than suggestion, but that was okay for now. "This is fine. Too dangerous to go on without good light."

All the way up Killbird there were deep ravines, sheer fissures in the mountain that dropped off unexpectedly. This was the first level clearing they had reached and darkness would be falling within the hour.

"We're about halfway up, aren't we?" he asked.

Vanessa dropped her own pack and followed it down, stretching out full length on her back, hands cushioning her head. "Man, I hope so! My calf muscles are screaming."

He sat down beside her on the rock's surface, slid one hand underneath her leg and massaged the muscle there for a minute. She groaned appreciatively. "Oh, yeah…other one, please."

He complied and she felt the tightness relax beneath his fingertips. "Higher?" he asked.

She sat up, almost too quickly and scooted out of reach. "Uh-uh, that's okay."

Clay smiled. "Why so skittish?"

He knew why and he knew she knew it. Massaging her thighs was not a good idea. A deliciously provocative idea, but not a good one.

She ignored his question, began plundering inside her backpack and asked one of her own. "Hungry?"

"Not yet. You go ahead, though."

She tossed him a candy bar. "Me? I like to start with dessert."

"You wicked girl." He tore off the wrapper, took a bite of the chocolate, then handed the rest back to her.

She munched on the candy while taking a last look around them before darkness made it impossible. Better get their minds back on the case. "Think James knows we're after him?"

"I doubt he's spotted us since we've been under cover of the trees most of the time. Tomorrow could be different."

Vegetation would grow sparser as they climbed higher. Fewer trees, more rock. Visibility would be greater.

"This is the safest way up and probably the way he came, but we haven't seen any sign of him," Vanessa said, uncapping her bottle of water. "That makes me think he's being careful not to leave any obvious tracks."

She took a swig, wishing the water were ice cold instead of lukewarm. She offered him some and he took it, grimacing a little after he tasted it.

"Maybe he's psychic," Clay suggested, and not in a facetious way. "Many people have feelings they don't recognize as being extrasensory and act on them instinctively. Or maybe he's paranoid."

"Which doesn't mean we're not out to get him," Vanessa said with a dry laugh.

Clay smiled with her. "How do you do it?"

"Do what?" she asked.

"Lighten everything up the way you do. Even in the tensest situations, you seem able to find a little dash of humor. Look at you now, as relaxed as if this were merely a stroll up the mountain to enjoy the fall foliage."

He shook his head and glanced around them. "Look at the colors, how they're beginning to turn. I wish that really was why we were here."

"Me, too." Vanessa lay back on the rock and took another bite of the candy bar. She chewed for a minute. "Whatever I do must not be a conscious thing. I wasn't aware of it anyway. I guess joking around is a defense mechanism to keep from getting too wound up."

He reached for the candy, his fingers brushing over hers as he took it from her. "Maybe the secret's in the chocolate."

"Cures what ails you," she said with a grin, snatching it back and finishing it off.

"You have a little…" He leaned over and stroked the corner of her mouth with one finger, a slow sensual caress that fired all her senses at once.

Before she knew what she had done, Vanessa touched his finger with her tongue. Their gazes locked, darkened faster than the sun had slipped behind the mountains.

He traced her lips, pressing the bottom one lower, opening her mouth as his descended on it. Just like that, they were kissing. Again.

Chapter 9

Vanessa sighed deep and long, drawing in his scent, damn near desperate for it. His sound of satisfaction hummed through her. It was just one of those golden moments that didn't need sunshine to make it so.

Any second, she expected him to draw back, tell her how they couldn't do this, that it would tangle up their lives, that they had to stop. Only he didn't. Instead, his arms snaked around her and cushioned her back from the rock on which they lay. One large hand cradled her head as he deepened the kiss, changed the angle, devoured her.

She felt herself floating, then realized he was lifting her off the rock. Seconds later, he lowered them both to the grassy ground. Vanessa realized then that she would have to be the one to call a halt to this if they were to stop at all.

If he had not arranged her on top instead of beneath him, she knew she wouldn't have said a word. As it was, he had more or less put her in control. She felt obligated and oh, so reluctant. With another sigh, this time of regret, she moved back, her arms propped on his chest and looked down at him. She could hardly see his features clearly now in the deepening twilight. "Almost got away from us, didn't it?" she whispered.

He released his breath slowly and ran his hand over the side of her face, letting it come to rest on the curve of her neck. It lingered there, warm, comforting, possessive. She knew he could feel her pulse going ninety to nothing. "Yeah, it did."

She noted he didn't apologize for it this time. Neither would she. If she was sorry about anything at all, it was that her common sense had kicked in when it had. She wanted him so fiercely even now, she could hardly keep from kissing him again to let him know how much.

"Gotta get up from here or it might yet." She pushed off him and sat back on the grass, running her hands through her hair and resting her elbows on her knees.

Neither she nor Clay needed this complication, they both agreed on that. This "it" they were fighting grew like summer crepe myrtle, branching out in all directions at once and making a huge tree before you knew it if you didn't keep cutting it back. Maybe it was time to dig it right out of the ground. She knew how to do that. She would use a blunt shovel.

"Look, Clay," she said, "you want me because I make you feel more Indian. No, don't deny it," she said before he could get a word out. "That's the draw right there. That's the whole deal. All your life, you've played at being red, haven't you? Studied the languages, the customs, even wear your hair that way to enhance your features. You do look the part, I'll grant you that. But inside, you're mostly white and you know it. It eats at you."

He cleared his throat. She could tell he was facing away from her when he spoke. "Get to the point."

She had hit a nerve, big time. "All right. You want to deny

that white part, but if you do, you know you'll have to become some sort of totem for the rest of us, right? That's the way you're made. You'd have to do something in the way of setting things right. In other words, you wouldn't be working for the very government who took away the lands and rights and customs you would profess to own."

He issued a grunt, then a short laugh. "That's without a doubt the most patently ridiculous thing I've ever heard you say. Where is this coming from?"

"The heart," she said, sounding a little too flip, or more so than she had intended. "As for me, my motive for wanting you is a lot less convoluted. You're hot as a firecracker."

He laughed outright, the soft sound blending with the wind in the trees. "Vanessa Walker, what am I going to do with you?"

"Nothing," she stated baldly. "We are not going any further with this, Clay. Get over the Indian thing. You are half and that's all you'll ever be."

"So are you," he said, still not angry the way she wanted him to be. "What about that Italian mother of yours? If the Cherokee are so matriarchal in their lineage, then you're technically Italian."

Vanessa rolled her eyes. "You are so damned literal, Senate!"

"And *hot,* don't forget that. Hot as a firecracker." He chuckled. "I like that. Might put it on my résumé."

She sensed him stretch, could even see the vague silhouette of him as he did. "I'm serious. This is going nowhere."

"Might," he argued. "But I won't push."

"Promise?"

For a long time he said nothing. "Maybe you're right," he said finally.

Right about this going nowhere or right about his motive for wanting her? Vanessa couldn't bring herself to ask and what did it matter anyway?

He dragged both their packs down off the rock and set hers next to her.

Vanessa felt around, then unbuckled the pack straps that secured her rolled-up blanket. In moments, she was snugly wrapped inside it with her head resting on the pack. Clouds obscured the moon and stars completely. She should have checked the weather. The mountain was as dark as the back of a cave and you could almost smell the rain.

Clay startled her when he settled right next to her with his back flush against hers. Not a lot of safety in that, but she supposed it was more prudent than cuddling spoon-style.

"Buona notte, volpe piccola," he said with a smile in his voice. *Good night, little fox.*

"Good night, White Eyes," she replied.

Somehow she'd thought he would be a lot more sensitive about his heritage, that her insults would put him off big time and solve their problem. Instead, he seemed to find everything she'd said amusing.

And he hadn't really promised when it came to not pushing for something to happen between them. It was almost as if he knew something eventually *would* and, like it or not, neither of them could do a damn thing about it.

Vanessa tried like crazy to squelch that eager, wicked little voice inside her that screamed a fist-pumping, Snoopy-dancing *Yes!*

Surely her brain was suffering a dearth of oxygen at this elevation. All right, maybe they weren't that high up yet, but it was definitely laboring under the deliciously combined scent of fresh mountain air and essence of Senate.

At any rate, she wouldn't sleep a wink with that magnificent blue-jeaned butt pressed smack against hers. That was the last conscious thought before exhaustion overtook her.

However, late in the night, she did wake long enough to

realize it wasn't his back that snuggled next to her, but his front. One strong arm surrounded her, his hand resting lightly on her forearm. If his breathing hadn't been so deep and regular, she might not have willed herself back to sleep.

Clay woke to a sound he recognized only from the murky depths of his vision. Quietly so as not to disturb Vanessa, he moved away from her and rose as stealthily as he could. Dawn was just breaking. He released the safety on his pistol and crept nearer the rock outcropping a little less than thirty feet away from where they'd slept.

Again he heard the high-pitched growl and identified its position. Just above him on the enormous rock, which projected straight out of the ground like a small mountain in itself, crouched a panther.

Clay froze in firing position. He had fifteen rounds, surely enough to bring down a cat of any size. This one was not enormous. One shot to the head, right between the eyes. But if he missed? Better aim for the heart. The nine-millimeter H&K had stopping power.

Shots would alert Hightower and lose them the element of surprise. He had always been told not to make eye contact with a dangerous animal, but Clay had always done that with the two-legged variety and that had saved him more than once. A subtle flicker of the eyes signaled the next move of a man, so why not a beast?

He met the animal's narrowed amber gaze, heard the warning growl, then a huh-huh-huh sound. Fascinated, he watched the panther open its mouth, twist its head and look off to its right. Then it gazed back at him with a steady, non-threatening regard. It repeated the action.

Then Clay watched it turn slowly and silently disappear down the far side of the large outcropping of rocks.

For several minutes he remained locked in position, unable to move. Or maybe unwilling to move. He had felt no fear. His adrenaline had kicked in there for a minute, but in a positive way.

He had no desire to go after it, to kill it, though that would have made perfect sense. It could return and attack, track them and take them when they were vulnerable. Hell, it could have killed at least one of them before the other could have gotten a weapon out if it had attacked while they slept.

"That was *so* amazing!" Vanessa whispered as she approached him from behind. "There are so few sightings."

Clay turned, lowering his weapon. He saw that she had hers out, too, holding it down by her side now. "Shots would have warned Hightower," he said, thinking to justify why he hadn't fired.

She smiled indulgently. "Don't be silly. You knew better than to shoot your spirit guide. What kind of Indian would that make you?"

"Don't make fun of it," he said, a little riled that she was finding humor in this.

"I'm not." She tucked her weapon into the holster attached to her belt and snapped the cover. "Ah, but you're embarrassed, caught listening to a painter? Well, don't be."

"Painter?"

She nodded. "That's what the old folks call them." She looked off in the direction the panther had looked and pointed. "I guess he was telling you to go that way."

Clay didn't argue. Maybe she was teasing him, maybe she wasn't. Though she had encouraged the vision thing, he couldn't be absolutely sure she really bought into it. Maybe she thought he was faking it all, and just wanted to see how far he would take it.

But the big cat had looked him directly in the eyes and Clay had sensed something in the exchange. If not an actual communiqué, then *something*. Wouldn't Mercier, with his telepathic obsessions, freak out over this one?

In any event, the way the panther had signaled was as good a way as any. It led up, and the top of Killbird was the most likely place to find their prey. "So let's go," he said with a shrug. If she was poking fun at him, and the panther didn't eat them somewhere along the way, he would have the last laugh.

They lingered long enough to consume a couple of the MREs her grandfather had packed for them. Clay had forgotten how truly tasteless the military meals-ready-to-eat were. It had been a while since he had had one.

Mr. Walker had a case of the things on hand for emergencies such as getting snowed in. Apparently living off the land and eating berries and bugs held little appeal, even for a former soldier. The eggs-and-ham thing Clay had opened wasn't a great improvement over that, he thought as he chewed.

"Ketchup?" Vanessa asked, her voice brighter than it had any right to be first thing in the morning. She tossed him a small packet, obviously filched from a local fast-food place. He squeezed it on the concoction he was eating while she prepared the coffee. A small can of Sterno heated the tin cup full of instant that they would share.

He toasted her when it was his turn to drink. "To MREs. Yet another reason to get this over with and get back down the mountain."

She appropriated the cup and drank her share as if it were special brew. "You're a city boy at heart, aren't you? Remind me never to invite you on another camping trip. Bitch and moan. Bitch and moan."

Clay couldn't suppress a laugh. "Busted. So I like my

comforts. Too many days in the field weaned me off all the primitive pleasures."

Her eyes flared comically. "Well, not *all* of them, I guess."

He silently agreed as he gathered up the used packets, tucked the trash away in a special container and stuffed it in his pack to dispose of later.

Vanessa capped the Sterno, rinsed out the coffee cup with a bit of water and put both away. "Ready," she said, standing and shouldering her backpack.

Clay led the way again, keeping a sharp eye out for signs of the panther as well as any indication that Hightower had passed this way.

He wished he could make Vanessa understand him. To her credit, she wanted to, but he knew she never could. Her analysis had been right as far as it went. His greatest wish was to belong, but he would never risk opening himself up enough for that. Too much rejection already, he guessed.

The white/Indian conflict within him had not been an issue for years. At least he hadn't thought it was. Whites saw him as Indian. His doing. Indians saw him as white. His father's doing. The truth was, he was an American, a soldier at heart, a man who simply wanted to make a difference. A good difference in the society in which he lived.

He hadn't given the race thing any thought lately until this last vision. For the first time in his life, he had felt truly Indian and he had liked that. Liked it almost too much.

If he read Vanessa right, she was trying to make him angry and he knew why. She felt something strong for him that she did not want to feel. So why did he keep trying with her? Why not just leave her the hell alone?

Maybe because he felt the same thing and couldn't help himself. But was she right? Was it Vanessa the woman or was it all she represented that drew him like a lodestone? Until he could answer that question truthfully, he wouldn't touch her again.

They had climbed steadily for an hour when thunder rumbled in the distance and clouds quickly enveloped the mountain. Visibility dwindled immediately. "We have to stop," Vanessa called just as Clay's back disappeared. "Wait! I can't see you."

She ran smack into him, bounced off and landed on the ground. He reached down to help her up. "Talk about pea soup. You can't see your hand in front of your face. I guess we sit here until we can."

The cloud that surrounded them either drifted or lifted, impossible to tell which. The ground sloped so much where they were, she was afraid they would slide back down the mountain when it got wet. And it was definitely about to get wet.

Thunder boomed. Lightning struck nearby almost simultaneously. A tree cracked and they heard it fall. The sharp odor of ozone filled the thin humid air. Sudden, driving rain drenched them within seconds. "We have to find some shelter away from these trees before we get fried."

Unable to see more than six or eight feet ahead through the rain, Vanessa took the lead since she knew the terrain better than he did. "This way," she told him. "Hang on to my pack in case we get clouded again. She felt the tug as he gripped it.

Carefully, she picked her way around rocks and through the scrubby ground cover. She spied a dark shape marring the rock face just ahead. "There! Is that a cave?"

"Let me check it out first," Clay ordered, stepping around

her. Vanessa moved to one side to let him pass and the rocks beneath her feet gave way.

At first, she thought they had only shifted on the ground and she tried to step over them. Her foot met thin air. She screamed as she fell sideways, unable to find a foothold.

Her breath cut off with a jerk as the straps of her pack yanked her shoulders back. She hung suspended on a rock face. Below her was nothing but rain. Terrified to move, even to breathe, she did manage a low-pitched moan that sounded something like Clay's name.

"Stay still!" he cautioned. "I'll get you. Snake your hands up and grab on to your straps. Hold tight. I'm going to lie down and drag you back up, okay?"

She made another sound that wasn't quite a word. Inch by careful inch, expecting to fall free at any instant, she lifted her left hand. The right arm wouldn't move. Pain knifed through her shoulder every time she tried. With a death grip on her left strap secured, she sucked in a slow, deep breath to tell Clay about her arm. But suddenly the pack moved and she dropped a few inches.

"Hold on!" he demanded. "I've got you. Relax now. Don't struggle. Just grip it tight with both hands."

"Can't!" she cried. "My right shoulder's out."

She heard his curse. "Okay. All right. Just take it easy," he said, his voice calm again, trying to reason with her panic. "Turn to your left slowly. I'm twisting the pack so you can face the rocks. That way maybe you can get a toehold and help me lift you. Can you do that, Vanessa? Try to do that. Go, now," he ordered.

She turned as best she could. The pack was above her head, only the shoulder straps now beneath her arms holding her. The chest strap was beneath her chin, nearly choking her.

Her shoulder screamed all on its own and she fought

fainting for all she was worth. Grunting with effort, she moved her feet slightly and felt the toe of her boot connect with the rock face. She dug onto it, managed to push herself up a few inches. There!

The purchase defaulted and she swung free. Rocks tumbled, clacking and bumping below her for what seemed forever. It had to be a long way down and there was no splash at the bottom. Only the pelting rain and no place to put her feet.

Tears filled her eyes, washed away just as quickly as she shed them. God, she was going to die. No way Clay could lift her dead weight and a thirty pound pack up this vertical drop.

"Vanessa!" he called. "Stay calm. I've still got you. You with me? Say something!"

"Help?" she managed, feeling ridiculous as the word popped out. "I can't do anything!" Anger suddenly pushed the fear down. She had to do something. But her right arm was useless, there was nothing beneath her feet and her left hand had already gone numb from gripping the strap.

"Here we go," Clay said. "I'm backing up, pulling you a little higher. When I stop, try to feel around with your feet again. Can you do that?"

"Yeah," she gasped, wishing she didn't sound so… helpless.

Inch by grueling inch, she felt him drag her a little higher. The rain felt merciless, threatening, never-ending. At last he rested. Vanessa gingerly toed her boots forward and felt both catch on something. "Got it," she shouted. "Pull and I'll push. Pray it holds!"

She heard him grunting and tried her best to propel herself upward. The pack above her shifted to her right and she could see his hand above her.

"Another foot, Van. One more push if you can make it. You're doing great, sweetheart. Don't give out on me now."

She bent her knees one at a time and slid her toes over the rocks. Finally she found a crack wide enough to hold the entire toe of her left boot. She tested it as much as she could without resting her whole weight there. It felt solid.

"If I straighten my leg, I think I can raise myself close enough for you to reach my hand," she said in a rush.

"On three, go for it," he said. "One…two…three!" He pulled and she pushed. Vanessa cried out with relief when his strong hand clasped her left wrist.

"I have to cut you free of the pack so I can get you up here," he told her. "Steady now. I'm slicing through the straps. Don't panic when it falls free."

She felt him slide the blade of her grandfather's hunting knife beneath the chest strap, then the one on her right shoulder. Biting her tongue to keep from crying out, Vanessa groaned. The pack swung from her left shoulder now, wrenching it painfully, rendering it almost as useless as her right. He quickly sliced through the last strap and it fell away. She heard it bump the rocks on its long way down.

Now she was braced with one toe in the crevice and Clay gripping her left wrist.

"Try another toehold," he commanded. He didn't have to tell her to hurry. She knew he must be exhausted by this time.

She felt around with her free foot and gained a small fissure. "Ready," she told him. She moved her foot out of the first hold and pushed hard with her right.

A mad scramble followed as Clay clutched her jacket with one hand, held onto her wrist and somehow got the top half of her body on the ledge where he lay.

"Rest a minute," she gasped. Vanessa lay there for a long few minutes dangling half over the edge while they recovered. Then he grasped the back of her belt and pulled her up completely, rolling her away from the precipice and into his arms.

He gripped her so hard it hurt, but she relished it, burrowed into him and cried like a baby.

"Shh. You're all right now. You're fine. You're safe," he crooned, running his hands over her, smoothing her hair out of her face, pressing his mouth to her temple, her eyes, her forehead. "God, that was close," he groaned. "But you're fine. Just fine."

She wasn't fine. She hurt like hell and the true extent of the terror was only now coursing through her. But Clay was here, holding her, saving her. She cried some more, un-ashamed. She was so damned glad to be alive.

Once she calmed down a little, he released her and sat up. "We'd better see about that shoulder. I'll get you down the mountain and to a hospital."

"When the rain stops," she said. "We don't want a replay of this." They were both covered in mud and debris, soaked to their bones and thoroughly spent.

She thought about James Hightower somewhere up here on the mountain, planning to detonate his bombs from this remote location. They couldn't let that happen.

Clay stood. "Stay here a minute. I'll see if that really was a cave we saw. He grabbed up his discarded backpack, glanced around as if trying to orient himself, then loped off into the rain.

Her adrenaline rush was dwindling and she began to feel really shaky. Her body shuddered as she stared at the crumbled edge of the cliff and the muddy evidence of their struggle.

The full impact of what had just happened to her and where she would be right now if Clay had not been here hit her full force.

Against all odds, he had saved her. She owed him her very life.

* * *

The cave proved even larger than Clay had hoped. He saw evidence of human habitation. Someone had left the remnants of a fire near the entrance. It was too wet there now from the rain blowing in to kindle one on the same spot, but maybe farther back. He dropped his pack and fished out the flashlight to check for any four-legged occupants that might resent company.

When he found it safe, he rushed back out to get Vanessa. She lay curled on the ground, either asleep or unconscious. He scooped her up and carried her back into the cave, depositing her in a dry spot away from the opening. "First order of business is getting you dry and warm," he muttered, not really expecting her to answer him.

Her backpack was at the bottom of the gorge so they only had one dry change of clothing, one Mylar blanket and half the food and water. However, her grandfather had packed two large Ziplocs with the bare essentials, one in each of their packs.

He began to strip off her wet, muddy clothing. She groaned and he stopped, remembering her injured shoulder. Gingerly he probed it and exhaled sharply with relief when it didn't appear to be dislocated or broken. "Probably pulled a muscle or tendon," he told her.

Gently, he removed her jacket and her shirt. Her skin was chilled. He pressed his fingers to her neck and checked her pulse. Rapid. Her breathing was shallow and jerky. He feared she was already in shock. It wasn't that cold, but hypothermia was still a possibility. She was soaking wet and probably traumatized to hell and gone.

"Let's dry you off," he crooned, patting her down with the extra T-shirt from his pack. "You'll be just fine. I'll get a fire going soon as I get you wrapped up."

He cocooned her in his dry shirt, snuggled the Mylar blanket around her and gently laid her down on her side. In minutes, he had the fire going, burning the brick of fire starter from his pack. Unfortunately there was nothing else to burn within the cave. The brick would burn for a while, but wouldn't throw off much heat.

Well, he would have to use what warmth was available. Shucking off his own wet clothes and drying the best he could with the shirt he had used as a towel, Clay then brought her closer to the fire and lay down next to her. The crinkly Mylar barely covered them both.

She burrowed closer and he felt her begin to shiver. After a while, she relaxed, sighed and slept.

Clay remained awake, unable to ignore the soft, sweet body pressed to his. Though he didn't move, he did let his imagination wander all over the place. All over her.

Several wonderful, torturous hours passed before she awoke. Her left arm stretched out and she arched her back. "Strangely enough, I feel pretty good."

Oh, she felt good, all right. *Way* too good. She had joked about his being hot as a firecracker. If she only knew.

"I should go out and wash off some of the mud while it's still raining," she said after a while.

"How's the shoulder?" he asked as she pulled away from him and he helped her sit up.

She looked very young bundled in his large shirt. She was such a strong presence that at times he forgot just how small she was, a full foot shorter than he was and so slender she almost appeared delicate. He knew she wasn't that. Not Vanessa. This girl had strength, grit and an indomitable will to survive. She never gave up, never gave in.

She tested her shoulder, rotating it slightly, and winced. "Hurts, but at least I can move it."

Clay ran his hand over it several times to reassure himself she wasn't downplaying the pain. "I'll get you some ibuprofen from the first-aid kit and some water."

He retrieved his tin cup, took it outside the cave and let it fill with rainwater for her while the rain beat the mud off him. When he heard her laugh, he opened his eyes and turned around. She stood nearby, naked as he was, face upturned to the skies.

"Get back inside!" he commanded, pointing to their shelter. "I just got you dry and warm!"

She opened her mouth to catch a drink. "Worrywart, I'm okay now."

Okay didn't begin to cover it. Clay couldn't help but stare. Pale copper skin, high firm breasts with nipples like juicy berries, long slender legs braced to steady her in the driving rain, she provided a vision like none he had ever seen. Her hair streamed over her shoulders and back, clinging like dark wet silk. Her lips were slightly parted now and her eyes closed as they met the continuing downpour.

Rain goddess, that was what she was. A more beautiful sight would be impossible to imagine. Clay simply stood there and relished it while he could, knowing it was a moment that would live in his mind and heart forever.

He didn't realize he had moved until he was right in front of her, nearly touching.

She opened her eyes then and smiled. "We could be the only two people in the world," she said. "Doesn't it feel unreal?"

He couldn't speak. He couldn't even nod. He knew exactly what she meant. He had almost lost her. They were together, impervious to any outside forces, isolated from all regulations and rules, alone with the elements. Nothing else in the world mattered.

She seemed to float as she closed the small distance that separated them. When her hand touched his face, traced the wet surface of it with her fingers, the contact erased any qualms Clay had ever had about possessing her. He slid his arms around her, lifted her gently and took her inside the cave.

Chapter 10

Vanessa reached up for him as he knelt above her.

"I should check on the fire," he muttered, his mouth so close to hers, she could feel the warmth of his breath on her lips.

"Yes…fire," she agreed. She had felt embers glowing in her midsection even before he'd mentioned it and now they were a crackling blaze even the driving rain couldn't quench. She met his lips and took them with a hunger she had never known with another man.

He suddenly broke the kiss and looked down at her. "I am not making love to you here."

"Talking to me or yourself?" she whispered, smiling her wickedest smile.

He smiled back. "Both. I just want to hold you."

"Liar," she groaned. His resolve was obviously stronger than hers in this instance and she knew he was right. This was neither the place nor the time.

Swiftly he pulled the blanket up around them as they lay side by side.

As simply holding went, he was a master at it. He embraced her as if he'd never let her go. "God, I thought you were a goner," he muttered, kissing her ear, her hair where it was plastered to her head by the rain. His lips were warm against her cheek.

Gently, he massaged her arm, then higher, still checking for damage to her shoulder, but he did it in the guise of soothing her. She relaxed and ignored the aches and twinges of pain in her muscles.

He had wonderful hands, a magic touch. If he wasn't a medicine man, he should be, she thought with a smile. If only he would unbend enough to make love to her, Vanessa knew she would feel better than ever. But he seemed determined to play the gentleman.

"Why won't you take me at my word?" she asked, her voice lazy with contentment. "I'm not even considering COMPASS. We could—"

"No, we can't," he argued softly. "You could change your mind. You *should* change your mind. I couldn't be objective about my recommendation if we were lovers, you know that."

"You can't be objective now," she accused, but without the heat of anger. "What does it matter?"

"It matters to me," he told her gently. "I want you to have every opportunity."

Except the very one she wanted most right now, Vanessa thought. But she closed her eyes and relished the comfort of having him next to her. He made her feel sheltered, treasured. He did care and didn't mind if she knew it. Maybe he wasn't as much of a loner as he thought he was.

"You're a prude, you know that? A big old sanctimonious prude!"

He sighed and nuzzled her neck. "And you're a wanton little witch trying to goad me into something that's not good for you." He pressed his lips against her throat. "If I ever make love to you, I want it to be perfect, soft lights—"

"The fire's pretty low," she interrupted, snuggling closer.

"Sweet music…"

"Crickets will do. And the wind."

"Satin sheets…"

She kissed him back. "Two out of three…"

"Hush. I am not making love to you in the wild. Stop tempting me."

She cradled his face in her hands. "I want you, Clay. More than anything I've ever wanted in my life. In the wild. Right here, right now."

His mouth covered hers, devoured her with a passion she had only guessed at before. With nothing held back, he consumed her whole and left her breathless and wanting when he pulled away.

She expected him to protest again, but instead, he slid his hand up her rib cage and over her breast, his caress gentle yet possessive. His palm felt cold against her warmth, but heated her even more with the contrast. She ached for him. Burned.

"I wish I could see you," he whispered, breathing into her ear, exciting her to fever pitch. "All of you."

His wickedly talented hands ran over her body as if memorizing every inch of her skin. She relished the sounds he made in his throat, deep growls of pleasure mixed with frustration. His shadow loomed above her, a dark silhouette that she welcomed, wanted to become part of. He brushed her mouth with his and kissed her again, deeply and thoroughly, his tongue mating with hers, demanding and giving, even as she knew his body would.

She rose to meet each powerful thrust, gloriously lost in

their kiss. They melded into one with a sharp rush of satisfaction, a culmination that should have been only the beginning. Her body shuddered and contracted against and around
him, drawing a deep satisfied groan from him that she echoed
with one of her own.

He smiled against her face. "Satisfied now?"

"If I had breath to purr, I would. What do you think?"
she gasped.

"Short and incredibly sweet," he whispered. "You owe me
time."

She liked it that he didn't apologize. No reason to since he
hadn't jumped the gun. She had.

"Next time, my way," he promised.

"What way is that?" she managed to ask, her breath still
coming in fits and starts.

"Slowly and in a more romantic setting. Like a bed."

She laughed and pinched his behind where her hand was
resting. "Candy-ass."

He held her for a while longer, their bodies still joined.
When he withdrew, Vanessa was half-asleep, her entire being
as warm as melted butter. She gave a sigh and let her palm
slide down his arm. He took her hand, interlaced their fingers
and she drifted off, replete.

Clay stirred the fire and added a few sticks he had located near
the back of the cave. He should be cursing himself for wrecking
her chances at the COMPASS job. Maybe he hadn't. Mercier
might understand and assign someone else to evaluate her.

Clay didn't even consider lying to his supervisor about
taking advantage of Vanessa. His feelings for her were
probably branded on his forehead like a big scarlet V. He had
a feeling she had marked him for life.

Now he needed to think about damage control. Surely when

she succeeded in capturing or killing Hightower, that would work in her favor, no matter what his report about her said. The proof was in the pudding, so to speak. Her op would succeed.

One thing he knew for certain: sex with Vanessa was definitely not enough to assuage whatever it was he felt for her. Even if their interlude had lasted all night long, it wouldn't have been enough.

He wanted more. He wanted her there when he woke every morning and when he retired every night. He wanted her laughter, her tears, her love, her children. God, he was hooked on her, pure and simple.

He only prayed he hadn't messed up her career. She would say she didn't care about that right now, but he knew better. When her blood cooled in the cold light of day, she would hold this against him.

Vanessa had made it very clear she wasn't looking for a long-term relationship, much less marriage. She was a career woman through and through, as elusive and difficult to capture as quicksilver.

She had wanted him and he had given in. All pride aside, he would give in again before he left her if she would have him.

With that in mind, he left the fire and went back to their little nest to hold her while he could.

When she woke, she seemed reluctant to talk about what had happened. Clay decided not to push it. Maybe she just wanted to forget it had happened. No question that it shouldn't have, but he was damned if he would apologize for something he would repeat if given half a chance.

"Thanks for saving me," she murmured. "Hope it doesn't have to become a habit. I'm not usually such a klutz."

He brushed his palm down her arm and back up to her face and caressed it. "Klutz? You climbed that cliff like a little mountain goat. Some would have given up, but not you."

"I lost half our ammo," she reminded him. "Also half our supplies." No way could she have climbed up with that extra weight on her and he had known that. Disentangling the straps and pulling it up first might have sent her tumbling to the bottom of the gorge.

"I was the one who cut it loose," he reminded her. "We'll make do with what we've got. I have a feeling Hightower's not that far ahead and he has no reason to hurry unless he's spotted us following him."

"Which is not impossible. I probably made enough racket when I fell to alert him. He could be waiting out there for us in the morning and pick us off as we go outside."

Clay released her and sat up, propping on one arm as he looked into the fire. "Then I'll need to go after him tonight."

"And how will you find him? He grew up around here and knows this area like the back of his hand, Clay. The only way we're going to get James is to either corner him somewhere or lure him to us."

"You think he would bite?"

Vanessa shrugged with her uninjured shoulder. "I expect he wants my hide badly enough to take the time. And he has two days to kill before the festival if that's what he's waiting for."

"Let's try it the other way first. I'd rather approach him out in the open than get cornered in here." Clay knee-walked over to the fire and stoked it a little with a stick. He had placed some of the wet wood from the old fire pit around it to dry out. Now he added the smaller bits that were dry enough to burn. "We'll leave here before daybreak."

"I'll take the first watch," Vanessa offered. "I'm not sleepy."

To her surprise, he let her. She checked her weapon and positioned herself near the mouth of the cave to stand sentinel.

Clay might be a little overprotective, but he did trust her

and knew she was capable. Her self-confidence badly needed the boost after her slip on the cliff and she knew he had somehow sensed that.

In the hours that followed, she would be protecting him.

Hightower had seen the two on his trail. He had to stay hidden until the festival the day after tomorrow and it came time to detonate, but he couldn't let himself be captured even then. He could either avoid Vanessa and the fed she had with her, or get rid of them. This was a good place to do that.

He would die before going back to prison and he sensed Vanessa might find a way of proving his guilt if he let her live long enough. Besides, he had already decided that she should die for what she'd done. And that federal lapdog was sticking to her like glue so she must have convinced him of her theories. As long as the bodies weren't found, he'd be okay.

So his first order of business was to eliminate these two chasing him and have his revenge on the woman responsible for his losing everything. He would lay a track anyone with half sense could follow and set his trap.

When it was all over, he would convince Lisa Yellowhorse to furnish him with an ironclad alibi. After pointing the finger at him the way she had, she owed him. Now everyone was primed to believe her when she admitted how she had tried to set him up because of a lover's spat. He might even let her live. Or not.

Yeah, he had all the bases covered.

Clay and Vanessa left the cave just before first light and trekked upward on Killbird Mountain. They had been at it for less than an hour when they found the first real clue to Hightower's presence.

"Look at this," Clay said, pointing out a broken branch

about waist high. "And there." He motioned at the clear outline of a boot print on the ground.

After several more blatant clues, he commented, "I don't like it."

They continued, finding more prints and signs. "A clear trail," she agreed. "He knows we're after him and he's setting us up."

Clay stopped and rested his hands on his hips. "I want you to go back and wait at the cave."

"Like hell. We've already had this argument," she said pushing past him.

"Wait." He slid his hand around her elbow and stopped her. "With that shoulder injury, you won't be in top form during a confrontation. I'd rather you sat this one out. Be reasonable, Vanessa."

"I am. You can see I'm fine." She rotated her shoulder to show him she could. Clay noted the beads of sweat that broke out on her upper lip and the wince she was hiding behind suddenly firm lips.

"The ability to follow orders is just as important as how you function on an assignment. Surely I don't need to tell you that."

She yanked her arm out of his grasp. "Don't patronize me, Clay! Mark it against me in your little assessment book if it makes you feel better, but I'm not bowing out of this. I don't care about your appraisal or about the COMPASS job. Got it? I plan to stay on this and do what I do. This is my assignment. You're only here to assist me or did you conveniently forget that?"

He huffed. "Give it up, Vanessa. You're not going any farther up this mountain if I have to tie you to a damn tree."

For a long moment, she glared angrily. Then she looked away, glancing up, then back down the way they had come. She chewed her bottom lip for a minute then shook her finger thoughtfully. "You know, neither of us should. He's expecting that. I think we ought to set a little trap of our own and make him come to us."

Clay considered her suggestion. "What if he ignores us, stays up there and detonates as planned?"

She shook her head, then leaned against a nearby tree, crossing her arms over her chest. "He needs to get rid of us, me in particular. Say he goes through with his plans and decimates everything below. How's he planning to get back down the mountain and get away if we're waiting for him. And whether those bombs go off or not, he knows we'll be waiting."

"What do you have in mind?" Clay asked. So far, she had thought everything through very carefully, but this was an off-the-cuff impulse. It would be interesting to see how swiftly she could devise a workable scheme. He felt very proud of how neatly she had let go of her anger and suggested an alternate plan of action.

"The cave's a good place to stage it, I think," she said. "James couldn't have seen what happened to me on the cliff because of the low visibility. You and I could barely see each other."

"True. What's your plan? If the visibility's good when he returns, there's no place to hide but in the cave."

She grinned. "We stage another accident. This time *you* will be the one who's out of commission. Or better yet, out of the picture altogether. Then when he comes in to finish me off, we'll grab him."

Clay saw several flaws in the plan. "What if he keeps his distance and picks you off?"

She shook her head. "No. I know him. He'll want to gloat a little, up close and personal."

"Maybe you're right. He's not a great shot. According to his service record, he didn't even make expert on the range."

"So it's a pretty good assumption that he'll come in close.

But I don't think he would risk that unless you weren't a threat. You're the unknown quantity for him."

"What about you? Surely he's aware of how capable you are. You don't get through FBI training unless you have top-notch skills. You took him down once."

She smiled. "He would never admit that had anything to do with skill, even to himself. James believes females are subhuman."

Clay pursed his lips and thought about it. "What about little Dilly? He obviously feels differently about his daughter. He wanted to see her."

"Ha! Don't bet on that," she said with a bitter chuckle. "He's decided he has some use for her. Or maybe he was just curious to see if she looked anything like him. He constantly accused Brenda of having affairs, which she never did. I wish she had. I wish, by some stroke of luck, James really wasn't Delinda's father. If he ever got his hands on her, I shudder to think what her life would be like. After the way he treated Brenda…" She shook her head and shivered, rubbing her arms briskly with her palms.

"Don't worry about that," Clay said, stepping closer, trying to reassure her. "He'll never get near her. We'll see to it, right?"

She nodded, then took a deep breath and smiled. "Absolutely. Now, we need to get back to the cave and decide how to set up something that will boost James's confidence and get him in close."

She moved around Clay, careful not to brush against him, and started walking back the way they'd come.

They were both being so cautious today, trying to prevent the current that arced between them each time they drew near one another. Avoidance wasn't working. Being so close and not touching only made him want her more. He would never get over this. He'd never get over her.

She marched swiftly now on her downhill path, all business. "I'm thinking we should stage something similar to what happened to me. Only you wouldn't appear to be as lucky as I was. What do you think?"

"You want me to go over the edge? That's pretty risky. What if I can't get back up fast enough?"

She shrugged. "We'll stage it right and see that you can. If he thinks I'm alone and unprotected, he'll go for it and try to take me out."

"It could work," Clay admitted. It seemed a pretty good plan as far as it went. If it fooled Hightower. If not, at least they would be on familiar ground when things went down.

"The timing's crucial," she warned. "He's going to have to see you go down or he probably won't approach."

Clay agreed. They needed to wait until Hightower came back down this far to see why they hadn't taken his bait and followed him.

"I'll take care of that," Clay assured her. He examined their path and the surrounding area very closely. When Hightower returned, he would have to come this way since it offered the only access. He would have to be within fifty yards of the clearing in order to see if they were there.

When they reached the best vantage point that would offer Hightower a view of the clearing, Clay stopped.

"Hold up a minute." He knelt, fished through his pack and came up with a small sewing kit he'd seen tucked in one pocket. He removed the spool of dark thread and strung it across the path between two trees about waist level. Then he let the rest play out through his hand, tying another skein onto the end as it ran out, then another. He had just enough to almost reach the clearing. He secured the end to his tin cup, which he set on a high rock nearby.

"The thread's thin enough he won't notice it when he trips

it," he told Vanessa. "It should dislodge the cup, but it won't make much of a clatter and is far enough away that hopefully, he won't notice. Should be enough to alert us, though. The cup's visible from where we'll be. If it disappears off the rock, he'll be in place, watching."

She clicked her tongue. "Yeah, and what if your cat comes back this way and trips it accidentally?"

He smiled. "That's why I strung it high. It would take something the height of a bear on his hind legs to snag it. If one of those happens along, I'd just as soon know about it, wouldn't you?"

They hurriedly set up the scenario, tying the climbing rope to a sturdy tree and snaking it along the cliff to the carefully chosen spot where Clay planned to go over the edge.

He rappelled down and checked it out. There was an undercut to the rocky edge where he could brace himself easily enough. He could be back up in a couple of minutes. He practiced several times until he was confident.

To be on the safe side, he secured the thin cable to his right wrist. Sitting on flat rocks near the edge, they ate, checked their weapons and talked in hushed tones, tried to prepare for every possible contingency that could take place when Hightower approached.

Clay marveled at Vanessa's energy. Her ability to set pain aside and focus on the job impressed him. Mercier couldn't do any better if he wanted a dedicated agent for the COMPASS team. She just needed a little more convincing. Maybe success on this op would do the trick.

Clay kept the cup in his peripheral vision. He hoped the trip thread worked, but there was a possibility it wouldn't. It could hang on rough bark and break without dislodging the cup. He couldn't think of any alternative warning system, however, so he watched, waited and hoped it was successful.

At mid-afternoon, they had almost given up the wait when a slight clink alerted Clay. The cup had fallen, making almost no noise at all.

"The cup fell off," he whispered to Vanessa. "It's showtime."

"Ready," she said. "Go for it."

Clay stood up and stretched, careful to keep the rope running along his right side so it wouldn't be visible. He made a great show of tucking his pistol in the back of his belt.

"I'm going to walk around and scout the area," he said loudly, backed a few steps toward the cliff's muddy edge and cried out as he slipped on purpose.

Vanessa scrambled toward the edge on all fours, issuing a scream that would wake the dead.

Clay had grasped the rope and swung into the side of the cliff, yelling, letting his voice trail away, as if plunging to his death.

Several feet below the edge, he braced inside the concave section that formed a niche. He pulled the rope tight and felt it cut easily into the muddy edge of the cliff. The grasses and mud would conceal the rope.

Vanessa was screaming his name, sounding truly panicked, crying out loud. "I'll call for help!" she cried. "Clay, answer me! Can you hear me? Oh, please don't be dead!"

He heard her scrambling around up there and moaning, "The phone. Oh God, I need his *phone!*" He heard her running for the cave.

Clay smiled. The girl had missed her calling. She sounded terrified and, as they had planned, she sounded alone and vulnerable.

He inched sideways to brace himself more securely in the niche and wrapped his left arm around a small projection of rock to rest that hand from the cut of the rope. He hadn't worn his gloves. That might have given away the ruse since the weather was too mild to require them for warmth.

He flexed his left hand, then his right, one finger at a time, as he held onto the rope secured to his wrist. His toeholds were solid. He pressed his chest against the rock and leaned into it. Thank God there was no wind to speak of. Normally, it would have been a great day for climbing if that was the sport of choice. While it definitely wasn't Clay's, he still felt confident.

Now all he had to do was wait for Vanessa's cue for him to climb up. As soon as Hightower entered the cave, she would scream the man's name.

A few minutes later, Clay heard slogging footsteps above him. A deep growling chuckle told him it wasn't Vanessa returning.

Clay felt certain he wouldn't be visible if Hightower simply looked over the precipice. Unless the man lay down on the ground and hung his head over the edge, Clay's position was hidden. Hopefully, the rope had bitten into the mud deeply enough that it wouldn't be noticed.

Suddenly the belaying rope that had been secured to the tree on the cliff above went sailing right past Clay's head and dangled uselessly from his right hand.

He shifted his weight and the rock below his left foot broke away, tumbling down the cliff and dislodging others as it fell. Left hanging by one arm and braced with only one perilous foothold, he barely managed to stifle a curse.

What the hell would he do now? Clay wondered that just as he heard Vanessa scream, "James!"

Chapter 11

"Put down the gun, Vanessa," Hightower ordered. He held one of his own in his right hand and a remote-control device in his left. It looked like a garage-door opener and he had it pointed toward the outside as he stood just inside the cave's entrance.

"Even if you get off a lucky shot, I will still press this and blow our precious little res to kingdom come. Drop the gun and kick it over here."

Vanessa squatted and carefully laid the Glock on the ground. She stood up and nudged it with her boot. James was standing with his back to the entrance. If Clay jumped him from behind, she wanted the pistol where she could get to it quickly.

That scenario worried her. Sunlight flooded most of the cave floor now. It would be difficult for Clay to surprise James if he threw a shadow inside as he approached. They should have accounted for that. Hopefully, Clay would realize it before he acted.

"I said kick the damn thing over here! Kick it hard!" he shouted, his voice reverberating off the cave's walls.

She kicked hard. The pistol flew past him, out of the cave, out of their reach. Maybe right off the cliff outside. "There!" she said with a huff. Now her job was to keep James facing her, his back to the entrance.

He cursed. "Sit there by the wall, right where you are."

She sat. Now she was totally unarmed.

"That was a nice little bit of playacting. Might have worked if I hadn't watched you two set it up. But I cut the rope your boyfriend was dangling on out there," he told her with a laugh. "Help is *not* on the way. I heard him fall."

Vanessa's breath caught in her throat. Shock held her immobile, speechless. Had Clay fallen? James would never have left him out there clinging to the cliff.

Snatches of memory flashed through her mind. Clay's scent, the smooth glide of his palm over her skin, the yearning in his eyes that he couldn't quite hide. She felt a wail of denial billow up from inside her and barely contained it.

She would *know* if he were dead. She would feel it like a dreadful weight, a sudden vacuum in her soul. No, he was out there, she told herself. He couldn't possibly be dead or she would know.

James kicked the open backpack that lay near the fire pit. The contents spilled out. He stamped on Clay's cell phone until he crushed it.

"I think you should join your friend," James said conversationally, smiling his evil smile. "I couldn't have arranged a better end for you two. So thanks for cooking this up!"

Clay was alive. She knew he was. The only thing she could do was play for time and hope he could climb to safety. The trick was to keep James talking as long as she could.

She took a deep breath and clung to hope. "You won't get away with it. They suspect you already."

"No, they suspect you have it in for me," he retorted. "I'll have a rock-solid alibi, don't worry about that. There are terrorists to blame for the bombs at the festival. What reason could I possibly have for blowing up the fairgrounds? There's no connection, see? No motive. At least not one they could know about."

"Don't kid yourself. They know you stole the C-4. They found the bomb you put under the judge's car."

"No, they don't know it was me. I covered my tracks just like I'm doing here. No physical evidence at all. You and the fed at the bottom of that gorge will be classified an accident if they ever find you. Bad weather, poor climbing skills."

"And you're so good at arranging *accidents,* aren't you?" Vanessa said. "Brenda could attest to that. Does she haunt you, James?"

His eyes narrowed. He clenched his jaw and made a grunting sound.

"She does," Vanessa murmured, nodding. "She comes to you in your dreams, doesn't she, James?"

"No! And don't say her name!" He shook his head vehemently and his hand tightened on the pistol he held, a cheap .22 caliber Saturday-night special, she thought. Unless he managed a head or heart shot, she would probably survive a bullet, maybe two. Could she take him down before he killed her? At least whoever found her body would know it was murder.

She got to her knees and started to stand, her gaze probing his. If she launched herself at him…

"Don't try it," James warned, waggling the remote device he held in his other hand. "It's too soon to get the desired results from the festival explosion, but there are others that ought to do what they're supposed to do. This little gem should work from here, I think. One wrong move and we'll soon see if it does."

"Why are you doing this, James? I can understand your being angry with me, and even with the judge who sentenced you, but why would you want to kill innocent people?"

"Innocent?" he spat. "How many of those innocents looked the other way when my old man beat the hell out of me and sent me to school all banged up, huh?"

"That was years ago. You could have blown the whistle on him any time and you know it."

"I tried!" he insisted. "No one would listen. And how many of them jumped right on the bandwagon when I was accused? I saw it in their eyes in that courtroom. Hell, I heard them say it! *Chip off the old block,* they said, didn't they? *Just like his white-trash daddy,* with the emphasis on *white.* Just because I look like him—"

"Oh, come on, don't play the race card, James. Abusers come in all colors and you know it. You *did* beat Brenda," she reminded him. "I saw the bruises."

He scoffed and rolled his eyes. "Yeah, well, she was too much like Mama. She kept reminding me, you're either the hammer or you're the nail. Damned if I was ever gonna be the nail again! But I wouldn't have killed her if it hadn't been for you. *You* told her to leave me."

Vanessa nodded, hoping to reason with James if she accepted his blame. "She loved you. In spite of everything and even after she decided to leave. Brenda wouldn't want you to do this."

"Don't say her name!" he ordered again. She saw tears in his eyes and, for a few seconds, Vanessa clearly recognized the man her cousin had once cared about, handsome, vulnerable, lost and lonely.

"But she was going to leave me anyway," he muttered. "Because of you."

"James, please think about what you're doing. This is so wrong."

Rage suddenly altered his features. "Don't you preach to me, Vanessa Walker. You busted up my marriage, made me kill my wife and helped them steal my kid. I spent four years in a freaking prison laundry fighting off perverts because of you! Now, get outside!" He turned sideways and waved the pistol toward the entrance of the cave.

Vanessa got up slowly. Should she attack now and make him detonate? That would do less damage today than it would when the fairgrounds were crowded with people there for the festival. Or could she depend on the four EOD people and their one dog now searching to find everything James had planted? Could they locate and disable the bombs before the crowds arrived?

Maybe the remote wouldn't work from inside the cave. Did she dare risk that? What would Clay do?

James would shoot her if she jumped him, she had no doubt. A bullet would tell those who found her that she hadn't simply fallen off the cliff. If she were ever found.

Clay, where are you? She cried out in her mind for him and prayed that he could somehow hear her.

As she neared the entrance to the cave, she heard the distant, mournful cry of the panther. Warning, reassurance or goodbye? she wondered.

Time had run out. She had to act now.

Clay had dropped the useless rope and hung on the small outcrop of rock until he found another just above it with his free hand.

He called up the meager rock-climbing training he'd undergone as a teenager and found it sorely lacking. Never overly fond of heights, he hadn't pursued the sport any further than a couple of outings, trying to conquer mild acrophobia. That done, he'd gone on to other activities. Now he sorely wished he had excelled in it.

The basics had stuck. He tested his new handhold the best he could, then lifted his foot and sought purchase to propel himself upward. Slowly, by inches, mindful of slippery earth and loose rubble, he managed to make it to the muddy edge.

He could see the cut end of the rope lying a couple of feet away but couldn't reach it. What he feared most was crawling over the lip of the cliff and the whole thing sliding away, taking him with it. The edge that had seemed stable before now felt treacherous.

Voices emanated from the cave some ten feet away, but he couldn't understand the words. At least Vanessa was still alive. Keep him busy, he warned her mentally.

Though he firmly believed in telepathy and had seen it work on the job, it wasn't one of his talents. A couple of the other agents he worked with were experts on that and had been able to read him on occasion. He could open his mind enough to receive general warnings, but nothing specific the way they could. He projected now for all he was worth, trying to connect with Vanessa's mind. Keep him busy!

Clay felt so distracted by his present predicament, he doubted if anyone could get more than a weird jumble of emotions even if he was successful.

Willing himself to keep calm, he reached out and grasped two fists full of thick weeds. One clump came away as if rooted in soup. He flung it down and grabbed again.

Well, he couldn't hang here all day. Vanessa needed him. He took a deep breath and decided to risk all and push up with the one foot he had lodged on a minor bump of rock and pull on the patch of weeds that did seem to be holding.

Head and chest over the edge, he grabbed out for the rope.

He caught it only to have it slip from his grasp. Fingers clawing for purchase, he slipped back a foot before catching another clump of weeds. He toed his way up, huffing and spitting mud.

Finally, he lay flat on the ground on his stomach, breathless and spent. But he couldn't afford a minute to rest. He rolled to his side and swiped at his mud-coated face with one hand. His eyes felt gritty. He opened them wide and resisted blinking until they teared up and cleared a little.

Vanessa was inside the cave with Hightower. She was holding her own, but he could tell by the tone of her voice that she was trying to reason with the man. That meant Hightower had the upper hand.

Clay got to his knees, then to his feet. He drew his weapon out of his belt. It was covered with mud like the rest of him. He wiped it off and chambered a round.

At that moment he heard the remote cry of his feline mascot. Think big cat, he told himself. Stealth and cunning.

He approached from the side of the cave's entrance and was still a few feet from the opening when Hightower shouted. A shot rang out. Clay dashed inside.

"Van!" he shouted as he saw her fall.

A bullet whizzed past his ear, the report echoing in the small cavern. Instinctively, he whirled and fired just as Hightower rushed past him. Clay grabbed for him and they went down together, Hightower on top.

Clay rocked backward, tossing his attacker against the cave wall, then forward again to gain his feet. By the time he turned, Hightower was halfway up, still clutching the gun. Clay kicked out, disarming him. The gun hit the rocks and bounced out of reach. Clay raised his own weapon.

"I'll blow it!" Hightower cried. "I'll blow everything if you move!"

Clay froze, noting the object Hightower held in both hands now, his thumb moving nervously over the button. Would it work from inside here? The opening of the cave was large, the cliff's ledge outside eroded. There might be an unimpeded signal path from here to the town. Hard to tell.

Vanessa stirred slightly. Clay stole a glance. The left side of her head was covered with blood. For a split second, he wanted nothing more than to kill Hightower and damn his threats. But those were Vanessa's friends and family in peril down there.

Hightower moved to the cave's entrance, carefully staying out of Clay's reach should he kick out again.

Clay held the gun on him. "Give it up, Hightower. Every badge in the southeast will be on your tail within the hour."

"No way for them to know. I got rid of your phone." He nodded at the backpack near where Vanessa lay. "You toss the piece over here, Fed. If you don't, I push this button." He held the remote just outside the cave, pointed toward Cherokee.

Clay figured Hightower wanted to wait until tomorrow so his bombs could do the optimum damage when the festival got underway, but it was clear he would do it now if pushed. And who knew how many other places he had wired to blow?

"You use that and I guarantee you won't live to hear the blasts," Clay promised.

"But you will," Hightower taunted. "And all those deaths will be on your conscience, won't they!" He inclined his head to Vanessa. "She'll blame you, too. If she lives."

Vanessa was lying there bleeding from a head wound. She needed immediate help.

"Shoot me and my reflexes will trigger this, Fed. Let me go and you'll have about eighteen hours to find me." He smiled and began backing out of the cave. "*If* you can find me. I'm counting on you to *try*." Then he darted out of the cave and disappeared.

Clay let him go. Helping Vanessa was first priority. He could catch Hightower later.

He knelt beside Vanessa, raked back her hair with one finger and examined the wound. A bloody gash rather than a bullet hole, thank God. Hightower must have butt-stroked her with the pistol after he'd fired. That made sense. He wouldn't want to shoot them unless he had to.

She was groaning now and trying to sit up. He grabbed the water bottle from the scattered items of the backpack and wet her face, daubing the worst of the blood off her with the T-shirt he had used as a towel earlier.

He picked up his flashlight and turned it on for a closer look. "Open your eyes and look at me," he coaxed. The skin on her forehead was broken, but the wound itself looked minor. However, with the goose egg forming around it, above her eyebrow, she could easily be concussed. "Let's see those pupils," he murmured.

She blinked at him for a few seconds, then collapsed back with a moan. "He hit me!"

"Lucky he didn't shoot you. Look at me now. Follow my finger."

"Wh-where is he?" she demanded.

"Got away, but I'll get him. For now let's get you squared away."

Clay rummaged around for the first-aid kit and found gauze and antibiotic ointment. He poured some water over his hands, splashed some on his face to clear off the worst of the mud and dried off on the shirt. With one of the antiseptic wipes, he cleaned his hands more thoroughly and treated her wound. "I don't think you have a concussion. Eyes look okay. How do you feel?"

She sat up then, a hand to her head as she shook it gently. "Brain scrambled. We need to get some more searchers up here."

"Can't. He destroyed the phone."

"Oh yeah." She sighed, remembering. "Without the phone, there's no way we can call in and report that we found him and verify that he's the bomber. If he manages to kill us like he plans, there's nothing but my accusations and the circumstantial evidence provided by Lisa Yellowhorse to tie him to the bombs."

Clay ran a hand over her arm, caught her hand in his and nodded at Hightower's .22, which lay several feet away. "Well, he's unarmed now unless he has another weapon wherever he's camped. I'm thinking if he had anything better than that cheap pistol, he would have been using it."

She rested her head on her hand and drew up one knee to prop her elbow on it. "We have to find him and we'll need the element of surprise. You can bet he'll be waiting somewhere he's sure that detonator will work."

Clay agreed. "That also limits the area we'll have to search."

She turned her head and smiled thinly. "Look for the silver lining, huh?"

Clay heaved a sigh, sat down beside her and drew her into his arms. "That optimism of yours is contagious, I guess."

She clung to him and he held her tight, relishing the warmth of her body, thankful beyond everything that she was still breathing. She had escaped death yet again. How many times was this now? And how long would her luck hold?

"Twice I almost lost you, Van."

"You, too. When he told me he cut your rope, I almost shut down and gave up. But I knew somehow you would make it."

"Borrowed some of your luck, I guess. I wish I could carry you back down this mountain and stash you somewhere safe until all this is over."

"As if I would let you," she replied. "This is my case and

I'm not about to hand it over because of a bump on the head. Quit trying to play knight in shining armor when you look like a giant mud pie."

"Good camouflage," he said, setting her away reluctantly and noting how dirty he had gotten her. "How about if you rest here for a little while and get your wits together. I'm going out to take a look around."

She was standing up before he was and brushing off the seat of her pants. Clay realized he wasn't going to go anywhere without her unless he butt-stroked her back into unconsciousness. "You are one hardheaded woman, Walker," he snapped.

"Lucky for both of us," she quipped as she picked Hightower's weapon off the floor of the cave and checked it for damage. She searched for her Glock, but it was nowhere to be found. "My weapon's gone and his is empty." She tossed it onto the pack.

"We might as well gather up what's left of our supplies and head out before his trail gets cold."

Clay just hoped there was a trail to follow. Hightower was much cannier than they'd figured. With a little luck, he could destroy everything he planned to, get rid of the only two people who could point the finger at him and walk away from this unscathed.

Clay kept thinking about the part of his vision where the earth fell away and he experienced that sinking feeling of failure. Could he turn that around?

"We're going to stop him," Vanessa declared, as if she had read Clay's mind. Maybe she had.

"You bet." He smiled at her, admiring her grit and determination. And her hardheadedness, he admitted. She might frustrate the hell out of him, but he wouldn't change a thing about her. Not a blessed thing.

He was going to recommend her for COMPASS no matter

what she said, and beg Mercier to hire her if he had to. Mercier could convince her to leave the Bureau.

If nothing else, that would get her to McLean where Clay could see her often. As it stood right now, he didn't think he could give her up, even if that meant he had to change jobs and move near her.

Vanessa tried to ignore the pain in her head that was almost blinding. The going got rougher the higher they climbed and there was not as much cover. More rocks and fewer trees. Surprising James grew a lot less likely.

"We should stop and go on after dark," she suggested. "It's more dangerous, but I don't think we have much choice."

Clay looked at her, his expression concerned. "You're not feeling up to this."

She patted his arm, giving it a squeeze, just because. That no-touching rule hadn't lasted long. He had been ignoring it, too, soothing her with a palm to her back, on her waist as they walked.

"He's going all the way to the top," she said. "We don't need a trail. It's solid rock up there so he can see all around him. And he'll have a clear path with nothing but air between that damned remote and everything below. I honestly don't know what approach we can use."

"There will be a trap between here and there. I feel it," Clay said. "Question is, how elaborate is it? He hasn't had much time to construct anything sophisticated."

Clay lowered the pack, leaned against a tree and drew her against him, cushioning her body with his as he held her. "He's had ranger training. That's scary right there."

"He's not so tough for a ranger. However, he has tramped these mountains since he was a kid. He'll know all the possibilities."

She rested her hands on the arms that surrounded her and took comfort from Clay's strength. Pressing the back of her aching head against his chest, she closed her eyes. If only they could stay this way for a while, just be together like this and relax.

She felt him brush the top of her head with his chin and knew he placed a kiss there. It reminded her of her father whom she could barely remember. He used to kiss hurts to make them better. The memory made her smile.

She could not afford to forget that they had a job to do here, a critically important task that might save countless lives. Lives of people she had known well all her life and truly cared about. Her people.

"Let's camp till dark," he said, moving her gently away from him. "I'll get you something for the headache."

"How do you know my head hurts?" she asked, looking up at him as she turned.

"That little line right between your eyes," he said, tracing it with one finger. "And your frown." He trailed down to the corner of her mouth. "You almost never frown." His voice had dropped to a near whisper. "I love your smile."

He lowered his mouth to hers and kissed her so softly she could barely feel it. When he drew back, she saw something in his eyes that almost frightened her with its intensity. "Don't make me love you," she whispered. "Please don't."

It wasn't in the plan. Her life was all worked out and she didn't have a place for anything permanent with a man. Instinctively, she knew Clay was the sort of man who would require more than she could give. Like *everything*.

She knew how precarious relationships were in her line of work. And his. An enormous amount of trust was necessary. They would need double that to have any success at all.

"You know it wouldn't work."

He shrugged slightly and removed his hands from her

arms with a gesture of surrender. "I'll find the pills," he said, crouching to open the pack.

Just like that, he was giving up? Vanessa grasped her hair with both hands and turned away, amazed at the wave of disappointment and frustration that washed through her.

Well, what had she expected, that he would kiss her within an inch of her life, overcome her every objection and sweep her off her feet and into blissful domesticity?

She snatched the pills when he held them out and popped them in her mouth.

He smiled knowingly as he handed her the nearly empty bottle of water. She upended it and swallowed, nearly choking.

"Any chocolate left?" she snapped.

He tossed her a Snickers before the words were out. How could a man covered in dried mud look so damned appealing? And so darn smug?

Yeah, he knew it was too late. She already loved him.

Chapter 12

Darkness fell, the moon finally rose, and they were on their way again. Clay knew there were problems ahead that weren't related to the present situation with Hightower. Personal stuff would have to take a back seat for now. They had a killer to catch.

Vanessa cared about him, more than she wanted to. He'd give anything to know what was going on in that head of hers. She acted angry. He knew it was the result of her injury, frustration of the job and finally, predominately, her feelings for him.

He wished he could show her that giving in to those wouldn't limit her in any way. Or would it? If they were involved, could he stand to wave her off on an op, not knowing whether she would survive it or not? Could she bear to do that with him if she loved him?

Given how hard it was now to even let her accompany him up this mountain and face a man who wanted to kill her, he had to wonder. Maybe she was right to fight this thing that was definitely escalating between them.

Clay dreaded what would happen during this final confrontation with Hightower. He couldn't feel any optimism. The vision kept plaguing him, that part about his gut-wrenching feeling of failure. He had always believed that approaching a project, whatever it was, with the expectation of success was key. Somehow he couldn't muster that this time.

"Damn the vision," he muttered as he stumbled slightly on a rock.

Vanessa placed a palm on his back, more in a gesture of mental support than physical. If he had taken a tumble there was no way her small frame would keep him upright. The true meaning of her touch didn't escape him. She was there for him. She loved him. He knew it as well as he knew his own name.

While that love made his heart swell to bursting, he couldn't dismiss the worry that he had little to offer her. Good sex, yes. A learned skill and one that had always come naturally. His protection. He would give his very life for her without pausing to think about it. But hell, why would she welcome that? She thought she could protect herself as well as he could.

She had told him outright she didn't want anything permanent. Unless he left her alone altogether, he knew he could never settle for less with her. Even if he talked her into marriage, there was the issue of children. Given how she loved little Dilly, she would surely want some of her own someday. How could he ever be certain what he might pass on to their progeny when he knew nothing of his maternal lineage? Genetic problems? Mental illness? At the moment he didn't feel too stable in that regard. How could he ask this brave, beautiful woman to be a part of his life?

And how could he not? She had changed him so radically

in the past few days, it was as if she already owned part of him, maybe the best part.

"Gotta stop," she said, her breath coming in little pants.

Clay halted immediately and turned, taking her up in his arms. She was such a little featherweight. He carried her to a small clearing off to their right. When he had settled her on the ground, her back to a half-buried boulder, he sat down next to her. "Let's get you rehydrated and down for a nap. How's your head?"

"Pounding," she admitted, then checked the LED on her watch. "It's nearly 3:00 a.m. I'm slowing you down. Maybe you should go on without me."

"Can't leave you here. I won't," he said. "If you pass out, you'd be fair game for any predator, two- or four-legged."

"I'll stay awake," she promised. "You have to stop James."

He put the water bottle to her lips and helped her drink. "He won't detonate until the fairgrounds are full. We'll have until midmorning, I figure."

"God, I hope our little EOD team has located all the explosives."

"Unfortunately we can't bank on that. That map of the fairgrounds could be a diversion. What if he's rigged something else, like the museum or the other shops?"

"Or the vehicles of those he's sure will attend the festival. Several bombs in the parking lot would take out a big portion of the crowd," she said. "It's impossible to search everywhere."

"So we take that detonator away from him before he uses it," Clay said.

She nestled against him. "I'll be okay in a few minutes, then we'll go on. It's not far to the top."

Not far at all. Clay looked up where the ragged summit blocked out half the sky. The harvest moon was full and gave off enough light to cast shadows of the trees and rock formations. He debated whether he could safely leave her here. No, she would be too exposed, too vulnerable. "Rest. We have plenty of time," he said softly.

The mountain was probably riddled with caves. If only there were another nearby, that would give her some protection. He left her sleeping and scouted the area nearby. Nothing but rocks, trees and a deep ravine cut by eons of spring runoffs.

Just as he was returning to Vanessa, his eye caught a tiny flicker of light from above, not at the summit, but closer by. He stopped and stared at it. It blinked out for a split second, then reappeared.

Clay hurried over and shook Vanessa gently. "Wake up. Have a look."

She grumbled for a second, rubbing her eyes, then sat up straight and peered at the spot he indicated.

Clay slid his arm around her and massaged her shoulder. "At first I thought it was a flashlight, then saw it flicker. It's a fire. Would he risk pinpointing his location this way?"

She snorted. "He's not that stupid. The weather's too mild to demand warmth for survival. He wouldn't build a fire to cook a meal. It's a trap."

"Needs to get rid of us so he lures us up there." This was her operation and she was in charge, he reminded himself. "Any ideas on how to approach?"

"He'll be waiting." She thought for a minute. "Let's split up. You're strongest so you circle around, come in behind him. I'll go straight in and try to keep him distracted."

Clay was already shaking his head. She might not like him protesting her plan, but he did it anyway. If he had to, he'd pull rank on her. "We'll have to reverse that. He knows you were injured. I might make him believe I've left you down there, either dead or recovering, and come up alone. If we do it your way, he'll be expecting me."

She agreed rather than arguing the way he had expected. She might be bullheaded, but she was also smart. "Let's do it then."

Clay handed her his pistol. "Take this."

Vanessa wished for her Glock, but it was probably at the bottom of the gorge after that mighty kick she'd given it. And the .22 was useless without bullets. All they had now was Clay's service weapon.

"You keep it. I'm not letting you go up there bare-handed!"

"I have to. He'll have his finger on that button and make me toss it anyway. Get in position. If you can get off a shot that will take him out, take it. That will be our best and maybe our only chance. We have to do this now. Even if he detonates, there won't be as many casualties below as there would be during daylight hours."

"But there could be some and even one is too many." She took the weapon and peered up at him. "However this goes down, Clay, I want you to know I did everything I knew to do."

He caressed her face, gently brushing a lock of hair off her bruised forehead. "Right by the book. You're the best agent I've ever worked with."

She gave a rueful chuckle. "This sounds too much like we're saying farewell."

"Well, we're not! We don't do farewells. No goodbyes, no good lucks, just see you later and buy you a beer to celebrate."

"See you later then," she said, stretched to loosen her muscles, winked and took off.

Clay heaved a sigh and a fervent prayer and began his climb toward the tiny, ominous flicker of light.

The ravine he'd noted earlier lay just to his left, a narrow fissure that snaked its way up. It seemed to beckon him nearer, probably a residual compulsion left over from his long-ago bout with acrophobia.

His breath grew shaky and he willed it to steady. Reluctantly, he recalled edging up to another precipice, closer and closer, unable to resist the lure of it, when he was a child. He remembered the wild fluttering of fear in his heart as death called to him. *Here, here, come and meet me…*

He shook it off. Conquered that, he assured himself, staunchly denying the seconds of panic he'd endured when Hightower had cut that damned rope and left him hanging on the side of the cliff.

Self-preservation had him putting a few extra feet between him and that dark ribbon of danger. There would be enough peril to face once he encountered the mad bomber who was waiting for him. Hightower was insane, that was clear, and his compulsion was a hell of a lot more critical than a simple fear of heights.

The plan was to get Hightower talking, to distract him while Vanessa got in place to take him down. Clay just hoped Hightower didn't have another weapon besides the empty .22 he had dropped in the cave.

Clay trudged on, purposely taking his time to allow Vanessa to make her longer route around. His gaze kept flicking at the fathomless ravine.

Vanessa stopped to catch her breath, her eyes never leaving the point of destination. Clay would give her time to get in place. He knew her injuries had weakened her. Thank goodness she wasn't concussed. She felt a little shaky, but her aim should be true if she could find a prop of some kind to steady her hands.

Clouds were moving in, intermittently covering the bright full moon that had guided them so far tonight. Now she could hardly see. She made herself go on.

She wished for moccasins. Her feet would have bruised in those, but she could move soundlessly if she had some. Instead, she had to watch her steps. Her hiking boots would break fallen branches, crunch leaves, make noise that might give her away.

At last, she drew close enough to see James moving against the firelight. She was a good thirty yards away. At twenty-five, she would feel confident of a hit that would kill all his reflexes. If only she could close in just a bit. He straightened suddenly and disappeared behind rock cover just beyond his fire.

She watched as Clay entered the circle of light cast by the flames. "Hightower?" he called, his voice deep with fury. "I'm here to make you pay for what you did to my woman!"

Without warning, shots rang out and Clay fell. Vanessa couldn't catch the small cry that erupted. Oh, God! James *had* brought another weapon! Sounded like another Saturday-night special, best she could tell, but she couldn't be sure. How many times had he fired? Four? Five? How many times had Clay been hit? She couldn't think about that.

Summoning all her training, Vanessa beat back the urge to run to Clay, to save him if she could. Other lives depended on her, too. James had come out from behind the rocks, brandishing the pistol in one hand, pointed directly at Clay. He clutched the detonator in the other.

She crept closer. There was no place to brace her hands, no way she could trust her aim. Her entire body shook like a leaf in the wind. Clay could be faking it, but James would find out and finish him off if she didn't do something now!

If she fired, it would distract him, but unless she could kill him instantly, he would detonate the bombs he'd set and probably shoot Clay again as well. Then he would come after her. Closer in, she could take him out, but it would be too late.

He kicked Clay's side while aiming the pistol directly at him. Then he raised his head and looked around, scanning the darkness. "You out there, Vanessa?" he shouted. "Lover boy's down for the count! Might not be dead yet. Show yourself or I'll shoot him again!"

She held her breath. If she opened fire and blasted him with all the rounds she had, Clay might catch ricochets off the rocks behind them. And James's reflexes could tighten his thumb on that dreaded button. Maybe she could draw him away from Clay, somehow get him closer. Sucking in a deep breath, she let out a throaty moan.

Hightower tensed and turned in her direction. She groaned again. He took several steps, trying to see where she was.

She knew he might have spotted her if the clouds weren't blocking out the moonlight.

"I...c-can't...move!" she groaned, sounding more like the panther's yowl than herself. Where was that beast when Clay needed him?

She watched as James glanced back and forth between Clay, who still lay unmoving, and where he thought she was hiding. She coughed and cried out as if in great pain. Not much pretending to that, either. Her bum shoulder was giving her fits.

He started toward her, turning his back on Clay. Vanessa almost shouted with glee as Clay promptly rolled to his feet and rushed James from behind. She took off for them at a run and stumbled.

When she regained her footing and looked back at the clearing, they were gone, had disappeared like magic. Without slowing, she tore through the gorse and scrambled over piles of rock until she reached the circle of firelight. She could hear them grunting, cursing and wrestling, but they were nowhere to be seen.

"Get *off!*" she heard James scream frantically. "I'll blow it! I will!"

"Go ahead," Clay shouted. "Do it!"

Vanessa rushed for the wide crack in the ground that bypassed the fire and threw herself on her stomach. She flicked on the flashlight and shone it down on the writhing figures a good fifteen feet below.

Clay had James pinned in the deep V of the crevice, grasping both his wrists. James still held the remote in one hand, his pistol in the other.

"Clay, were you hit?" she cried.

"He's got one round left! Get back!" Clay shouted.

James struggled, trying to angle the barrel of the pistol at Clay who banged his arm against the rocks. The gun discharged and the bullet zinged past her head. His other hand worked frantically, pressing the button on the remote control device over and over.

"Changing the channels in hell?" Clay scoffed. "Give it up, man. It won't work down here."

With a loud bellow, James bucked Clay off him and hit him hard in the temple with the detonator. Before Clay could recover, James scrambled off down the bottom of the ravine and disappeared into the darkness.

Vanessa couldn't let him get away, not with that detonator in his hands. If he climbed out of that ravine farther down the mountain, he still had a good shot at making his plan work.

She shone the flashlight in the direction he'd gone, saw movement and opened fire. When the clip was empty, she moved farther down the edge and saw him. Or at least she saw his hands and the top of his head.

"James!" she cried out, unable to do anything to help.

He looked up at her, terror in his eyes. His mouth worked frantically. "Van, the baby...look after..."

His fingers scrabbled for a hold, sliding and grasping at the muddy edge where the base of the ravine dropped off to an even deeper crevice. He roared, a cry of pure rage, then fell as the soft ground gave way. His fading scream ended abruptly a good two seconds later. The aperture must be very deep, she thought, wincing.

Sadness pierced her, knowing James's final thoughts were of his little daughter, a child he had never even seen. Way too late for him to show concern for anything but himself and his vengeance.

She played the light around the irregular floor of the ravine and saw the remote device. It lay harmless and broken, surrounded by a small pile of stones and the batteries that had spilled out of it.

A wave of relief washed through her, quickly replaced by renewed fear for Clay. Exhaustion almost claimed her, but she fought it. She had to help him.

A few minutes later, she had him in sight again, playing the beam of her light along his body. He had collapsed and rolled to his back, but she could see the rise and fall of his chest. Inches below his collarbone, blood oozed from a bullet hole.

Less than a foot from his hip and leg lay another deep fault in the ravine floor, much like the one that had claimed James. "Don't move, Clay," she warned. "Stay right where you are. Can you hear me?"

He tried to raise his arm.

"Okay. That's all right. Just lie still and save your strength."

How the hell was she going to get him out of there? She had lost her phone along with her backpack and James had crushed Clay's to smithereens, so there was no calling for rescue. He couldn't climb up. She couldn't climb down. He would bleed out if she left him there to go get help.

As if on cue, it began to rain.

Vanessa left him to plunder through James's gear for anything that might work. She scattered items right and left, discovering another flashlight and a coil of rope. She stuck the light in her pocket and uncoiled the rope, measuring by guess. Knotted for climbing, it would be too short. But there was nothing else.

She thought of rolling rocks into the ravine to build the floor of it high enough for him to climb out. Even if she found strength to dislodge enough of them to make any kind of difference, their weight could erode the edge of that fissure. He didn't appear able to climb anyway. Not an option.

Huffing with effort, she grabbed the rope, ran and secured one end to the nearest tree and prayed it would hold. Putting in the least number of knots she figured she could get by with, Vanessa went over the side of the ravine and rappelled down to where Clay lay. She had to turn loose and fall the last three feet.

Soaking wet and slogging on her knees in the mud, she reached his side and checked his wound with the flashlight. It looked small. When he tried to sit up, she ran a hand behind his shoulder and felt for an exit wound. There was none. God only knew how much internal damage the bullet had done. Twenty-two calibers tended to enter and bounce around. "Any other hits?" she asked, trying to sound crisp and professional instead of waterlogged and terror stricken.

"Don't think so," he gasped. "Do something for me?" he added.

"Anything I can," she promised, sheltering his face from the rain with her body.

"I…I've been trying to…contact…help."

"You have? Any luck?" she asked, thinking he must have begun hallucinating. They had no phones, no way to communicate. She figured her best bet was to try to drag him down the ravine to a place where the bottom of it might be shallower than here. If she didn't get him out, find some shelter and treat his wound, he would probably die. And if the ravine stayed this deep, she would die right along with him. The rain pelted her back, chilling her through and through.

His fingers settled around her arm. "Agent Eric…Vinland. He's…psychic. Can read me sometimes. But I can't…think straight. You try."

Vanessa swallowed her hysteria and tried to humor him. "Okay. Tell me what to do. I don't have much, uh, experience with this." And didn't believe in it, either, but she wouldn't tell him that. "You do, right? You've done this before. Many times?"

His head moved in a jerky nod. "Believe. Concentrate. Send north. Call to him. He…can locate. Homing…implant in my shoulder."

Vanessa expelled a breath, blowing away the rainwater collected on her lips. Clay was making no sense at all. But she did recall his telling her about some of the agents he worked with having certain talents when it came to psychic phenomena. Maybe he was making a strange sort of sense after all.

She had run out of options and was willing at that point to try anything. "Okay, got it," she told him. "Eric Vinland. Concentrate. North. Call in the cavalry."

"Go…up," he ordered, his voice grating. A thin stream of blood trickled from the corner of his mouth and his eyes clenched shut.

Vanessa almost lost it when she saw that. Definite internal damage, probably his lung. "Going," she told him. "I'm going up!" She gave him her flashlight. "Light my way, then keep it on. I have another one in my pocket for when I get up there."

She stood and cast the light up to the rope's end, which

dangled a couple of feet above her head. When she grabbed it, it slid right out of her hand.

Moving as quickly as possible, she dragged a few loose stones over beneath it and stood on them. They scattered, but held in place just long enough for her to get a better hold on the rope.

Three tries at it and she was on her way up, her boots slipping and sliding, the treads finally grabbing on the wall of the ravine. Time crawled as she climbed.

Finally back on solid ground, she looked back down at Clay. The flashlight had rolled to one side, out of his hand, and he looked unconscious. "Hang in there!" she called down in case he could hear her. "I'll be back soon as I can."

She fished her flashlight out of her pocket and took off for the summit. Her legs felt like rubber and blisters lined her palms. If her pounding head didn't roll off her shoulders, she would be surprised.

"Let this be for real," she prayed. "Please let this guy be for real and let me find his hotline."

When she reached the highest point she could navigate, Vanessa paused, leaned over with her hands on her knees and heaved. Her stomach was empty and she felt she was turning inside out.

What a leap of faith, she thought, unable to believe she was really doing this. Maybe she was the one hallucinating, out of her mind with exhaustion and fear.

Soon as she caught her breath, she sucked in all the oxygen she could and stood tall. She faced north and cleared her mind of everything but a heartfelt plea and shouted as if her words could reach Virginia. "Help us, Eric Vinland! Send help. Clay Senate is hurt. He might die. Help now!"

She waited, wondering if she should expect an answer. Then she laughed bitterly, felt extremely stupid to be standing on top of a mountain, calling to a total stranger a thousand miles away as if he could hear her.

In spite of that, she tried again, putting every ounce of her energy into thinking it, shouting it, pleading with the unknown. And the known. She added a fervent prayer to any deities who might possibly care to listen and heed.

"I love this man!" she shouted. "Do *not* let him die. Not this way. He does not deserve this! Help me save him!" She added a groaning, "Please!" and fell to her knees, clasping her hands around the flashlight and letting her tears mix with the rain as she sobbed and whispered, "Don't let him die."

She had been away from him for at least half an hour, maybe a bit more. It would take her another twenty minutes or so to descend. Unwilling to leave him alone any longer, Vanessa trudged back down the mountain as swiftly as she could and still keep her footing.

She went directly back to the rope and began lowering herself down to be with him.

The rain had abated to a drizzle some time ago and now had stopped completely. And though it cast a dimmer light than before, the moon was back. That was a good sign, wasn't it? Maybe some higher power had actually heard her.

But when she reached the end of her rope and dropped the rest of the way, Clay was no longer there.

Chapter 13

Clay held on, but he was already losing hope. He realized, now that he couldn't make contact, how he had come to depend on his fellow agents. No, they were not only that. They were his friends.

Eric, the trickster hiding his kindness behind a devil-may-care facade. Holly, whom he trusted in spite of his lifelong wariness. Her husband, Will, the quiet one, the one who saw too much. Joe, the good ol' boy who would go to the mat for any of them. Yes, even Jack Mercier. Jack could be a real hard-ass, but he was fair and always willing to listen.

Yeah, he had underappreciated all of them, held himself apart, trusting them with his physical self, but rarely with any confidences.

It had taken a little snip of a woman with her laughing attitude and boundless energy to yank him out of his shell. He looked around the weak pool of light cast by the flashlight he had dropped. Here he was, lying in the pit of a mountain, not even a remarkable mountain at that, ruminating over the part of his life he'd misspent. And she was up there somewhere sending her thoughts out like smoke signals just because he had asked it of her. She probably thought doing that was as useless as blanketed puffs of smoke, too. Maybe it was.

Well, he ought to do something besides bleed. He touched his wound and thought maybe it had stopped. Carefully, he rolled to his side, hoping to shift himself upright before she got back. Maybe his head would clear.

The ground beneath him sank under his weight. Clay slid rapidly, unable to catch onto anything solid. Mud slithered through his hands and over his face as he descended at a steep angle into what must be hell. A wet, engulfing hell of darkness. Hope died completely on the way down. He had failed her, failed himself, failed his friends and those he had tried to help Vanessa protect. Hightower had escaped.

With an overwhelming sense of déjà vu, he realized that portion of his vision, earth falling away and a pervasive sense of doom.

"Clay!" he heard her scream. With the last desperate breath of effort he could manage, he called to her.

Vanessa crawled toward the sound, half groan, half shout. He had fallen into the crevice. She directed the light down and saw him immediately. Thank God there was not a steep drop-off here in this ditch within a ditch, but it was still too deep for her to reach him. If she slid down, too, she knew she would be trapped.

There was nothing for it but to go for help to get him out and pray that he survived long enough for the rescue. She picked up the flashlight he had dropped and shook it. The batteries were dead. Hers were good, though, and should last until daylight.

She looked up at the wide ribbon of sky visible over the walls of the ravine. "It'll be dawn soon, Clay," she shouted down to him. "I'm going to start down the mountain and get a rescue team. All you have to do is stay alive, you hear me?" When he didn't answer, she stuck the light in the mud and braced it with some stones so he would have light. "Hang on. We'll get you out soon." She hoped with all her heart it would be soon enough.

Vanessa had gone less than a quarter mile when she heard the thump, thump, thump of a chopper. Damn! She had no flashlight, no way to signal them. The one she had left in the ravine with Clay was shining down on him and might not be visible from above. No way to light a fire, either. Her clothing wouldn't even reflect if they used a searchlight. The rain had thoroughly doused James's fire.

She started back up, hoping they would keep hovering around the mountain until she could reach that flashlight and beam it up. Wildly grabbing at bushes and trees to help propel her faster, she scrambled toward the ravine.

What was the helicopter doing here anyway? Maybe her grandfather had gotten worried and called someone in to search. God bless him, he had wanted to come, too. She wished now she had allowed it. He would know exactly what to do.

Almost there, she told herself, though she knew she still had a ways to go. The sound of the chopper faded. "Don't go!" she cried aloud. "Please don't go!"

She got up and ran, stumbling the last fifty feet, threw herself on her stomach and retrieved the flashlight. Shining it up through the clouds, she prayed it would be seen, even as she realized there was no sound from up there now. They had abandoned the search.

Choking back her terror, she rolled back to the edge and lit up the ravine where Clay lay. "They're searching!" she called down to him. "Hang on! They'll be back!"

When he didn't move or acknowledge her in any way, Vanessa lay back and switched off the light to save the batteries. Her eyes kept closing and she feared she would pass out from exhaustion and miss signaling if they did another flyover.

Had to stay awake. She couldn't let him die. To remain conscious, she began chanting a song of hope, one in the old language. Her grandmother had taught it to her years ago. Somehow it held despair at bay, so she repeated it. On her third repetition, she heard the chopper again and sobbed with relief.

She switched on the flashlight and aimed it for the sound. Just as the batteries were weakening, the searchlight from above shone down on her. Vanessa waved her arms wide in welcome as the aircraft hovered. Unable to stand, she watched someone rappel down a rope and land a mere fifteen feet away in the clearing where James had built his fire.

"Vannie?" someone called, running toward her. "Is that you?"

Her grandfather? "Du-da?" she whispered, then called louder to him. "We have to get Clay! He's been hit and he's in the ravine. You can barely see him. Hurry!"

He used a collar mike and spoke with those in the rescue chopper and told them an agent was wounded. Immediately, another man slid down the cable and joined them. She recognized Sam Wolf, of the emergency rescue team she had worked with when she'd been a guide. "There's no place to put down," he said. "We'll have to reel him up." He looked at her. "You hurt, Van?"

"I'm okay. Just go get *him*," she ordered, pointing into the ravine.

Sam put a hand on her shoulder, thankfully her good one. "There's no room for all of us but we've called for another chopper and they have your coordinates. If you can wait, I'll go up with the victim."

Victim? He was calling Clay the victim. Vanessa pushed to her feet. "Agent Senate will need blood. He's lost a lot."

Sam nodded and began rigging the cable and giving orders to whoever was operating it from the chopper. She and her grandfather moved out of the way. He held her close while they watched and worried.

"They almost gave up," her grandfather said. "Then we saw something on the rocks up there. Thought it was you, Clay or maybe Hightower. When they beamed the searchlight down, it was the panther." He pressed her head to his chest and comforted her as he had when she was a child. "I knew you and Clay were near when I saw it. We followed it with the light until we saw your flashlight."

"His spirit guide protects him," Vanessa said softly and looked out across the mountain.

"You, too," her grandfather assured her. "Maybe because you will belong to him. Think so?"

Vanessa couldn't answer that. In her heart, she did belong to Clay, but she knew it was much more complicated than that. Sex didn't necessarily make them a couple. Neither did these strong feelings they had for one another. There were large issues in Clay's life that he had to deal with before he shared it with anyone, even a woman who loved him. She just prayed now that he would live to work things out.

Before they knew it, Sam and Clay were ascending on the cable that looked too skinny to support two men. She finally sucked in a deep, cleansing breath and released it in a rush once they disappeared into the chopper. It veered away, taking her strength and her heart with it.

"He's in good hands now," her grandfather said gently, patting her back.

"Thanks, Du-da," she sighed and collapsed in his arms.

When she regained consciousness, Vanessa wondered who had beaten her black and blue. Her arms and hands were a mass of scratches and bruises. Her legs felt like rotten rubber and she couldn't get her mind around what had happened. It seemed someone had questioned her and she had answered, but she was still a little fuzzy on that.

She was lying in a hospital room. Only her grandmother was with her. "Where are we?"

"Finally, you're awake! You've been out if it for nearly eight hours. Want some water?" She held a straw to Vanessa's lips. "We're in Asheville. They brought you here in the second helicopter. You were pretty much out of it. There were no apparent injuries except for bruises, but they're keeping you here a while for observation. Do you hurt anywhere, dear?"

"No, ma'am. Clay? How is he?"

"In ICU. Don't worry, he'll make it. The bullet did some muscle damage, but was fairly close to the surface. Loss of blood was the worst of it. They fixed that. Every lawman in three counties volunteered to replace it with theirs." Her grandmother smiled. "But they were preempted by those agents from McLean. Four of them flew down here. Apparently, your young man inspires great loyalty in his friends."

"He's not *my* young man," Vanessa argued with a wry laugh.

"But you wish he was, don't you, dear?"

Vanessa nodded and lay back, wishing that, and also that she could see him, just to assure herself that he was recovering.

The door opened and a tall, dark-haired man entered the room. He wore a business suit, a boring tie and a look of angry concern. "You are Vanessa Walker?" he demanded.

She drew her lips to one side and gave him another once-over. "Says so on my chart, I expect. Who wants to know?"

"Jack Mercier. I work with Agent Senate." He nodded to her grandmother and asked politely, "Would you mind if I spoke to Ms. Walker alone?"

"If you will be brief," her grandmother answered, not at all intimidated by the man's tough demeanor. "She has been through quite an ordeal." She left when Mercier agreed.

Their brief exchange had given Vanessa time to collect herself for what could be a confrontation. The man looked angry. "You mean Clay works *for* you, right? You're the agent in charge of Sextant."

"Yes. Did he tell you he was sent here to recruit you?"

Before she could answer him, three other people walked in. What was this, Grand Central Station?

Mercier looked around, obviously not altogether pleased to have an audience, yet he didn't order them out. "Agents Griffin, Griffin and Vinland," he said by way of introduction.

"How do you do?" Vanessa said, going for formality.

Mercier cleared his throat. "So, you knew that you were being recruited?"

"I did. Agent Senate was very forthright about it."

"He was to assist you in completing your mission, as well."

"Which he certainly did," Vanessa stated.

"It appears that you distracted him. As a result, he has been severely wounded."

Vanessa tried to keep her cool. This was Clay's boss. He was upset that his man was hurt and wanted someone to blame. She could understand that. "I let him get shot. Yes," she admitted. "And I assume full responsibility. If I had killed Hightower when I had the chance earlier in the day, Clay would have been safe." She inclined her head and looked up at Mercier. "However, if I had, he would have detonated all that C-4 he planted and there might have been a number of innocent lives lost. If you think I feel no guilt about the man I love lying critically wounded, think again. I wish it were me and I'm sure you wish that, too."

"Well, well, she took the wind right out of your sails, didn't she, boss?" The beautiful black woman with short cropped curls, long red nails and a matching designer suit stepped to the foot of the bed and winked as she spoke. "Way to go, hon. Jack's got a mad on, so you'll have to excuse him. See, he has a real soft spot for Clay." She looked around, then back at Vanessa. "For all of us, if you want the truth. You doing all right?" She patted Vanessa's foot through the sheet.

"Fine, I think," Vanessa said, noting the two male agents behind Mercier. One was a tall, buff blonde who would have looked more at home on a surfboard. He was smiling at her with secrets in those electric-blue eyes. The other was good-looking, too, in a Wall Street kind of way. He appeared a little impatient with the proceedings.

Mercier cleared his throat again, meaningfully, as he glared at the woman. Then he addressed Vanessa again. "We have rules about our agents becoming involved. I will have to withdraw any offer Agent Senate might have made you concerning employment with the COMPASS team."

Vanessa laughed bitterly and wagged her head. "You think I *care?* Do you honestly think I'd be bothered by that when Clay is lying upstairs struggling to live? Get out of my room, Special Agent Mercier, and take your stupid *job* with you." She shook her finger at him. "And if you think I'm going to back off Clay Senate just because *you* think we don't suit, you know where you can go! And I don't mean back to McLean!" She crossed her arms over her chest and glared at him.

He pursed his lips and turned to the others. They peered

back at him as if waiting for his response. "She'll do," he said with a nod and calmly walked out of the room.

"Well, damn!" the woman at the foot of the bed said and raised her perfect black eyebrows. "Looks like you're in, honey."

"In what?" Vanessa looked from one to the other of the agents.

"COMPASS team. I'm Holly Griffin with Sextant," the woman told her. "Married to this big ol' rascal right here," she said, giving the dark-haired agent next to her a backhanded knock on the chest. "This is my Will. The kid over there is Eric Vinland. He wants a few words with you. We'll be outside."

Vanessa muttered something in the way of goodbye, nice to meet you and threw a questioning glance at Vinland. His name was all too familiar, one she had called from a mountaintop in an hour of madness. "What?"

He grinned and stuck out his hand to shake. Vanessa took it.

"You did call to me," he said. "Came through loud and clear, too. Got me right out of a hot tub where I was about to get lucky with my new wife. I forgive you, though, and she will, too, eventually."

Vanessa stared. "You *heard* me?" Then she shook her head and withdrew her hand from his. "That can't be. My grandfather called in our location and got the choppers there." At his pointed smile, she asked, "Didn't he?"

Vinland leaned against the bars of her hospital bed and reached for her hand again. "I got your message almost word for word. Clay has a homing device implanted in his shoulder—Jack likes to keep tabs on our whereabouts—but we lost track. Figured he was underground somewhere, but his last transmission was on that mountain. I called your grandfather and he verified that's where you and Clay had gone after Hightower. We arranged local rescue and you did the rest with that flashlight. Clay's alive because of you, Vanessa."

"You *heard* me?" she asked again, unable to get past that.

He laughed merrily. "Sure did. Surprised the hell out of me, too! That's the first mind-to-mind connection I've had in over a year. Thought I'd lost the knack. It's also one of the strongest I've experienced, ever."

"So you are all this way?" Van asked, trying to recall what Clay had said about it. It hadn't been much.

Vinland smiled. "These skills are Sextant and COMPASS's secret weapons, so they aren't discussed much, especially not when evaluating a prospective agent and trying to determine her own talents." He continued. "And if you think Mercier doesn't want you on the COMPASS team, you're bad wrong. He knows you're telepathic now and you can pretty much name your salary if you're greedy. All that guff he gave you was just his version of a test. Trust me, he wants you. Today I can read his mind like a teleprompter."

Vanessa thought she must be dreaming. "But I'm not telepathic. All I did was what Clay told me to do. I didn't even believe it would work. I still can't believe it." She scrunched up her forehead and blinked really hard to clear her mind. "It didn't really. Did it?"

"Yep. After setting up the rescue, we jumped on the plane and got here as quickly as we could. All present except Joe, who's minding the store." He held out his hands, palms up. "So welcome to the HSA family."

"I can't think about that right now. All I want is to see Clay and make sure he'll be all right."

"No can do. At least not right now. They're very strict about only one visitor at a time, and as long as he's unconscious, he has to have an agent with him." He glanced at his watch. "Right now, that would be Danielle Sweet. She's with COMPASS."

Vanessa saw red. "You have a female agent named *Sweet* in his room?"

"Yep," Vinland said with a wiggle of his eyebrows. "Dani's a looker, too. Are you jealous?"

"Perfectly green," Vanessa admitted. "Get these bars down for me. I'm going up there. When he wakes up, it's not going to be to a pretty face. It's going to be to mine!"

Vinland laughed out loud. "You're gonna fit right into that bunch Jack's hired."

He did just as she asked, then took her arm to help her up. "First, let's get some of the mud out of your hair and wash your face a little better. Don't want to scare the lad to death, do we?"

"Oh, my God!" she cried when she saw herself in the mirror over the sink. Her hair looked like a fright wig. A huge bruise darkened her eye and one side of her face where James had butt-stroked her. And she was wearing a faded hospital gown several sizes too large and hanging off one shoulder with snaps missing. "Help!"

"I intend to," Vinland told her seriously. "If you'll wait right here, I'll be back with the necessary equipment."

"What equipment?"

"Leave it to me. Disguise is my forte. When I finish with you, you'll raise his pulse to danger level."

Vanessa couldn't believe this guy who looked more boy than man. "Are you reading *my* mind now?" she asked.

He smiled a secret smile. "No, I wouldn't be that rude." Then he cocked his head and seemed to reconsider. "Well, maybe I would, but I was actually busy checking out Clay. He's dreaming about you right now."

"What? What's he dreaming?" she insisted, caught up in the novel idea of getting inside someone's head. No, not just anyone's head. Clay's. Call her interest prurient, call it intrusive. But she just *had* to know.

Vinland teased her with a minute of silence, fingering his chin and squinting at her. Then he shrugged and spoke. "Clay must have some wild fantasy thing about you and the rain."

Vanessa poked him in the arm with her finger. "Stop that this minute! Don't you dare intrude on—"

"Hey, peace, Van! I'm off it, okay? I only wanted to see if he was sleeping normally or in a coma or something. Now, dunk your head in that sink and be washing out some of that grime while I go steal some makeup and a hair dryer."

Vanessa wasn't altogether sure she wanted him giving her a makeover. Not while she was trapped in a backless hospital gown and naked underneath. Oddly enough, she felt comfortable with Vinland, though.

"Yes, I'm perfectly harmless," he said with an exasperated roll of his eyes. "I'm well married and never one to poach on a friend's woman, even when I was single. Okay? All I want to do is get you looking decent."

"Thanks, but you are a *guy*. Shouldn't my grandmother or your friend Holly be doing this for me?"

He cocked an eyebrow and pinned her with an exasperated look. "Hey, do you want to look merely *cute* or sexy as sin?"

Vanessa snickered and tapped her temple. "Read my mind, Ace."

Chapter 14

Danielle Sweet welcomed her with a smile when she entered Clay's room. "Hi, Vanessa. Since you're here, I guess I can take a break. He's been pretty heavily sedated, the nurse says, but should be coming around soon."

Eric had been right. Danielle was a looker. An amber-eyed, brunette. And single, judging by the lack of a ring on her finger. She looked very professional in her silvery-gray suit and low-heeled pumps. The girl could pass for a news-caster or maybe a real-estate salesperson, but didn't look tough enough to fight terrorists. She looked…sweet, like her name.

She paused beside Vanessa and held out her hand. Her grip was firm. "I'm Dani Sweet. Eric tells me you'll be coming onboard with us. Just want you to know how pleased we are. COMPASS includes only Cate Olin and myself right now, but we have another candidate hired. He'll be joining us when he finishes his training. Clay gave you a glowing recommendation when he spoke with Holly on the phone."

"Well, Agent Mercier might have more to say about that. It's far from a sure thing," Vanessa said, "but thanks, Dani."

"See you around," the agent said and, with a final glance at the sleeping Clay, stepped out of the room and closed the door.

Vanessa took a seat in the chair beside Clay's bed and waited for him to wake up.

Clay fought through the fog of pain. Hightower was getting away and he had to stop him.

"Clay? Can you hear me?" He felt a warm palm brush his brow.

"Vanessa?" he whispered and forced his eyes open. "Are you all right?"

"I'm great. How are you feeling?"

"Fine," he lied. He raised a hand and closed his fingers gently around her forearm. He needed the contact to make certain she was real, not a dream. "What did I miss?"

"Well, in case you don't remember, we got Hightower. They haven't found his body yet, but I heard him fall. The remote device is out of commission for sure and they're still searching for the bombs. Danger's passed now and the op's all over except for doing the reports and the debriefing."

He exhaled through his teeth as relief poured through him. "You…you look…different," he said, squinting up at her and wondering whether his eyes were damaged. Her hair shone like satin and was caught up in some kind of Lara Croft slicked-back braid. She had on enough makeup for a Broadway production. "What happened?" Then he guessed. "Eric's here, right?"

She giggled. "So you really are psychic."

He winced as he looked up at her. "No, I just recognize his brush strokes. Next time, just say no."

Again she laughed, the delighted sound, music to his ears. "He said you'd like it."

Clay reached up and touched her lips. "Think you could stand losing some of that lip gloss if you kiss me?"

She leaned over the bed rail and touched his mouth lightly with hers. "Later we'll do a serious lip-lock. I just needed to see you for a minute. You should sleep now and get well."

He grasped her hand to keep her from leaving. "Wait. I need to marry you."

She gasped and her eyebrows flew up. "And you are obviously on some seriously heavy drugs."

Clay knew that hadn't come out right. He had thought and thought about it while lying in the bottom of the ravine, expecting to die. If he lived, he had promised himself, he would have her and to hell with everything else. Somehow he would convince her that she would lose nothing by becoming his wife. He had to make her see that.

"I need you. I love you." There, he couldn't go wrong saying that. Or maybe he should have put the love first. He meant the love first. "No, I love you and I need you," he muttered. "Yeah, that's right."

She patted his hand and pulled hers away. "What you need is rest. I'm going now and I'll be back when you sober up."

When he opened his eyes again, she was gone. Eric was there, dozing in the chair beside his bed. "Hey kid," Clay said. "Where's Vanessa?"

Vinland jumped up and leaned over the rail. "You must have scared the life out of her. She came out of here crying and shaking her head. I couldn't get a word out of her, but she's confused, man. Real confused. Couldn't make heads nor tails out of her thoughts. Pure chaos. I ordered her not to drive if she was leaving the hospital, but she said she wasn't.

I think she went to the chapel. Her grandmother went with her."

"I asked her to marry me," Clay said. "I think."

Eric rolled his eyes. "You *think?* Oh man, I should never have let her in here when you were so doped up on pain meds. Did you…mean it?"

Clay frowned at his friend. "Hell, yes, I meant it." He closed his eyes and sighed. "But I'm not sure I said it right."

"What did you say? Exactly?"

"I don't remember. Exactly."

Vinland thought for a minute. "Okay, let me go do some damage control."

"Wait! Don't help me, Eric. Please?" Vinland was too famous for his practical jokes and this was no time for that nonsense.

"Hey, what are friends for, huh? I'll square it with her and she'll be back in here in a minute ready to plan the wedding."

Clay groaned. He had IVs in both arms, the plastic oxygen thingie up his nostrils, electrodes attached to his chest and was pretty well anchored to the bed. There was nothing he could do but hope Vanessa had gone home with her grandmother and that Eric couldn't find their house.

He punched the button for an extra spurt of morphine. He hurt like hell and had probably lost any chance to hook up with the woman he loved on a permanent basis. Damn.

Vanessa couldn't believe Clay had really asked her. Would he if he had been lucid? Probably not. Should she take advantage of it? It wouldn't be fair, would it?

Her grandmother sat with her in the chapel and held her hand, saying nothing, letting her mull it over in her mind and decide how to handle this.

"What should I do?" Vanessa asked her finally, needing some advice.

"What your heart tells you. You love him. He loves you. I see no problem here."

"But he never once mentioned marriage before, not when he was thinking straight. I know he thought that getting serious with me would compromise my chances at the new job, but I told him I didn't care about that."

Her grandmother placed a hand over hers and squeezed as she leaned closer. "His worry goes deeper than that, Vanessa, and has probably affected every relationship he has. You know what has bothered Clay all his life. If he found his place in the world and got centered, he would feel more confident about sharing himself." Her grandmother pulled an envelope out of her purse. "You were right to ask for my help. I think this will do it. It's the information you wanted me to find."

Vinland interrupted them, tapping her on the shoulder. "Our boy's going nuts in there waiting for your answer. If it's not yes, I think he'll die."

"Liar!" Vanessa scoffed. "He sent you, didn't he?"

Eric nodded. "I'm here to tell you, Clay's not one to make any offers lightly. I've never known him to date a woman twice, much less propose to one."

"Well he's never dated *me* at all, not even once," Vanessa replied. "Now he drops this proposal on me with no warning?"

Vinland smiled sweetly. "It's his way. He's not smooth, I grant you that. But he is totally sincere. So sincere we worry about him all the time. Now it's your turn. Marry the man and give us some relief, will you?"

Her grandmother gave her a nudge, the closest thing to interfering with Vanessa's decision that she was likely to offer.

"Both of you let me be alone for ten minutes?"

They left together, Eric already plying her grandmother with broad hints for a visit to her home.

Vanessa opened the envelope and began to read. After scanning only half of it, she refolded it, her decision made. This couldn't wait ten minutes. Clay had been waiting too long already.

"Hi," she said, offering Clay a smile. "I have something for you, a get-well gift from my grandmother and me."

Clay looked at the envelope. "Get-well card?"

"No. Information. You are White Mountain Apache," Vanessa told him proudly. "How about that? My grandmother has many contacts and she used them all. She and my grandfather have attended powwows all over the country and met many of the People. They have formed e-mail loops you wouldn't believe, a countrywide grapevine."

"So someone admitted they knew a woman named Margaret in this tribe you mentioned?" Clay asked, obviously unwilling to believe what he was hearing. Or maybe afraid to believe.

She took his hands in hers and placed the envelope in them. "It's true, Clay. Your parents met in Arizona at the Sunrise Ski Resort, where she was working as an instructor. He married her in a traditional ceremony on the res, then took her back to Boston with him."

Clay shook his head. "How is it I missed getting this? I checked there and everywhere else. Investigated for all I was worth. No records existed of any marriage that might have been theirs. I've worked on this for years!"

"Unrecorded marriages happen all the time. Unless your mom tried to claim something of his, such as in a divorce settlement or social security or something of that nature, she would not have needed documents. People attended. There were witnesses aplenty, but unless they were called on to help her in that way, they wouldn't have volunteered the information."

"Why in the world not?"

"She died, Clay. You told me yourself that your people do not speak of the dead. They won't even touch things belonging to the deceased. It's custom. If you went there asking about a woman named Margaret, they probably said there were many named that, right?"

He nodded, looking thoughtful. "Yet they told your grandmother?"

"She knew the questions to ask and how to phrase them. She inquired about a gray-eyed child who was taken by his white father after his mother was lost. She took it from there. Apparently, your mother died in an accident at the ski resort. Fell from a precipice. Your father came and took you away. He didn't want you living there, obviously. Your grandfather is still alive. And two of your aunts."

She saw she had rendered him speechless. But the excitement in his eyes spoke volumes. How he wanted a family of his own. He had even been thrilled to share hers for a little while. "Now you have a tribe," she said softly, smiling up at him. "Will you go to Arizona for a visit?"

Clay had closed his eyes and the look on his face was sublime. "You have to ask?" Then he opened them and gazed at her with such love. "Will you come with me?"

Vanessa drew in a deep breath and released it along with his hand. She turned away so he wouldn't see the longing in her eyes as she refused. This was something he needed to do alone. "I can't."

"Why not?" he asked softly.

Why, indeed? Vanessa asked herself. What was preventing her from giving him the support he wanted? She knew why. "Because I want you to love me for myself, Clay. You once admitted you weren't sure if it's me you love or what I represent to you."

"That's not true any longer," he assured her. "It is you, for yourself alone, Vanessa. Marry me, Vanessa. Or at least come with me to McLean where we can be together. Think of the advantages we could give little Dilly there. She is so bright and needs to be in a challenging school where she'll shine."

Vanessa was already shaking her head. "We've already had this conversation, Clay. What do you think my grandparents, not to mention Cody and Jan, would say to that plan?"

"They would miss her, of course. Bring them, too!"

"Listen to yourself, Clay," Vanessa said gently, patting his hand as she might a child in need of counsel. "You are thinking exactly the way your father thought. That our life here with the people is not good enough. That our culture is lacking somehow. I assure you it's not. I would never take Dilly from the home she knows and loves. It will be her decision to stay or go when she comes of age, just as it was mine."

"Oh my God," he said, pressing his thumb and forefinger to the bridge of his nose. "It must be the morphine."

She smiled down at him. "No, it's your protective instinct kicking in, just the way your dad's did. You need to get a better understanding of what went down when you were seven, Clay. You need to forgive your father. And you need to forgive yourself."

"Me?" he snapped. "What for?"

"That guilt that's making you crazy. I don't know. Being half white, maybe? Accepting a privileged lifestyle? Being angry with your mother for dying and leaving you? I can't answer for sure because I'm no psychiatrist and it's not up to me to analyze you. You need to do that on your own. Go to Arizona. Meet your family and your tribe. Find what you've been searching for all this time." She shrugged. "Seek another vision."

His gray eyes pleaded with her, told her he loved her and

wanted her with him. But she knew he wouldn't ask again and risk another refusal.

"I just want you to be sure," she insisted, feeling like the worst hypocrite in the world because she wanted so badly to go with him wherever he went. "Find your grandfather. Find yourself, Clay. Then if you still want me, come back and we'll see."

"You'll wait?" he asked.

Vanessa nodded. "I promise. Besides, that spirit guide of yours would eat me alive if I messed around, right?"

One corner of his mouth kicked up in a half smile. "Right. I'll give him orders."

"Speaking of orders, I expect mine any minute now. I have to go back to Cherokee today and see about wrapping this up. We have to recover James's body and that remote, find and account for all the C-4 he took, then there'll be all the paper-work. Eric told me they're airlifting you to Bethesda first thing in the morning so I might not see you again while you're here."

He nodded and gave a long sigh, his eyes filled with longing that nearly erased her resolve. "Then could you just come here and let me have that lip-lock you promised? I've been dreaming about it."

Their kiss in the rain. She would dream of that magic moment, too, and all that followed.

Vanessa kept this kiss fairly chaste in spite of his demand. She didn't want to weaken now that she had done the right thing.

Was this a goodbye kiss? Would he come back to her?

Chapter 15

Clay rotated and stretched his shoulder, cursing the month it had taken to get it that mobile. Two weeks in Bethesda navel hospital had seemed like a lifetime. At least he had completed his report and been debriefed while he was there. Now he was recuperating further at his grandfather's home.

Mercier wanted Vanessa on the COMPASS team. He had conveniently overlooked Clay's personal involvement in light of Vanessa's success, obvious suitability and remarkable record with the Bureau. Of course, it didn't hurt that the boss continued to be intrigued by her incredible escapes and the fact that she had been able to transmit psychic messages to Eric Vinland. Yeah, she was definitely in, if she wanted to be.

Clay would remain with Sextant, so they would not be working together directly. He wondered if he could convince her to take the job. If she showed the slightest reluctance, he had decided to transfer out of Sextant, much as he loved the work, and ask HSA for an assignment closer to her home.

Unless she had changed her mind. He had called her frequently, but she had remained noncommittal, waiting for him to iron out his personal life. He hadn't pushed her. Maybe she had a few doubts she needed to settle in her own mind. He did come with a lot of baggage and she might be having second thoughts about getting involved.

It had been an interesting couple of weeks here, he thought with a smile, but it was time to go. Saying goodbye to this place was not as easy as he'd thought it would be.

He patted the pinto who danced eagerly beneath him and gazed out at the vista he now considered home. It was rough country, stark and beautiful.

He couldn't live here, but at least he had a home base now, a foundation he recognized. Much of his early years had come back to him through his grandfather's stories. They had not seen one another for nearly thirty years, but the old fellow acted as if Clay had been living with him all along. No strangeness existed between them or with the two aunts he had met. They'd welcomed him with open arms. Clay felt he knew his mother better through her sisters.

She had loved his father, but had been unable to adjust to his lifestyle in Boston. Apparently she had encountered more prejudice and curiosity than she could handle and wanted to get Clay away before he was old enough to experience that, too. His father had let them go for a visit to her family and she had refused to return.

Clay deduced that he had either witnessed his mother's fall or perhaps had seen it in one of his early visions and had blocked it from his mind. That would account for his acrophobia.

He now had a firm grasp on all that had happened and was okay with it. How self-centered he had been all this time, thinking only of how events had affected him and not considering what his parents had endured. Neither of them had been prepared for dealing with the problems associated with a mixed marriage. Love had not been enough. Maybe if his mother had lived longer, they would have worked something out, but Clay didn't think so.

Was *he* ready for marriage? "Damn straight I am," he muttered to the horse. Clay's things were packed and ready. The new truck he had purchased in Tempe for his grandfather was gassed up. They would drive to the airport where Clay would fly to Vanessa. He was good and ready.

A yowl in the distance spooked the pinto. Clay calmed it as he searched the landscape. Far away on a large boulder, he spied a flash of tan. He eased closer and the cry came again. A panther. The horse reared and Clay almost lost his seat. When he got control and quieted the animal, he looked again for his spirit guide, but the big cat had disappeared.

"Thank you, brother," Clay said sincerely. "I am on the right path now."

He urged the pinto into a gallop that would speed him back to his grandfather's house and then on to his beloved. That's what the old man called Vanessa when referring to her, *your beloved*. A fitting term for the woman who had changed Clay's life.

Vanessa scanned the horizon where Mr. Tanner had indicated. Clay's grandfather had shown no surprise when she'd arrived an hour ago. He had merely smiled and called her granddaughter. After a nice chat, in which she'd done almost all of the talking, he'd told her Clay would ride in from the west and it was time to watch for him.

She almost danced on her toes in anticipation. From the first day she'd seen Clay, she had imagined him riding across the wide open spaces on a horse, his hair flying in the wind, his strong legs gripping the animal and guiding it where he wanted it to go.

"There he comes!" she cried, laughing and pointing. "Oh my goodness, he's a daredevil! Look at him go!"

The old man chuckled, his weathered face a study in pride. He reminded her so much of his grandson. Though his stature was much shorter and his eyes were dark brown, they shared many features and even gestures as they spoke. He had that deep timbered voice and a way of speaking that made a person stop and listen to every word.

She couldn't wait to hear Clay's voice, but right now she so enjoyed just looking at him. It was just as she had imagined, only he wasn't half-naked. He wore a brown shirt, jeans and boots. But his hair flew free, streaming out behind him as he leaned into the ride. Her imagination provided the feathers, leather and paint. "What a warrior," she whispered in awe.

He reined in and dismounted before the horse's hooves stopped moving. In a flash, he swept her up and kissed her soundly on the mouth. Nothing chaste about this one, she thought, as she got really into it. The old man would just have to look somewhere else if it embarrassed him.

"I was coming to you," Clay murmured into her mouth as he renewed the kiss from another angle. "Today I was coming."

"I know," she answered when she could catch her breath. "but I couldn't wait."

"We are destined to be together. Thank God you realized that," he said, hugging her to him with a fierceness that stole her breath. "Nothing could keep us apart for long."

"Nothing!" she agreed. "I could hardly stand to give you this much time."

"It was enough. Everything I ever wanted, I have now,

thanks to you." His eyes softened, glistened in the sunlight, and she thought he might be holding back a couple of tears.

"I love you, Clay, more than my life." The admission came so easily it surprised her. She did love him. More than the life she'd had planned for herself. More than anything. She knew, too, that he would never require her to give up anything she really wanted to do. He would even help her continue her work with young people, broaden the scope of it, no doubt. She kissed him again for good measure, putting her very soul into it.

"Marry me now?" he asked, but it came out more of a demand.

"Absolutely," she answered. "Now. Today if you want."

Mr. Tanner cleared his throat to get their attention, and they reluctantly broke the kiss and looked at him.

"What is it, Grandfather?" Clay asked, love gentling his voice, giving it a quality devoid of the wariness. Vanessa had hoped he would lose that, and at least here, it was missing.

"I will take the truck and go to your aunts. We will make the plans. Today is soon. We will do this the day after tomorrow," his grandfather said with an incline of his head.

"Not soon enough," Clay said, laughing. "But I guess we'll survive the wait. What should we do to get ready for the ceremony?"

"Stay here. Welcome your beloved. Then bring her to Nohwike Bagowa when it is time. We will have what you need."

When the old man had left them there alone at his simple two-bedroom house, Vanessa looked up at Clay. "What is that place he mentioned?"

"House of our footprints," Clay explained. "Cultural museum. Looks like we might have a very public wedding." He leaned down and kissed her lightly on the forehead.

"What kind of hello is that, you Apache rascal? Grandpa told you to *welcome* me!"

Laughing out loud, he scooped her up in his arms and carried her inside.

Clay's bedroom was outfitted with a wood heater, a cushy old recliner and a double bed. Clay put her down on it.

"Cozy," she replied, shrugging out of her jacket and skinning out of her sweater. "Warm," she added, reaching for the snap of her jeans.

"Allow me," he growled. "My duty is to make you comfortable." He tugged off her boots, socks, then her jeans. She lay in her new pink satin bra and panties. His hot gray gaze took in every inch of her. "Pretty as these little silk things are, the silk beneath is what I want." He slid them off, trailing the sensuous fabric over her skin as he dispensed with them. "My, you do look relaxed now. Have to fix that."

He kicked off his boots, popped the snaps on his shirt and tore it off. Vanessa watched, her gaze languid and appreciative as he pulled down the zipper of his faded denims and stepped out of them. "My, how *cowboy* of you," she said with a soft chuckle. "No underwear."

"As if I knew you were coming and wanted to save time," he replied with a grin. "Actually, it was all packed except what I planned to wear on the plane. Didn't want to greet you with odor of horse sweat."

She rolled her eyes. "Go ahead, dash all my illusions."

"No illusions. No pretense. Nothing between us but truth." He came down over her and embraced her fully, his hair drifting over her face and neck as he kissed her softly. "I love you, Vanessa."

"And I love you," she whispered back. "I think I have since the minute I first saw you, before either of us knew who you were." She swallowed hard and felt tears creep down her cheeks. "If you don't take me right this minute, we're going to have our first real fight."

He smiled down into her eyes as he entered her slowly. "I take you as my wife. We will be forever."

"Forever," she repeated fervently, holding him within her without moving, feeling their oneness completely.

Clay stirred inside her, then began to move, his body lifting slightly to withdraw and enter again, as if to reclaim that rush of initial bliss. Vanessa cried out with the joy of it, knowing no one could hear but her other half.

He braced above her, his gaze holding hers as they loved, slowly, sensuously at first. When pleasure built so keen, so high she thought she would fly apart, he rode faster, harder, higher. Lightning flashed around and inside her as the storm broke over them together.

Clay's groan of completion mingled with hers as they soared from the precipice and glided to the ground, replete, gasping for breath and holding one another tight. The oneness remained, stronger even than before.

Yes, forever, Vanessa thought as she lazily stroked his back. "I feel *so* married," she whispered, loving the sensation of his lips against her neck, the sweet sage scent of his skin, the beat of his heart against her body.

That day and the next, Vanessa lived as an Apache. She shared the cooking and chores with Clay, and shared the bed whenever it suited them.

It was almost with regret they left the little house of his grandfather for their wedding ceremony. Vanessa wore the navy suit she had packed to wear home and Clay wore his gray pin-stripe with a red tie. Not exactly wedding attire. She had always sort of thought she'd have a wedding dress of some kind.

"Do you know what to expect?" she asked him as she parked her rental car near his grandfather's truck.

"Not a clue. I guess we'll share a blanket."

Vanessa giggled. "Already done that. Does that mean we're already hitched?"

"Guess not," he said, seeing his aunts approach with a gleam in their dark eyes and a bevy of women in tow. "Looks like they have plans for you."

Vanessa went with the women after he introduced them. Mary and Janetta took her to a dwelling down the road belonging to one of the other women and showed her what she was to wear. Apparently this had become a community project.

"How many horses will Clay give for you, I wonder?" Mary said with a cheeky grin as she braided Vanessa's hair. "I think he only has the one his grandfather gave him. It is not a very good bride price."

Vanessa got right into the spirit of the gentle teasing. "I'll see that Clay gets him a truck with many horses under the hood. My grandfather will welcome the trade, I expect."

"Are you so much trouble then, little bride?" Janetta asked. "Is our Clay in for a wild ride all his life?"

"Absolutely!" Vanessa said, laughing with the women. "Can't let the boy get bored!" The giggling went on until she was dressed and ready to go. She loved these women with their easy humor and wicked little grins. Clay was lucky to have found them and she knew they would be good for him. She wished she could have known his mother.

Soon Vanessa was decked out in a butter-soft white doeskin dress and cape decorated with shells and quillwork. Her feet were encased in moccasins that must have taken weeks to make. She felt as grand as any bride draped in white satin. Her hair was plaited and the braids wrapped with soft fur. Two dots of rouge highlighted her cheeks. If only her grandparents could see her now.

When she entered the cultural-center building and saw

Clay standing there in the lobby, she couldn't help sighing. He wore an off-white tunic and leggings with knee-high Apache boots to match and a colorful woven belt. His midnight hair hung shiny and straight, bound only by a solid red headband. He held out his hands to her and she joined him before the holy man.

After they were led outside and properly smudged, covered in fragrant sage smoke to purify them, they were ready to proceed and taken back inside the center. A few curious tourists had gathered, but it was chilly November and off season, so most of those present were Apache.

"We decided the ceremony should be here," his grand-father told everyone. "There is good medicine in the old things we have kept of our ancestors." Vanessa understood this exception to their custom of avoiding the possessions of those who had departed. All spirits would wish them well today.

Clay's elder aunt, Mary, stood beside him in his mother's place while Vanessa wished for her father or someone she loved to stand with her.

A commotion nearby made her turn slightly and she saw her grandparents approaching, all smiles. Behind them came Cody, Jan and little Dilly. The women and Dilly wore tear dresses and the men had on their ribbon shirts, the traditional Cherokee dress.

Behind them strode Jack Mercier, Holly and Will Griffin and Eric Vinland. Even Dani Sweet had tagged along. She gave Vanessa a little wave and a smile.

"Jack flew them in!" Clay whispered to Vanessa. "I owe him for this."

Vanessa felt a rush of gratitude toward Clay's associates. They were the best. She embraced her family while Clay greeted his friends.

Her grandmother carried blue blankets to drape around her and Clay for the ceremony. Without delay, she accepted hers and watched Clay don his.

Her grandfather held one of her grandmother's intricately woven baskets that contained ears of corn. Vanessa knew she was to give this to Clay. His aunt handed him a ham of venison, the traditional gift to the bride.

"I give you this with a promise to love you and provide for you as my wife for as long as we live," he said quietly.

She took it and handed it off to her grandfather, then placed the basket in Clay's hands. "I give you this corn to symbolize my vow to love and care for you as my husband for all of my days," she said sincerely.

They exchanged the wedding gifts as happily as they swapped the silver rings his aunts provided. The entire ceremony was a wonderful mix of old traditions and a few new twists, like the rings, that made it truly theirs.

Once the gifts had been dealt with, the holy man said his words in the language of Clay's people and then bound her hands to Clay's with a crimson wrapping, symbolically tying them together for a lifetime.

They were offered the sacred pipe next. His aunts had explained that it was the holy object in which both the men and women had a hand in making. The men carved the pipe itself and the women decorated it with bands of quillwork.

Vanessa took a few small puffs, surprised at the flavorful taste of the sacred tobacco. Clay blew his smoke so that it mingled with hers.

The blue blankets were removed and folded as the holy man placed a white woolly robe around them both. He raised his hands and declared them wed.

Clay kissed her soundly and everyone present seemed to sigh as one. Their wedding had blended the traditions of her people and his so beautifully, she knew their marriage would do that, as well. As they had improvised throughout their wedding, they would improvise their way through life, employing what worked best from three cultures for them as a couple.

The hoopla would begin now. She heard the drums strike up outside. Still Clay would not release her until she gave him a slight push and laughed. "Shall we dance?"

And dance, they did. And feasted. And met so many well-wishers she began to see all the faces in one long blur. The day wore on and they endured the crowd until they could politely sneak away.

Someone had constructed a large new tipi for their wedding night and that's where they went. The small, traditional Apache wikiups stood like little stick-and-wattle sentinels around the spacious, more modern dwelling many now used for temporary lodging when attending powwows. He lifted the flap for her and she saw the wonderful effort carried out on their behalf.

There was another basket from her grandmother containing fruit and little treats wrapped in cellophane. Stacked against one side of the bedding were other gifts still in their wrappings.

Little Dilly had added to the display with a framed crayon picture she had drawn of tipis, a feathered warrior, a spotted horse and the woefully misspelled caption reading Red Durt the Apace Brav.

"Wow! Would you look at this? Art, presents, furs, candle-light and the handsomest groom alive. What more could a bride ask?"

"Flattery runs in the family, I see. Dilly drew me even larger than the horse," he said, pointing at the picture.

Vanessa laughed out loud. "Hey, I'm not touching that line!"

"So what do you think tradition requires us to do now?"

he teased, running a long finger along the neck of her doeskin dress and playfully flipping up several of the cowrie shells.

"Shuck the corn?" She tossed off her cape.

"Not a chance." He untied the woven belt, tossed it aside and skimmed off his shirt.

"Cook that ham?" She untied her dress and let it drop.

"No way in hell." He loosened his leggings, let them drop and stood there in nothing but a loincloth. My, he was some sight to behold!

She pretended to wince at his size, then shrugged. "Well, I don't know about you, but I could sure use a nap."

Laughing, he grabbed her and tumbled her to their bed of furs. "Go on to sleep, then. I'll start without you."

"An empty threat if I ever heard one. Come here, you." She loved this playful side of Clay, one she suspected he had suppressed since boyhood. "I love your laugh," she told him as she lay beneath him, held his face in her hands and kissed the corners of his mouth.

"You taught me how, you little fox, but this is no laughing matter. I am *seriously* in need of comfort and you did promise to take care of me."

"And you, to provide what I need," she reminded him as she ran her fingers through his hair and looked at him with all the love in her heart. "All I need in the world is you."

"I am home whenever I'm with you," he said softly, all trace of humor gone. "If you want to stay near your people, I'll be there with you. Where I go will never matter to me as long as we're together."

Giving was his way and he made her want to give back. She would go with Clay to Virginia and work beside him. He had told her once that the world was their hunting ground and humanity their tribe. It was their mission to keep the world safe.

Wrapped in sumptuous furs inside their borrowed lodge, Vanessa held him and loved him throughout the night, this man who had turned her life around and would alter his own just to make her his.

In the distant hills of the White Mountain people, a big cat kept watch.

* * * * *

Be sure to watch for Lyn's next SPECIAL OPS *romance,*
SPECIAL AGENT'S SEDUCTION,
coming to Intimate Moments in January 2007.

*Experience entertaining women's fiction for every woman
who has wondered
"what's next?" in their lives.
Turn the page for a sneak preview of a new book
from Harlequin NEXT,
WHY IS MURDER ON THE MENU, ANYWAY?
by Stevi Mittman*

On sale December 26, wherever books are sold.

Ambience is everything. Imagine eating a foie gras at a luncheonette counter or a side of coleslaw at Le Cirque. It's not a matter of food but one of atmosphere. Remember that when planning your dining room design.

—Tips from *Teddi.com*

"Now that's the kind of man you should be looking for," my mother, the self-appointed keeper of my shelf-life stamp, says. She points with her fork at a man in the corner of the Steak-Out Restaurant, a dive I've just been hired to redecorate. Making this restaurant look four-star will be hard, but not half as hard as getting through lunch without strangling the woman across the table from me. "*He* would make a good husband."

"Oh, you can tell that from across the room?" I ask, wondering how it is she can forget that when we had trouble getting rid of my last husband, she shot him. "Besides being ten minutes away from death if he actually eats all that steak, he's twenty years too old for me and—shallow woman that I am—twenty pounds too heavy. Besides, I am *so* not looking for another husband here. I'm looking to design a new image for this place, looking for some sense of ambience, some feeling, something I can build a proposal on for them."

My mother studies the man in the corner, tilting her head, the better to gauge his age, I suppose. I think she's grimacing, but with all the Botox and Restylane injected into that face, it's hard to tell. She takes another bite of her steak salad, chews slowly so that I don't miss the fact that the steak is a poor cut and tougher than it should be. "You're concentrating on the wrong kind of proposal," she says finally. "Just look at this place, Teddi. It's a dive. There are hardly any other diners. What does *that* tell you about the food?"

"That they cater to a dinner crowd and it's lunchtime," I tell her.

I don't know what I was thinking bringing her here with me. I suppose I thought it would be better than eating alone. There really are days when my common sense goes on vacation. Clearly, this is one of them. I mean, really, did I not resolve less than three weeks ago that I would not let my mother get to me anymore?

What good are New Year's resolutions, anyway?

Mario approaches the man's table and my mother studies him while they converse. Eventually Mario leaves the table with a huff, after which the diner glances up and meets my mother's gaze. I think she's smiling at him. That or she's got indigestion. They size each other up.

I concentrate on making sketches in my notebook and try to ignore the fact that my mother is flirting. At nearly seventy, she's developed an unhealthy interest in members of the opposite sex to whom she isn't married.

According to my father, who has broken the TMI rule and given me Too Much Information, she has no interest in sex with him. Better, I suppose, to be clued in on what they aren't doing in the bedroom than have to hear what they might be doing.

"He's not so old," my mother says, noticing that I have barely touched the Chinese chicken salad she warned me not to get. "He's got about as many years on you as you have on your little cop friend."

She does this to make me crazy. I know it, but it works all the same. "Drew Scoones is not my little 'friend.' He's a detective with whom I—"

"Screwed around," my mother says. I must look shocked, because my mother laughs at me and asks if I think she doesn't know the "lingo."

What I thought she didn't know was that Drew and I actually tangled in the sheets. And, since it's possible she's just fishing, I sidestep the issue and tell her that Drew is just a couple of years younger than me and that I don't need reminding. I dig into my salad with renewed vigor, determined to show my mother that Chinese chicken salad in a steak place was not the stupid choice it's proving to be.

After a few more minutes of my picking at the wilted leaves on my plate, the man my mother has me nearly engaged to pays his bill and heads past us toward the back of the restaurant. I watch my mother take in his shoes, his suit and the diamond pinkie ring that seems to be cutting off the circulation in his little finger.

"Such nice hands," she says after the man is out of sight. "Manicured." She and I both stare at my hands. I have two popped acrylics that are being held on at weird angles by bandages. My cuticles are ragged and there's marker decorating my right hand from measuring carelessly when I did a drawing for a customer.

Twenty minutes later she's disappointed that he managed to leave the restaurant without our noticing. He will join the list of the ones I let get away. I will hear about him twenty years from now when—according to my mother—my children will be grown and I will still be single, living pathetically alone with several dogs and cats.

After my ex, that sounds good to me.

The waitress tells us that our meal has been taken care of by the management and, after thanking Mario, the owner, complimenting him on the wonderful meal and assuring him that once I have redecorated his place people will be flocking here in droves (I actually use those words and ignore my mother when she rolls her eyes), my mother and I head for the restroom.

My father—unfortunately not with us today—has the patience of a saint. He got it over the years of living with my mother. She, perhaps as a result, figures he has the patience for both of them, and feels justified having none. For her, no rules apply, and a little thing like a picture of a man on the door to a public restroom is certainly no barrier to using the john. In all fairness, it does seem silly to stand and wait for the ladies' room if no one is using the men's room.

Still, it's the idea that rules don't apply to her, signs don't apply to her, conventions don't apply to her. She knocks on the door to the men's room. When no one answers she gestures to me to go in ahead. I tell her that I can certainly wait for the ladies' room to be free and she shrugs and goes in herself.

Not a minute later there is a bloodcurdling scream from behind the men's room door.

"Mom!" I yell. "Are you all right?"

Mario comes running over, the waitress on his heels. Two customers head our way while my mother continues to scream.

I try the door, but it is locked. I yell for her to open it and she fumbles with the knob. When she finally manages to unlock and open it, she is white behind her two streaks of blush, but she is on her feet and appears shaken but not stirred.

"What happened?" I ask her. So do Mario and the waitress and the few customers who have migrated to the back of the place.

She points toward the bathroom and I go in, thinking it serves her right for using the men's room. But I see nothing amiss.

She gestures toward the stall, and, like any self-respecting and suspicious woman, I poke the door open with one finger, expecting the worst.

What I find is worse than the worst.

The husband my mother picked out for me is sitting on the toilet. His pants are puddled around his ankles, his hands are hanging at his sides. Pinned to his chest is some sort of Health Department certificate.

Oh, and there is a large, round, bloodless bullet hole between his eyes.

Four Nassau County police officers are securing the area, waiting for the detectives and crime scene personnel to show up. They are trying, though not very hard, to comfort my mother, who in another era would be considered to be suffering from the vapors. Less tactful in the twenty-first century, I'd say she was losing it. That is, if I didn't know her better, know she was milking it for everything it was worth.

My mother loves attention. As it begins to flag, she swoons

and claims to feel faint. Despite four No Smoking signs, my mother insists it's all right for her to light up because, after all, she's in shock. Not to mention that signs, as we know, don't apply to her.

When asked not to smoke, she collapses mournfully in a chair and lets her head loll to the side, all without mussing her hair.

Eventually, the detectives show up to find the four patrolmen all circled around her, debating whether to administer CPR, smelling salts or simply call the paramedics. I, however, know just what will snap her to attention.

"Detective Scoones," I say loudly. My mother parts the sea of cops.

"We have to stop meeting like this," he says lightly to me, but I can feel him checking me over with his eyes, making sure I'm all right while pretending not to care.

"What have you got in those pants?" my mother asks him, coming to her feet and staring at his crotch accusingly. "*Baydar?* Everywhere we Bayers are, you turn up. You don't expect me to buy that this is a coincidence, I hope."

Drew tells my mother that it's nice to see her, too, and asks if it's his fault that her daughter seems to attract disasters.

Charming to be made to feel like the bearer of a plague.

He asks how I am.

"Just peachy," I tell him. "I seem to be making a habit of finding dead bodies, my mother is driving me crazy and the catering hall I booked two freakin' years ago for Dana's bat mitzvah has just been shut down by the Board of Health!"

"Glad to see your luck's finally changing," he says, giving me a quick squeeze around the shoulders before turning his attention to the patrolmen, asking what they've got, whether they've taken any statements, moved anything, all the sort of stuff you see on TV, without any of the drama. That is, if you lon't count my mother's threats to faint every few minutes when she senses no one's paying attention to her.

Mario tells his waitstaff to bring everyone espresso, which I decline because I'm wired enough. Drew pulls him aside and a minute later I'm handed a cup of coffee that smells divinely of Kahlúa.

The man knows me well. Too well.

His partner, whom I've met once or twice, says he'll interview the kitchen staff. Drew asks Mario if he minds if he takes statements from the patrons first and gets to him and the waitstaff afterward.

"No, no," Mario tells him. "Do the patrons first." Drew raises his eyebrow at me like he wants to know if I get the double entendre. I try to look bored.

"What is it with you and murder victims?" he asks me when we sit down at a table in the corner.

I search them out so that I can see you again, I almost say, but I'm afraid it will sound desperate instead of sarcastic.

My mother, lighting up and daring him with a look to tell her not to, reminds him that *she* was the one to find the body.

Drew asks what happened *this time*. My mother tells him how the man in the john was "taken" with me, couldn't take his eyes off me and blatantly flirted with both of us. To his credit, Drew doesn't laugh, but his smirk is undeniable to the trained eye. And I've had my eye trained on him for nearly a year now.

"While he was noticing you," he asks me, "did *you* notice anything about him? Was he waiting for anyone? Watching for anything?"

I tell him that he didn't appear to be waiting or watching. That he made no phone calls, was fairly intent on eating and did, indeed, flirt with my mother. This last bit Drew takes with a grain of salt, which was the way it was intended.

"And he had a short conversation with Mario," I tell him.

"I think he might have been unhappy with the food, though he didn't send it back."

Drew asks what makes me think he was dissatisfied, and I tell him that the discussion seemed acrimonious and that Mario looked distressed when he left the table. Drew makes a note and says he'll look into it and asks about anyone else in the restaurant. Did I see anyone who didn't seem to belong, anyone who was watching the victim, anyone looking suspicious?

"Besides my mother?" I ask him, and Mom huffs and blows her cigarette smoke in my direction.

I tell him that there were several deliveries, the kitchen staff going in and out the back door to grab a smoke. He stops me and asks what I was doing checking out the back door of the restaurant.

Proudly—because, while he was off forgetting me, dropping by only once in a while to say hi to Jesse, my son, or drop something by for one of my daughters that he thought they might like, I was getting on with my life—I tell him that I'm decorating the place.

He looks genuinely impressed. "Commercial customers? That's great," he says. Okay, that's what he *ought* to say. What he actually says is "Whatever pays the bills."

"Howard Rosen, the famous restaurant critic, got her the job," my mother says. "You met him—the good-looking, distinguished gentleman with the *real* job, something to be proud of. I guess you've never read his reviews in *Newsday*."

Drew, without missing a beat, tells her that Howard's reviews are on the top of his list, as soon as he learns how to read.

"I only meant—" my mother starts, but both of us assure her that we know just what she meant.

"So," Drew says. "Deliveries?"

I tell him that Mario would know better than I, but that I saw vegetables come in, maybe fish and linens.

"This is the second restaurant job Howard's got her," my mother tells Drew.

"At least she's getting *something* out of the relationship," he says.

"If he were here," my mother says, ignoring the insinuation, "he'd be comforting her instead of interrogating her. He'd be making sure we're both all right after such an ordeal."

"I'm sure he would," Drew agrees, then looks me in the eyes as if he's measuring my tolerance for shock. Quietly he adds, "But then maybe he doesn't know just what strong stuff your daughter's made of."

It's the closest thing to a tender moment I can expect from Drew Scoones. My mother breaks the spell. "She gets that from me," she says.

Both Drew and I take a minute, probably to pray that's all I inherited from her.

"I'm just trying to save you some time and effort," my mother tells him. "My money's on Howard."

Drew withers her with a look and mutters something that sounds suspiciously like "fool's gold." Then he excuses himself to go back to work.

I catch his sleeve and ask if it's all right for us to leave. He says sure, he knows where we live. I say goodbye to Mario. I assure him that I will have some sketches for him in a few days, all the while hoping that this murder doesn't cancel his redecorating plans. I need the money desperately, the alternative being borrowing from my parents and being strangled by the strings.

My mother is strangely quiet all the way to her house. She doesn't tell me what a loser Drew Scoones is—despite his good looks—and how I was obviously drooling over him. She doesn't ask me where Howard is taking me tonight or warn me not to tell my father about what happened because he will worry about us both and no doubt insist we see our respective psychiatrists.

She fidgets nervously, opening and closing her purse over and over again.

"You okay?" I ask her. After all, she's just found a dead man on the toilet, and tough as she is that's got to be upsetting.

When she doesn't answer me I pull over to the side of the road.

"Mom?" She refuses to meet my eyes. "You want me to take you to see Dr. Cohen?"

She looks out the window as if she's just realized we're on Broadway in Woodmere. "Aren't we near Marvin's Jewelers?" she asks, pulling something out of her purse.

"What have you got, Mother?" I ask, prying open her fingers to find the murdered man's ring.

"It was on the sink," she says in answer to my dropped jaw. "I was going to get his name and address and have you return it to him so that he could ask you out. I thought it was a sign that the two of you were meant to be together."

"He's dead, Mom. You understand that, right?" I ask. You never can tell when my mother is fine and when she's in la-la land.

"Well, I didn't know that," she shouts at me. "Not at the time."

I ask why she didn't give it to Drew, realize that she wouldn't give Drew the time in a clock shop and add, "...or one of the other policemen?"

"For heaven's sake," she tells me. "The man is dead, Teddi, and I took his ring. How would that look?"

Before I can tell her it looks just the way it is, she pulls out a cigarette and threatens to light it.

"I mean, really," she says, shaking her head like it's my brains that are loose. "What does he need with it now?"

nocturne™

**WAS HE HER SAVIOR
OR HER NIGHTMARE?**

HAUNTED
LISA CHILDS

Years ago, Ariel and her sisters were separated for
their own protection. Now the man who vowed
revenge on her family has resumed the hunt, and
Ariel must warn her sisters before it's too late.
The closer she comes to finding them, the more
secretive her fiancé becomes. Can she trust the man
she plans to spend eternity with? Or has he been
waiting for the perfect moment to destroy her?

On sale December 2006.

In February, expect MORE
from

as it increases to six titles per month.

What's to come...

Rancher and Protector

Part of the
Western Weddings
miniseries

BY JUDY CHRISTENBERRY

The Boss's
Pregnancy Proposal

BY RAYE MORGAN

Don't miss February's
incredible line up of authors!

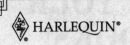

REQUEST YOUR FREE BOOKS!

2 FREE NOVELS
PLUS 2 FREE GIFTS!

Silhouette® Romantic

SUSPENSE

Sparked by Danger, Fueled by Passion!

YES! Please send me 2 FREE Silhouette® Romantic Suspense novels and my 2 FREE gifts. After receiving them, if I don't wish to receive any more books, I can return the shipping statement marked "cancel." If I don't cancel, I will receive 4 brand-new novels every month and be billed just $4.24 per book in the U.S., or $4.99 per book in Canada, plus 25¢ shipping and handling per book plus applicable taxes, if any*. That's a savings of at least 15% off the cover price! I understand that accepting the 2 free books and gifts places me under no obligation to buy anything. I can always return a shipment and cancel at any time. Even if I never buy another book from Silhouette, the two free books and gifts are mine to keep forever.

240 SDN EEX6 340 SDN EEYJ

Name	(PLEASE PRINT)

Address	Apt. #

City	State/Prov.	Zip/Postal Code

Signature (if under 18, a parent or guardian must sign)

Mail to Silhouette Reader Service™:

IN U.S.A.
P.O. Box 1867
Buffalo, NY
14240-1867

IN CANADA
P.O. Box 609
Fort Erie, Ontario
L2A 5X3

Not valid to current Silhouette Intimate Moments subscribers.

Want to try two free books from another line?
Call 1-800-873-8635 or visit www.morefreebooks.com.

* Terms and prices subject to change without notice. NY residents add applicable sales tax. Canadian residents will be charged applicable provincial taxes and GST. This offer is limited to one order per household. All orders subject to approval. Credit or debit balances in a customer's account(s) may be offset by any other outstanding balance owed by or to the customer. Please allow 4 to 6 weeks for delivery.

SILRS06

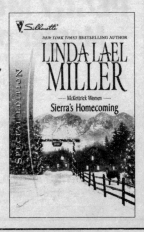

Silhouette Desire

**Don't miss
DAKOTA FORTUNES,**
a six-book continuing series following
the Fortune family of South Dakota—
oil is in their blood and privilege
is their birthright.

This series kicks off with
USA TODAY bestselling author

PEGGY MORELAND'S
Merger of Fortunes
(SD #1771)
this January.

Silhouette®

SPECIAL EDITION™

*L*OGAN'S *L*EGACY *R*EVISITED

**THE LOGAN FAMILY IS BACK
WITH SIX NEW STORIES.**

Beginning in January 2007 with

THE COUPLE
MOST LIKELY TO

by

LILIAN DARCY

Tragedy drove them apart. Reunited eighteen
years later, their attraction was once again
undeniable. But had time away changed
Jake Logan enough to let him face his fears
and commit to the woman he once loved?

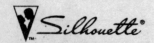
COMING NEXT MONTH

INTIMATE MOMENTS